PROOF OF LIFE

HAILEY EDWARDS

Edited by Sasha Knight
Copy Edited by Kimberly Cannon
Proofread by Lillie's Literary Services
Cover by Gene Mollica
Illustration by Leah Farrow

PROOF OF LIFE

The Potentate of Atlanta, Book 4

Hadley owes a wicked fae seven beating hearts, Boaz and Addie are coming for a visit, and her city is going up in magical flames.

Betrayal and heartbreak. Chocolate and sentient shadows.

Just another night in Atlanta.

I am enough

ONE

"...Three additional kiosks..."

Drowning in one of Midas's tees and a pair of my pajama shorts, I sat at my new desk, chin in palm.

"...break ground in six months..."

The redecoration of the apartment was going well, I thought, thanks to my shiny new bank card.

"...sales are up ten percent..."

All systems go for Addie's visit.

"...new employees hired..."

The one space Midas requested be left untouched was the loft, which suited me fine. And not because it meant one less room to redesign. The loft was *ours*, an end-of-day oasis, and not for guest consumption.

However, our perfectly good king-sized mattress perched on its perfectly good bedframe in our perfectly good bedroom was showroom ready. We even splurged on a reclaimed-wood headboard made by a packmate, plus matching his and her nightstands and a dresser with a framed mirror.

And yet, we still woke stuck together by our sweat on the cramped futon in the loft.

The problem with sleeping next to Midas, no sex involved, prior to mating with him, still no sex involved, was we had gone out of our way to establish a routine heavy on cuddles and not much else in the weeks leading up to the solidification of our union.

Out of mutual respect, we had conducted ourselves thus far as roommates rather than romantic partners. Now we were an official couple, and we were officially stuck in a rut. I wasn't sure how to reach the next level without making it weird between us or bursting our happy cohabitation bubble.

I loved Midas.

I respected Midas.

I also really, really wanted in his pants.

Frak.

I was a terrible person.

"Yes," Remy agreed, chewing with her mouth open. "You are a terrible person."

Swinging my head toward her, I scowled at her. "You read minds now?"

"No." She ate another square of Ambrose's chocolate, causing my shadow to coil like a serpent ready to strike her down for the insult. "You just mutter under your breath a lot." She balled up the wrapper and hit me in the forehead with it. "You also zone out during business meetings." She clucked her tongue. "Frustration does that to people."

"I'm not frustrated," I lied to both of us. "I'm fabulous."

"The looks you give Midas are illegal in several countries."

Tipping up my chin, I took the high road. "I don't know what you're talking about."

"I considered buying him a taser in case he needs to defend himself."

"What? Why?" The low road smacked me in the face. "I'm not going to molest him."

"Your mouth says that, but your eyes say different."

Note to self: *Purchase dark sunglasses at earliest opportunity.*

"I'm not having this conversation with you." I shoved away from the desk. "Are we done here?"

"Yeah, yeah." She gathered her papers into a folder. "I'll just forge your signature on any you missed."

"What?"

"Uh."

"Remy…"

"Do you smell that?" She sniffed the air. "I think I left my stove on."

Quick as a blink, she scurried out the front door and slammed it behind her.

"I've created a monster," I said to the room, and the room did not disagree with me.

A persistent buzzing reminded me I hadn't unmuted my phone when I woke alone at dusk.

Swiping my fingers across the screen, I exhaled long and slow. "Yes?"

"Did I call at a bad time?"

Reclaiming my seat at the desk, I couldn't fight the smile forming. "Midas."

"Are you too busy to talk?"

"No," I rushed to reassure him. "Just grumpy. I haven't had my café mocha yet."

"Bishop running late?"

Normally, he would have beaten down the door, grumbled about getting a key, and caffeinated me by now.

"I haven't heard from him," I admitted. "I've been in a business meeting with Remy."

Amusement dipped through his voice. "How did that go?"

"I have a hand cramp from signing papers for various business ventures, but I learned she's been forging my signature, so I can't imagine that will ever blow up in my face." I lowered my forehead onto the desk. "How's your night going?"

"All quiet on the Western Front."

Laughing softly, I shut my eyes. "I'm about to head to HQ. Need something before I go?"

We were short one beating heart for Natisha, but the witchborn fae coven wasn't making it easy on us to complete our collection. That worked in our favor, as I had yet to hit on a way to keep the viable hearts out of Natisha's hands while still fulfilling our end of the bargain with her. I patrolled each night until I limped home with nothing but blisters to show for my efforts. The sight helped, but it hadn't given me any *in*sight to where they laired. The ability to see through glamour was handy, sure, but not everything was hidden behind illusion magic. Some of it was just hidden period.

"Only for you to open the window."

Drawing myself upright, I pushed back my task chair then located the control for the blackout curtains. A soft whir rolled them aside, leaving me staring out at a breathtaking view of downtown Atlanta...and the equally breathtaking view of a golden-haired man with aquamarine eyes standing on the fire escape. Granted, his golden hair was skull shorn these days, but some guys can make any look work, and he was one of them.

Fumbling with the window lock, I set the remote aside and shoved open a pane. "Well, hello there."

"Join me for breakfast?" He gestured toward our outdoor nook where chocolate croissants in a glassine bag sat on my chair. A tray with two café mochas and two black coffees rested on the small table, and a container stuffed with crispy bacon rested on his chair. "I have a few minutes if you do."

"For chocolate—I mean, *you*—I will make time."

"I appreciate it." He took my hand as I stepped out onto the coarse rug.

"How is it you're here?"

"Mom is a big believer in early to bed, early to rise. We wrapped up our weekly security check-in around the time your alarm went off." He waited for me to sit before joining me. "I'm done for the night."

A tiny thrill zipped through me that he might patrol with me later. "What about post assignments?"

"Ford is handling it."

"Hmm." I dug in, and I groaned as the flaky pastry melted on my tongue. "And Bishop?"

A slow grin spread across his mouth, and I knew my guess was right. He was the reason Bishop was MIA.

"I heard a rumor he's too busy 3D printing various weapons to notice you're not on the roster tonight."

"Where did he get a 3D printer, I wonder?"

"Who knows?" Midas played innocent. "But he seems happy about it."

The ability to print whatever popped into his warped mind would entertain him for hours, if not days.

This scheme of Midas's explained why Remy had waylaid me at dusk with hiking Mount Paperwork too. She must have been tasked with keeping me busy until Midas arrived with the food.

"You seem to have everything planned out." I sipped my mocha, which was perfect. "Now that you have me all to yourself, what do you plan on doing with me?"

A crimson sheen rolled across his eyes, and he wet his lips. "I would like to take you out on a date."

"The courtship is over," I pointed out. "We're an old mated couple now."

Five days old, but who was counting?

"Our courtship wasn't what it ought to have been." He broke a strip of bacon in half then handed me the larger piece, waiting until I took a nibble before he dug into his food. "I want to make things right."

Squinting at him, I confessed, "I...can't tell if the other shoe is about to drop."

I had the unique ability to twist any seemingly innocuous phrase until it resembled a pretzel of insecurity.

"The mate bond is permanent." He grinned at that. "You're stuck with me."

"*Stuck* is not a great word." I tugged my earlobe. "It implies one or both of us doesn't want to be here."

Gaze traveling my face, he lowered his hands. "How do you think mate bonds are formed?"

"I figured it was reflexive." I squirmed on the spot. "Like you get within so many yards of your fated mate, and *bam*. A mystic bond is formed, and congratulations! You're mated."

"Then why didn't I mate with you the first time we met?"

Again, my mouth had its own ideas. "You're not an exhibitionist?"

"Stop deflecting," he chided me. "Why didn't the mate bond snap into place the first time we met?"

"I don't know," I muttered. "You didn't know who I was?"

The mixture of Amelie and Hadley, and Ambrose, might have confused his inner predator.

"Exactly." He tapped my knee. "I had to learn you to love you, to *choose* you."

A pleased flush spread through my chest, warming me and slowing my heart's frantic beat.

"This—" he gestured between us, "—is what concerns me."

"That I'm a person-shaped bundle of neuroses and insecurities?"

"I don't want you to doubt." He rubbed his palm over the stubble on his head. "Not me, and not us."

"I'm working on it," I said quietly. "I trust you, I do, but I've never not screwed up a good thing."

"There's a first time for everything."

The smile I attempted fell flat, but his faith in me—in *us*—worked its magic.

What we had was worth fighting for, every single day, every

single hour, whatever it took, and I...I would get better about believing I was worthy of his love.

"I don't want you to feel like you missed out." He crumbled another strip of bacon without eating it, a cry for help from a gwyllgi if ever I saw one. "I don't want our story to only be how I tricked you into a courtship then kept our mating a secret from you out of fear you would leave me." He wiped his hands clean on a napkin. "I want you to feel like you had a choice, not that I trapped you. Twice."

Oh, Midas.

Our neuroses and insecurities played so well together.

We really were perfect for each other.

"Midas." I slid onto my knees in front of his chair. "There are many things I regret, but you will never be one of them." I rolled a shoulder. "Our story is what it is. There's no rewriting the past." I tickled his ribs. "Plus, it's flattering that you were so desperate to have me you acted lowdown and sneaky to get and keep me."

Granted, he hadn't known what to do with me once he got me, but I had that effect on people.

"I did," he agreed, his voice a low rumble. "I do."

Resting my palms on his thighs, I relished the clench of his muscles in response. "So...a date?"

"Yes." He traced the ovals of my fingernails. "I rented Choco-Loco for the night."

"Whoa." I sat back on my ankles. "That place is crazy expensive."

I ought to know. That's where I sourced most of Ambrose's treats.

They sold human-friendly treats from noon to five, closed, then reopened around midnight. That's when they broke out the *real* goods.

"Chef Daaé too."

The pressure behind my breastbone increased tenfold. "You *rented* Chef Daaé?"

"For an hour," he clarified. "He promised that was enough to teach us how to make our own bonbons."

Squealing, I did a little dance that Ambrose joined in to mock me, but I didn't care one whit.

"I can't believe you did this for me." I flung my arms around Midas. "Thank you, thank you, thank you."

"I did good?"

"Better than good." I pulled back enough to brush my lips over his. "I'm a very lucky girl."

"Let me know if that ever changes." He kissed me back gently. "I want to make you happy."

"Same." I pressed my cheek against his. "This couple stuff is terrifying, right?"

"Yes," he exhaled, warm breath on my throat. "But I like it."

"Me too." Pushing off him to stand, I dusted crumbs off my palms. "What should I wear?"

"We'll be in the kitchen, so comfort over style."

"I like that you think I have style."

"We have about forty-five minutes." He checked his phone. "Can you be ready by then?"

Cramming the final croissant in my mouth, I tucked one mocha into the bend of my right arm then claimed the second with my left hand. Throwing a leg over the windowsill, I mumbled around my food, "Yeth."

"I'll clean up out here and meet you in the living room."

Straddling the wall, hands and mouth full, I nodded to him, dropping crumbs down my shirt.

A caffeinated skip in my step, I rushed into our bedroom and set my mochas on the new dresser, careful to center them on the delivery receipt rather than the gorgeous wood finish. While I pulled on a tight pair of skinny jeans and a cute blouse from the modest wardrobe I bought from Target to replace the clothes I lost in the fire, I stole gulps until I polished off both drinks.

"You look amazing," Midas said from the doorway. "God, you're beautiful."

The compliment struck me with the force of a blow, knocking the wind out of me, and I staggered a bit.

Midas had chosen to keep his sight. He saw through my glamour, past Hadley, straight to Amelie. And he still loved me, a woman whose truth lay somewhere in between who I was born as and who I was becoming.

"You're just saying that because I'm wearing clothes that don't have holes or bleach spots for a change." I slid on sandals and turned to dig a hair tie from my purse. "The contrast is confusing you. That's all."

Warm palms gripped my hips to hold me still, and calloused fingers spread heat across my stomach where Midas linked his hands at my navel. He ducked his head, burying his nose in my hair, and breathed me in deep.

"I don't care what you wear." His lips brushed the side of my throat. "As long as you're mine."

The urge to correct him—I was my own person, thank you muchly—faded when his teeth found my skin.

"I love the way you taste," he whispered in my ear, his voice husky and body hard against mine.

Dizzy from the potent words as much as the tender caresses, I asked, "Are you trying to seduce me?"

"Yes."

No hesitation. No indecision. No qualifiers.

Gulp.

"Oh," I said sexily, you know, if I were a frog croaking its mating call.

Hands sliding back to my hips, he turned me toward him. "Are you okay with this?"

The date, the seduction, or the chocolate, I don't know which he meant, and I didn't care.

Head bobbing, palms sweaty, I forced my mouth to work. "Yes."

"Ready?" He took my hand, but my brain had gone numb. "We don't want to be late."

The heat in his gaze caused my stomach to quiver and tingles to spread through my fingertips.

"Let's do it—*this*." I bit my lip. "Do this." I tried again. "Let's go make bonbons."

As Midas led me from the loft into the elevator, I got the impression my earlier wish to get into his pants was about to be granted. I was as stunned as Aladdin must have when the genie popped out of the lamp he had been rubbing.

Midas was seducing me.

And he was off to a damn fine start.

TWO

Outside the air-conditioned bliss of the Faraday, the night fell on the right side of lukewarm. Midas and I skipped the Swyft fare and walked the five blocks to Choco-Loco with our fingers meshed and our arms swinging like we were two teens out with our first crushes.

The city hummed around us, alive with traffic and voices and music, and I relaxed into the rare chance to spend time with him outside our jobs.

"Do you smell that?"

A few steps later, I sneezed into my elbow. "Smoke."

With the night off, we didn't have to rush into action, but it still made me twitchy.

"Call Bishop." Midas, who knew me too well, slowed his pace. "You'll feel better if you report it."

From there, Bishop could locate the origin and call the proper authorities.

"We're on a date." I already had the phone in my hand. "He would call if..."

An urgent flash lit up my display, and I groaned, letting my head fall back on my neck.

"It's okay." Midas released me. "Answer it."

The number was as familiar as my reflection. "What's up, Bish?"

"We got problems."

"I was about to call you anyway." I watched the blaze lighten the sky. "There's a fire—"

"Uh, yeah." He cleared his throat. "I don't think you and lover boy are having that date night."

Fear spiked in my heart. "What's burning?"

"Choco-Loco."

Standing beside me, Midas had no trouble following the conversation. "Daaé?"

There wasn't much gwyllgi ears didn't hear, which made cohabitation awkward to the extreme at times.

"We were meeting Chef Daaé." I started walking again. "Do you know if he was there? Or if he got out?"

"An anonymous tipster called in the fire," Bishop explained. "They didn't give details."

"We're almost there." I picked up the pace. "I can see the flames."

"Daaé's cell is going straight to voicemail," Midas reported. "No one is answering at the restaurant."

"I've ferreted out a home number for him." Bishop clacked a few keys in the background. "I'll start there and work my way up, see if I can get a bead on him."

"Let me know what you find out."

Tucking the phone into my pocket, I broke into a sprint, and Midas kept pace with ease.

Red and white lights strobed the night, bouncing off thick plumes, and sirens screamed bloody murder.

Chef Daaé was a vampire, a Last Seed, who had dedicated his immortality to chocolate as an art form. He was a local celebrity in foodie circles, a humble genius, and an all-around swell guy according to what I had gleaned about him during the past year.

The shadow I cast wilted as the potential ripple effects of the blaze on his sweet tooth hit Ambrose.

Two gleaming fire engines skidded to a halt across the street, and I didn't have to check the patches on the men pouring from them like militant ants—*ick*—to know Station Thirteen had arrived. As the unit responsible for responding to paranormal emergencies of the flaming-inferno variety, I wouldn't have expected anyone else.

Midas and I held our ground, our hands clenched in fists at our sides, giving them room to battle the fire.

An ambulance arrived minutes later, and a local coven of paramedics checked with the men then trotted over to us.

"Any injuries?" the young man asked. "Do you need medical assistance?"

"No," I answered for both of us. "We were on our way here for a date night when we saw the smoke."

A frown knit his brow. "Anyone else meeting you here?"

"Chef Daaé," Midas told him. "I booked him for a private lesson."

"Goddess," he breathed. "Let's hope he was running late."

"The crew just got here." I admired their valiant battle. "Have they had time to check the entire building?"

"Captain Gray says the place was empty." The young man ruffled his hair. "This will change things."

Daaé was old, *really* old.

A handful of ashes might be all that was left of him.

"Wait for the police." The man, who must be new if he didn't recognize either of us, backed up a step. "They'll want to talk to you."

Sentinels undercover with the Atlanta Police Department would respond, but they all knew me on sight.

"Sure thing," I assured him. "I'll do that."

Once he crossed the street, Midas and I got comfortable. I wanted to talk to Gray before we left, get his unofficial opinion on what started the fire. I was also curious how good a lion shifter's nose was on picking vampire ashes from other debris. As alpha of the

Kingsman lions, the newest predatory shifter pack to call Atlanta home, he had keener senses than most.

A buzz in my pocket had me fishing out my phone. "Any luck?"

"The Daaé clan's butler says the chef left for work at dusk," Bishop said. "I confirmed the drop off with his usual driver. He gave me the names of Daaé's four personal assistants. They're witches, and they all answered their phones. The general consensus is Daaé prefers handling private bookings solo. He genuinely enjoys teaching, and he feels an audience intimidates his students."

After checking Midas had overheard the update, I told Bishop, "Thanks for doing the legwork."

"See if you can't salvage tonight." He exhaled slowly. "You two might not be going out for a while."

Doubtful Midas and I could rekindle the mood, I made appropriate noises and then ended the call.

"I don't like this," Midas said at last, staring across the street, flames reflecting in his eyes.

Wrapping my arms around his waist, I rested my head on his chest. "Neither do I."

"Four people, including Chef Daaé, knew I was bringing you here tonight."

"You heard Bishop." I rubbed small circles at his spine with my thumbs. "He had assistants."

A high-end outfit like Choco-Loco would have kept schedules out the wazoo, particularly for their star chef and the handpicked assistants who orbited him like chocoholic moons. The chef and his assistants might have had the only copies, or they might have been available to management, or they might have been on an app or even an old-school bulletin board. There were endless possibilities, and none of them were helpful in narrowing down how this happened, tonight of all nights.

About three hours after we arrived, the fire was quenched or had simply run its course, the building's remains were smoldering, and a soot-smeared Captain Gray jogged across the road to greet us.

"I understand you had a date night planned." His grimace cut white lines through the grime on his cheeks. "That's bad luck."

"It's definitely something," I agreed. "The paramedic told us the building was clear?"

"No victims as far as we can tell."

A hit of relief spiked through me. "Does that include old-as-dirt vampires?"

"Sadly not." He wiped the sweat from his brow. "The cleaners are en route. They're calling in a specialist to take samples and test them. It will be weeks before we have conclusive evidence either way."

As treasured as Last Seeds were by their clans, we would have an inkling if Chef Daaé had survived before dawn by way of frantic calls made to the Office of the Potentate of Atlanta, the OPA, if he didn't come home once they realized who he was set to meet for a private lesson.

Midas found his voice. "Arson?"

"Looks that way." Gray leaned in, mouth stretched thin. "Aubrey says it tastes a bit like the fire magic he consumed in the clearing."

So, the coven had reared its ugly head yet again, uncaring of the collateral damage. Why was I not surprised?

"Thanks." I stuck out my hand. "I appreciate the work you do."

"You too." He shook it. "Let me know if I can be of any further assistance."

"I'll do that."

With our plans for the night blown, I returned my attention to Midas, whose brow remained crinkled.

Leaning back against him, I tipped my head onto his shoulder. "Do you think the coven is to blame?"

The question jerked him to attention, and he focused on me. "We declared war on them."

We hadn't made it official, the way the Society formally declared a blood feud, but yeah. We had carved out the hearts of six of their members and killed more than twice that. We had thrown down the gauntlet, picked it back up, and then smacked the taste out of their mouths with it.

The coven had declared war on innocents first, and that I couldn't ignore or forgive.

With a screech of tires, four white vans pulled up to the curb in a neat row. Men and women dressed in outfits that greatly resembled flame-retardant footy pajamas poured out onto the sidewalk. A red-faced man, who I hadn't seen since Bonnie Diaz had attempted to swallow him for barking orders at me, trundled across the street. Sweat dotted his balding pate, and dislike curled his lip.

"We have the area secure." He yanked on padded gloves. "There's no reason for you to be here."

"This is my city," I told him. "That's reason enough."

"Preliminary results will be uploaded into our database at our earliest convenience." His jaw might be grinding, but he was being civil. Bonnie really left an impression on him. A giant white gwyllgi with equally huge white teeth had that effect on people. "Until such time as we have completed our investigation, I ask you to leave so that my team has the freedom to perform their duties to the best of their abilities."

The Daaé clan must have thrown their considerable political weight around to get the cleaners out here so fast and in such numbers.

As much as this guy's attitude annoyed me, he was playing nice, so I would return the favor.

Pivoting on my heel, I started walking away from the chaotic scene, certain Midas would follow.

"We're banned from the crime scene, and Bishop has HQ in hand. Looks like the rest of our night is wide open." I linked my arm through his when he caught up to me. "What do you want to do?"

"Go home," he said, defeated. "We can order in, watch a movie."

We had nothing to do and nowhere to be, and I didn't want to waste the opportunity to spend time with Midas. We had put our lives on hold to cleanse Atlanta of the coven, and I refused to let shame eat him from the inside out for daring to take one night for himself. For *us*.

"This isn't your fault." I jiggled his arm. "You know that, right?"

His curt nod paid lip service to my reassurance, but I didn't press. It wouldn't do either of us any good.

"You're not getting out of taking me on a date." I withdrew from him. "I hope you have a Plan B."

"Hadley…"

"Come on." I grabbed him by the wrist and tugged him after me. "I have an idea."

The late hour meant getting creative, but there were plenty of para-owned businesses in town who kept Society hours to accommodate their nocturnal clientele.

"You don't have to do this."

"No, I don't." I yanked harder. "But I want to have you to myself for a minute."

Preferably one when the world wasn't burning down around our ears, but I would take what I could get.

"We're going to have guests soon," I kept going, filling the quiet. "We'll be stuck doing the tourist thing."

"We'll make it work." He exerted less pull against me. "Where are they staying?"

"They still can't decide," I admitted. "Oh, the joys of traveling with family."

While I was excited to see Addie and Boaz, I had a case of nerves about my faux father visiting, and I was doing my best to ignore that my biological mother would be sharing the same zip code with me.

"Let's forget about them." I skipped my gaze over the restaurant signs. "Let's focus on us."

The reminder Midas didn't know my whole truth was stamped on his face whenever I mentioned my family, but I had never told another soul about my mother. I wanted to tell him, but I didn't know how, and I was afraid he would treat me differently once all the pieces clicked into place.

Grier and Linus had witnessed her ambivalence toward me in my past life, but they didn't have a concrete reason to dislike her.

I could give them a metric ton of them, but not without that knowledge crushing me too.

"Okay." Sensing my mood, he leaned over and kissed my temple. "Us it is."

"I have an idea." I stopped in front of him. "It's not as great as yours, but it might do in a pinch."

Tilting his head, he glanced around us. "Do I get a hint?"

"It involves food."

"That's it?"

"That's it." I bounced on my toes. "Are you in, or are you out?"

"That sounds dangerously like a dare."

"I would never dare a gwyllgi."

"Mmm-hmm." He took my hand and shook on it. "I'm in."

"Excellent."

Keeping hold of him, I dragged him through the rear door of another restaurant that spat us out into the kitchen. An old man with weathered brown skin who hunched to avoid his shoulders brushing the ceiling stirred sauce in a pot on the stove. His limbs creaked when he twisted to see who had joined him, and the green leaves of his hair stuck out from under his chef's hat.

"Hadley," he rumbled, a smile curving the strips of bark that formed his lips. "Did you get turned around in the alley? The takeout window is up front."

And I made good use of it to get my grabby hands on his epic pies whenever the craving struck me.

"I have a *huge* favor to ask." I clasped my hands in front of me. "*Pleeease.*"

"A favor?" Knotty eyes fixed on me, he chided me. "After I haven't seen you in weeks?"

"Sadly," I confessed, the Choco-Loco blaze fresh in my mind, "business has been booming."

"I'm sorry to hear that." He turned slowly, his rootling feet long and thin. "What would you ask of me?"

Twisting my sneaker on the tile, I pressed my clasped hands to my chest. "Teach us to make pizza?"

The *us* made him curious enough to rake his gaze over Midas. "This is your boyfriend?"

"Her mate." Midas touched the small of my back. "I'm Midas Kinase."

"Kinase." The buds near his hairline unfurled, glossy and bright. "Tisdale's boy?"

Finding a genuine smile, Midas aimed it at the chef. "You know Mom?"

"Your mother and I are of an age." His grin exposed the dark age rings striping his teeth. "And her pack keeps me in business." He made a slight bow. "I'm Fergus Crann."

"Is that a yes?" I wheedled. "We wanted to do something special for a date night."

"I would have loaned you my Seanan even without the heir apparent." He checked on his sauce. "I hope that will suffice?"

"Thank you." I blew him a kiss that flushed his cheeks a muddy brown. "You're the best."

"Wait for her in the small kitchen." He turned back to his stove. "She'll be along shortly."

Hand in hand, we did as we were told. The small kitchen was the one original to the building. Fergus loved the old brick pizza oven and refused to part with it, so it was more decorative than anything these days. He kept it operational for parties where people, like us, wanted to learn how to make their own pie the right way.

Midas pulled out a chair at an empty table for me. "How do you know Fergus?"

"You'd be surprised how many trees are sentient." I kicked the leg of the chair opposite me, and it popped out for him. "Then again, being gwyllgi, maybe you wouldn't."

"We're taught to respect nature, but that doesn't mean nature gives up all its secrets to us."

That wasn't an answer, but just because he was part fae didn't mean he had taken everyone's measure.

"There were two kids tying firecrackers to a cat's tail then lighting them last Fourth of July." Humans, both of them. "The cat was understandably terrified and shot up a tree to escape them. His fur had caught fire, and it was a dry summer, so the tree wasn't far behind."

A growl built in Midas's throat, sympathy for the cat and the tree.

"It happened in Centennial Olympic Park, and I got lucky. I was able to dig a few large cups out of the trash to fill with fountain water. The cat didn't appreciate my efforts, or the trip to the vet's office, but what can you do?" I was amazed the scratches from the experience didn't scar. "Anyway, I saved the tree, and Fergus paid me a visit the next day with an offer of free pizza for life."

"I have noticed you eat a lot of pizza..."

"I'll have you know, even at my lowest, I didn't take him up on the offer."

Interest brought him in closer. "Why not?"

"I was doing my job." I rubbed my thumb across the glossy table. "No perks required."

"She saved the grove," Seanan told Midas as she joined us. "One wrong move from that cat, and the whole stand of trees would have gone up in smoke. Most weren't sentient, but we would have lost three elders who are meditating."

Behind my hand, I explained to Midas, "That means sleeping as a tree for a decade or two."

"It's not a bad gig, honestly." She anchored her hands on her hips. "I'm looking forward to my time."

From what I could tell, Seanan was a sapling compared to Fergus. Her skin was a warm brown, so were her eyes and her hair, but she wore a human glamour in front of customers that made it impossible to guess her true appearance. "When will that be?"

"Two centuries, give or take." She winked. "They make us earn our vacations around here."

While she built up the fire, Midas and I helped two of the waitstaff carry in the supplies for our lesson.

The evening didn't go as Midas had planned, but we had a good time. Seanan awarded me winner of the prettiest pizza, which wasn't saying much, then challenged us to a race to see who could eat their lopsided—but delicious—creation the fastest.

No surprise, Midas won. He was a gwyllgi, after all.

As we tidied up our workstations, Seanan reappeared with two boxes, one balanced on each palm.

"Dad made these for you." She presented the top one to Midas. "This is apple streusel." Then handed me the other. "This one is really just a giant chocolate chip cookie disguised as a dessert pizza."

"I would have asked for lessons sooner if I had known we got prizes." I leaned down and inhaled. "This smells amazing." Ambrose smoothed his hand reverently along the lid, and Midas mostly hid his jolt of surprise. At times, my shadow still managed to unnerve Midas when he popped in. "I've never seen it on the menu."

"There's not a big dessert pizza market," she confessed. "He makes them for family, but that's about it."

A wide smile blossomed across my face. "Now I feel even more special."

"Before your head gets too big to fit out the door, I should remind you that Midas's family orders our pie by the dozens." She turned to go. "Nightly."

"You're saying I'm only special by association?" I clutched my pizza tighter. "That's harsh."

Tossing a wave over her shoulder as she left, she chuckled. "That's small business for you."

Juggling his box, Midas removed two twenties from his wallet then placed them on the table.

You could tell a lot about a person by how they treated others, particularly those in the service industry.

Fergus would get his trunk in a twist over it, but Seanan had earned the tip for salvaging our date night.

Out on the sidewalk, I breathed in the cooling night air and the sweet hit of dessert pizza when Midas opened the lid on his.

"I had fun." He passed me a slice of his treat. "This was nice."

Answering before I took a bite required iron will, but I managed. "I'm glad you enjoyed yourself."

"You're amazing, you know that?"

"That's the carbs talking. Wait until after you see your food baby, then we'll see."

We had to walk past Choco-Loco on our way back to the Faraday, and we came to a stop together as if we had planned it.

All that remained was a charred husk, but despite the temperatures required to do that sort of damage, no other buildings had been harmed. That, paired with what Gray told us Aubrey mentioned to him, had me convinced the coven was behind this.

"We have plenty to keep us busy tomorrow." I forced myself to walk on. "We can't do a thing tonight."

The majority of the restaurant staff was human and would have gone home when the store closed at five. That didn't give them a pass, it just meant waiting until daylight to make calls, secure their alibies, and question them about Chef Daaé's last-known whereabouts. The after-dark crew would be mostly paras, and better informed, but we had to get our hands on a full list of employees before we started eliminating names.

Usually, I left potential arson up to the sentinels, but this case hit too close to home for me to ignore.

"We have enough time for a movie." A smile twitched his lips. "I noticed a copy of *It Came from Under the Kitchen Sink* arrived."

"You don't have to watch." I snorted. "I know you think it's lame."

"But you don't, and that's what matters."

Hank watched our approach from his position before the front doors of the Faraday. He kept his eyes on me, suspicious as always.

Or maybe he was just annoyed. Sheesh. I hadn't antagonized him in *days*.

"Ford was looking for you," he greeted Midas. "He mentioned a fire?"

Proof word traveled, and fast. "Ford knew where you were taking me?"

"I ran the idea past him. He told me to let him know how it went. He was thinking of taking Lisbeth."

The two of them had been getting closer, but their relationship was none of my business. I was too happy to have my friend back to ruin it with poking into his love life.

Hand on Midas's arm, I asked, "Do you need to check in with him before we go up?"

"He might worry if I don't," he admitted. "We've had a bad run with fire lately."

"True." I scrubbed my palm over his scalp. "Go fill him in, and I'll start the popcorn."

Leaning down, Midas brushed his lips over mine. "One day—"

"—we'll go on vacation far, far outside the city and leave our phones behind in our apartment."

"That's not where I was going, but I like your idea better."

"Give me your pizza." I smirked when he eyed me with suspicion. "Where's the trust?"

"Ask the pulled pork plate that vanished from the fridge last week."

"Do you think your pizza is in greater danger from me, who just ate and has another whole pizza, or Ford, who has been on shift all night and probably missed his lunch after he heard about Choco-Loco?"

"You have a point." He handed it over then placed his palm on the box top. "Don't eat it all."

"Shoo." I slapped him on the butt. "The faster you find him, the quicker you come home."

Home.

Our apartment.

I liked the sound of both.

With a spring in my step, I entered the elevator and mashed the button for the top floor.

Already debating if I had room in my stomach for another slice, I let myself into the apartment. All the lights were on, which was weird. Midas and I never did that. But Remy was weird about, well, everything. She didn't have a key to the apartment, but that didn't stop her from popping in when the mood struck her.

About to drop the pizzas on the kitchen counter, I noticed movement on my periphery and summoned Ambrose in a blink. Tossing the pies aside, I lashed out with my foot. A gratifying *oomph* rang out, and a body smacked the floor.

"What in the...?"

Whirling toward the familiar voice, I yelped, "Boaz?"

"Freaking hell." Sitting up, he rubbed the back of his head. "Who else would it be?"

Boaz was taller than me by several inches, but I held the advantage now. Milk-chocolate irises striated with lighter bands, like swirled caramel, glared at me. White scars, more than the last time I saw him, stood out against his tanned skin. His platinum hair, baby fine and impossible to style, was shaved on the sides and longer on the top. It was also currently hanging in his eyes thanks to his tumble.

Feminine laughter spilled from the loft, and I dropped my head back to find Adelaide sitting on the edge, dangling her legs. "I told you surprising her was a bad idea."

"You guys are here early." I pasted on a smile while my brain played catch-up. "Wow."

"We have a hotel across town." Addie stood and tread the stairs. "We'll be out of your hair in a minute, but the oaf wanted to let you know we made it in."

"The oaf has a concussion." He lowered his arm then shoved to his feet. "I'm seeing stars."

"You're fine." Addie pressed a kiss to his boo-boo on her way past. "He's such a whiner."

"This I know." I walked into her open arms. "It's good to see you."

Not to be left out, my brother wrapped us both in a bear hug that lifted us off our feet.

"I missed you too, doofus." I kissed his cheek. "A lot."

"Savannah isn't the same without you."

"Like you would know." I pinched his ear. "You're never home."

"She's not wrong." Addie slipped away from the huddle. "He's barely around enough to annoy me."

"She's desperately in love with me," Boaz told me behind his hand. "It's embarrassing, really."

A ballet flat hit him in the head and bounced off the wall behind him.

"I can tell." I smothered a laugh. "She's obviously smitten."

The knob twisted behind us, and the front door opened, transforming Boaz's smile into a frown.

He nodded a curt welcome to Midas then turned to me. "Did you leave the door unlocked?"

"I don't know." I scowled at him. "I was too busy being accosted in my own home to remember."

Midas paused between the door he shut behind him and me, and it opened a yawning pit in my gut.

Fear he would refuse to claim me in front of my family left a sour taste in my mouth. He could play this off easily as doing a security check on unannounced guests or wanting to touch base with me on city matters. With the locked status of the door in question, he could invent any excuse and leave.

As if reading my mind, Midas closed the distance, hooked an arm around my waist, and tucked me against him. Leaning down, he murmured in my ear, "Do they know?"

"Nope."

Addie knew I was shacking up with Midas—her words, not mine—but Boaz was clueless.

Things were about to get interesting.

Gulp.

"I didn't know you had a boyfriend," Boaz said casually, his gaze zeroed in on Midas.

"I..." I wrapped my arms around Midas like Boaz might try to take him away from me, "...don't."

"Then what's going on here?"

The words got stuck in my throat, and I don't know why, but I couldn't be the first to say them.

Understanding gentled Midas's expression as he wiped his fingertips over my cheek. "She's my mate."

"She's crying," Boaz pointed out the obvious. "Why is she crying?"

"He makes her happy." Addie popped him upside the head. "Look at them."

Unable to articulate why it mattered so much, I pressed my face into Midas's chest. "Thank you."

Boaz loved me, had always loved me. The purity of his love was part of the reason why I never allowed our mother to overshadow our relationship. What she did to me was apart from us. That didn't mean the stain didn't bleed between my carefully separated layers at odd times, like this one.

It was hard feeling worthy of love, so hard, when I had learned early that it wasn't given for free.

"You have nothing to thank me for." Midas cradled the back of my head in his palm. "This is nothing."

The tears started falling in earnest, and I strangled on old fear to say, "It's everything."

"You didn't cry like that when we got engaged," Boaz grumbled to Addie, unconvinced.

"I would have," Addie said wistfully. "If I had known what I was getting into back then."

"We were about to watch a movie." Midas kept me close. "Care to join us?"

Addie and Boaz groaned in unison and leaned into each other.

"Depends." She grimaced. "Who gets to pick the movie?"

With Midas holding me up, I found my own strength. "Our guests."

"Have a seat." Midas gestured to the living room, where one footstool was still wrapped in plastic. "We'll go make popcorn."

Addie's face lit up like a kid at Christmas. "Linus popcorn?"

"Yes," I said solemnly, aware it was a cult favorite for anyone who had tasted it. "Linus popcorn."

Granted, I wasn't nearly as skilled as him in the kitchen, but he had taught me how to make a damn fine bowl of popcorn by anyone's standards.

Under Midas's stare, I dug out my Dutch oven, cranked up the heat, and filled it with oil and kernels.

"I wasn't hiding you from them," I said when he didn't make a peep. "I wanted to tell them in person."

"I'm not upset." His warm palm cupped my nape. "I'm...confused."

"There are a lot of things about my childhood I haven't told you." I lowered my voice. "Or anyone else." He glanced over his shoulder to where Boaz watched us like a hawk. "I want to explain it, to you, but..."

"Take your time." He wrapped his arm around me again. "I'm not going anywhere."

Vision wobbly, I gave the popcorn my full attention before I burned it and stank up the place.

A throat cleared in the living room, and I rolled my eyes. "Neither is my brother."

"You could plead exhaustion." Midas gave me a look that pooled heat in my middle. "Send them away."

A smile tickled the edge of my mouth. "Do you really think that would work?"

"Probably not," he confessed. "Boaz is going to want to stare me down a while longer."

"That's what I figured too."

"How long does it take to make popcorn?" Boaz yelled right on cue. "Did you have to drive out to a field and pick the cobs yourselves?"

"Hush," Addie hissed. "She's a grown woman."

His grunt of pain led me to believe she had smacked, elbowed, or otherwise hit him.

Not gonna lie. Her violent streak was one of the things I most admired about her. She was going to need all the luck, and sucker punches, she could get if she hoped to beat sense into my brother. The boy had a head like a rock.

"Almost finished," I sang out sweetly. "I just need to toss it."

Once I finished dousing the massive batch in salt and butter, I poured it into two giant bowls. While I got sodas from the fridge, Midas carried our snack to the living room. Wisely, he handed Addie the first bowl then claimed a spot where I could sink down next to him and curl into his side.

"So," Boaz began as soon as my butt hit the cushion. "How long has this been going on?"

"Leave them alone." Addie crammed a handful of popcorn into his mouth then turned to me. "I'm happy you found someone who loves you as much as you deserve." She smiled warmly at Midas. "Remember, I might not be her sister by blood, but I won't hesitate to spill yours if you hurt her."

Choking on his popcorn, Boaz spat wet kernels across his lap. "What?"

"They're mated." Addie watched us. "That means he knows."

Faster than my brain could process, Boaz had drawn a dagger from goddess knows where and rested its edge against Midas's throat. He leaned over Midas, who held very still but showed no signs of concern.

Knuckles white, Boaz demanded, "You know who she is?"

"I do."

Arms folded across my middle, I confessed, "He knows what I am too."

"Goddess, Ame. Do you know how dangerous this is?" His eyes widened. "Does Linus know he knows?"

Tensing at the old nickname, I waited for the expected pain to hit, but only nostalgia filled me.

"Yes." I rested my hand on his. "He knows."

Searching my face, he kept his grip tight. "He's okay with it?"

"I'm still breathing, aren't I?"

Beside us, Addie blanched. "That's not as comforting as you maybe thought it would be."

The truth was rarely comforting. Linus was my fail-safe, my guarantee that should I go off the rails again, I would be put down before I turned into a monster to rival Ambrose. But it was hard to hear that, and for me to mean it somehow made it worse.

"I respect your concern for Hadley," Midas said, crimson rolling across his eyes. "I even appreciate it."

A shiver tripped down my spine, not fear of Midas but fear for Boaz.

"Lower the blade," Midas continued, calm and reasonable, "or I will do it for you."

"Boaz," Addie said quietly.

"This is our home." I put my foot down. "You're our guest, but I will kick your butt if you don't knock it off."

"You're the only little sister I've got." Boaz lowered his arm. "I worry about you, dork."

"Hadley will be the Potentate of Atlanta," Midas reminded him. "She can handle herself."

"You're Lethe's *little* brother." Boaz relented under Addie's warning glare. "Maybe it makes a difference, that you're the baby, or maybe it doesn't, but I worry about my sister."

Midas's gaze dipped to the scars crisscrossing his forearms, proof of how much he loved his sister, a story I had no intention of sharing.

No one else needed to know the depths of his love, or his pain. Everyone to whom it mattered already did, and I felt blessed to count myself in that small number.

Addie, however, watched me, the stand-in for the little sister she had lost, and she smiled gently.

"I think we all know how far we're each willing to go for those we love." She pulled Boaz down onto the couch beside her then draped herself half over his lap, which made him grin, but I suspected she was attempting to hold him down more than show affection. "Now that we've got that settled, let's get back to the popcorn."

Happy with the change in topic, I picked up the remote. "What movie did you guys decide on?"

"There's a new romcom." Addie winked at me. "Lots of love words, grand gestures, and smooching."

"That still trumps whatever creature feature Hadley had cued." Boaz patted her hip. "I'm in."

We rented Addie's pick with the press of a button, dimmed the lights, and settled in to watch a feel-good movie together. As a family. A year ago, I wasn't sure I had one anymore. This... I could get used to this.

Snuggled up to Midas, his fingers in my hair, his lips never leaving my brow, I forgot about the popcorn and the movie, and I watched us all instead. And when my eyelids drifted closed, I listened to Boaz and Addie whispering and laughing, to Midas's heartbeat and his every indrawn breath.

I had lost everything to get here. Everything and then some.

But goddess what a place to be.

THREE

Dusk brought a summons that required Midas's immediate attention, and he left Hadley sleeping under a quilt on the couch where he had woken. Boaz and Addie were gone, having let themselves out when the movie ended. The popcorn bowl on the couch sat empty even though neither Hadley nor he had touched it. Boaz and Addie had left their bowl on the coffee table, only bits and kernels, but it was sparkling clean now.

Ambrose, it seemed, had joined them for the movie, or at least for the snacks.

After Midas brushed his teeth, he glanced at his hair, what little remained, and dressed in fresh clothes.

The smell of black coffee hit his nose as he entered the hall and bumped into Ares.

"I have never been so tired in my life." She drank long and deep. "I hate when family visits."

"Liz has relatives in town?" He clasped her shoulder. "Have you made the big announcement yet?"

Liz, Ares's mate, was inching toward the end of her second trimester, and she was starting to show. Otherwise, given their struggle to reach this point, he wouldn't have been surprised if they kept it secret until the baby was safely in their arms to avoid jinxing their good luck.

"No." Yawning, she cracked her jaw. "I saw the visitor logs."

That didn't explain why she was tired, but Midas didn't push with her temper shortened by exhaustion.

"They wanted to surprise Hadley."

"There was a note on the log that said Linus cleared it. Boaz was the guy who dumped Grier, right?"

A warning prickle slid down his nape as he waited for her to make her point. "Yes."

There was no reason for her to draw lines between Boaz and Hadley, but with a Pritchard/Whitaker family visit looming, talk about him made Midas twitchy all the same.

"Can you imagine getting the girl but then being stuck with her ex in your life because the guy decided to go and marry your apprentice's sister?" She mashed the button for the elevator. "It's like he's stalking Linus." Her lips curved with glee. "Maybe he was obsessed with Linus and not Grier all along."

Relief sluiced through him, smoothing his hackles, and he joined her in the car for the ride to the lobby.

"Necromancy is a small world." Midas shrugged. "Society families are as close as pack."

"Boaz is Low Society," she said, as if testing her memory. "Addie must be too, right? And Hadley?"

"Yes."

"Ah." Ares gazed over the rim of her cup. "Boaz's love for Linus was doomed from the start."

Low Society necromancers rarely married up, and when they did, it was purely out of love to a High Society necromancer who could afford the indulgence. The lasting damage of such unions, in the Society's mind, was generational. The bloodline would thin, as Low Society necromancers had little to no magic, the loss of status would be catastrophic, and the financial implications could prove ruinous.

"I'll be sure to float that idea the next time I talk to Boaz."

"Oh, to be a fly on that wall." Knocking off the jokes, she studied him. "How did they take the news?"

"Addie was happy for us." He recalled the blade held at his throat. "Boaz was less thrilled."

"He's stepping into the big-brother role. Probably thinks it's his job to give you a hard time."

Ares had no idea how right she was, on both counts. "Any idea what's got Ford in a tizzy?"

The text from him was vague minus the part that specified Midas's presence was required downstairs.

"I worked last night and today." She chugged more coffee. "All I know is, I was sent to fetch you."

"Security?"

"Yep." She yawned again. "The Knoxville pack is in town for the week, and you know what that means."

"I forgot about that." He twisted his lips. "Hadley's family is here all week too."

"Your mom expects you both for dinner at least once. She wants to show off her new daughter-in-law."

Boaz's offhand remark about his proposal to Addie drifted to the forefront of Midas's mind.

Hand to his chest, he rubbed his breastbone. "Do you think Hadley expects a proposal?"

Coffee spewed from Ares's lips and sprayed the walls. "She's a necromancer, so I would say *yes*."

We're mated nearly popped out of his mouth, but one dark look from her silenced him.

Hadn't he told Hadley he had made a mistake in expecting her to conform to his customs without taking her beliefs into consideration? Hadn't he told her, only yesterday, he regretted how their story had begun? Now he was almost, *almost* fumbling again not twenty-four hours later.

"Mating is hard." Ares patted him on the back. "Mating outside the pack is better and worse. You get to learn a new person and experience life from a different perspective. But culture shock is real, and no one expects you to upend your beliefs in a day. Just be careful you don't grip your roots so hard that you rip hers out of the ground."

As happy as Ares was in her mixed-species marriage, he would be a fool to disregard her advice.

"Thanks." He exhaled hard. "Though I'm not sure how I'll pull off a proposal if I can't manage a simple date night."

But he would try. For Hadley, he would succeed. The right ring, the right words. Everything. All of it.

"Ouch." She winced. "I heard about Choco-Loco."

Eyebrows climbing, he cut her a look. "Did everyone know I was taking Hadley there?"

"Ford lost his ever-loving mind when he heard about the fire, so yeah. The whole break room—anyone on shift, really—knew you were supposed to be there." Quickly, she clarified, "I didn't know ahead of time, if that's what's worrying you."

"I didn't mean to imply I thought a packmate had anything to do with the fire."

"You broke a lot of hearts when you chose Hadley over every eligible female in the pack, but your mom has made it clear she accepts Hadley as her daughter and that any move against her will result in immediate punishment."

"I must have missed that memo."

"It was important the pack hear it from their alpha first." She cast him a pointed glance. "They'll want to hear it from their beta too."

A groan moved through him as his mother's intentions crystalized in his mind. "A pack potluck."

That's what she had dubbed the enormous meetings where the entire pack gathered while she made announcements that affected everyone. Gwyllgi hated meetings, so she shamelessly bribed them with food, dancing, and the occasional raffle basket, depending on the direness of the news.

"That's my guess." She grinned. "The next time your mom

mentions dinner, be suspicious. Very suspicious. And probably go ahead and write your speech so you can keep it in your pocket at all times."

They hit the lobby, and worries about how to proceed with Hadley took a backseat to the overwhelming scents of gwyllgi who were not pack. Familiarity with them didn't stop the low rumbling up the back of his throat. His inner beast felt its territory had been invaded, and the man wasn't far behind.

"You might want to dial that down," Ares murmured. "Here comes Claudia."

The crowd parted to allow the statuesque blonde a direct route to him, and they watched with interest.

"Midas." She sashayed up to him. "It's been too long."

"Claudia." He forced the barest smile. "Always a pleasure."

The Knoxville alpha knew better than to lay hands on him, though her fingers curled as if she wished to do just that. She had sticky fingers, no concept of personal space, and Midas usually counted on Ford to keep her entertained. With Ford spending more time with Lisbeth, Midas wasn't sure who else to palm her off on.

"Your gorgeous hair." She sucked in a sharp breath. "I can't believe you cut it."

That explained her twitchy fingers. "It will grow back."

"Ford told me the craziest thing when I first arrived." She bit her bottom lip. "He said you had mated."

"I have mated."

The coy amusement slipped off her face and shattered on the floor. "A necromancer, really?"

Hadley was so much more than a necromancer, but that was none of Claudia's business. "Yes."

Ford shoved through the gathering to reach Midas, all smiles for Claudia, but the strain already showed on his face. "There you are, darlin'."

"I came to hear the words from his own mouth." She pouted. "I can't believe he's off the market."

"He was starting to smell up the place," Ford teased. "We discounted him and hoped for the best."

"I would have paid full price." She lowered her lashes. "I don't mind if someone else took a bite first."

The growl in the back of Midas's throat revved louder, and her lips twitched in a knowing curve.

"I hate to break it to you." Ford pulled his *aww shucks* routine. "His mate isn't interested in a refund."

Laughing, she touched Ford's arm in a proprietary manner. "How will I know unless I ask?"

"Hi," an overly bright voice chirped from beside him. "We haven't met, but I signed off on your visit."

The gwyllgi who knew Hadley backed away slowly, except for Ares, who looked desperate for popcorn.

Nostrils flaring, Claudia cocked her head. "I don't understand."

"I'm Hadley Whitaker, the apprentice to the Potentate of Atlanta." She smiled, big and bright. "You required permission to enter my city, and I gave it."

Frown knitting her brow, she continued to stare at Hadley. "Thank you?"

"I would also like to mention, while we're chatting, that I will never, under any circumstances, grant you the same permission where my mate is concerned." Hadley took Midas's hand and unfurled his cramped fingers from the fists he had been making. "I would also really appreciate it if you guys could stop talking about him as if he were produce, let alone a bargain bin find."

"You're his mate?" Claudia sucked on her teeth. "Tisdale is wilier than a coyote."

There was value in allowing Claudia to believe theirs was an arranged mating, and Hadley must have clued in to it too. She didn't contradict Claudia, just let her make her own assumptions. His mother would cackle over them later, but rumors of negotiating such a match would boost her reputation in the eyes of the Knoxville pack.

"I need a drink." Claudia grabbed Hadley by the wrist. "Come with me?"

"It depends." Hadley shot Midas an uncertain glance. "Are you trying to get me alone to murder me so you can claim my mate for yourself?"

The deep belly laugh was too large for Claudia's thin frame, and it sounded more genuine than she had ever been with him.

"Murder you?" She yanked Hadley to her side. "Girl, I want to *learn* from you." Sliding her arm through Hadley's, she started dragging her away. "You landed the Prince of Atlanta. How did you do it?"

The women left, arm in arm, her pack trailing them, and Midas could guess which bar they would end up visiting. Claudia and her pack were banned from all but three, so it wasn't hard to divine their options.

Whistling low, Ford wiped a hand over his mouth. "That went better than expected."

"I'm confused."

"Women," Ford said in agreement. "They do that to a man."

"Claudia sounded ready to give Mom all the credit, but she changed her tune fast."

"Ah. That's one mystery I can solve for you."

Angling his head toward Ford, Midas waited to be enlightened.

"The political alliance aspect would have held water up until Claudia saw you and Hadley together." Ford smiled. "Hadley's not *possessive* of you so much as she's *protective* of you. The former makes sense, if your union is a gambit. The latter, not so much. She would only care if she, well, *cared*."

"Guys are so cute when they have no idea what they're talking about," Ares said from behind them.

Midas realized then exactly who had tipped off Hadley and sent her to his rescue. "What do you mean?"

"Hadley was throwing *I will chew off your arm and beat you to death with it if you touch my man* vibes."

"Huh." Ford rubbed his jaw. "I didn't get that."

"You're used to it." Ares rolled her eyes. "It's not like she pulls it out for special occasions. She's always rocking that vibe when it comes to Midas. She *is* protective of him, but you're nuts if you think she's not possessive of him too."

For some reason, that insight bolstered Midas's mood, and he was tempted to track Hadley down and make sure Claudia understood the feeling was mutual. Last night hadn't gone as planned, but he could try again. Or...he could use her momentary distraction to set a plan of his own into motion.

Yeah.

This impromptu girls' night out might just work in his favor.

The Knoxville pack's visit complicated things, as he was expected to mingle with his mother's guests. Hadley's family would eat up blocks of their time too, but this was life, and no life was perfect. They would always exist in stolen moments stuffed between the cracks of their responsibilities, but that didn't mean he couldn't pry those cracks wider.

Pulling his thoughts back on task, he asked Ford, "Claudia is why you texted?"

"Yes and no. I wanted to give you a heads-up the pack was here, and their alpha was waiting for you, but Captain Gray left a voicemail for me. The cause of the fire has been determined."

"Arson?"

"Magical in nature," he confirmed. "The cleaners are running tests to check the incendiary compounds against the various coven samples they have on file to see if they're a match."

Ares shifted her weight and folded her arms across her chest. "Who else could it be?"

"They've been targeting Hadley hard," Ford growled. "I don't expect this to prove otherwise."

The coven had hoped to add her to their collection so that a witchborn fae could wear her skin and seize control of Atlanta. That was the tune their elder sang when they fought on the outskirts of town just last week, but the notes rang false in his ears then and now. Had she truly been their primary target, they would have struck her down when they first arrived in the city.

Before Linus knew what happened, she would have been gone, and Midas never would have known her. The brutal attack on local shifters had united them, both Midas and Hadley, pack and OPA, against a common enemy. It was the one good thing to come from this tragedy. But grateful as he was for Hadley, none of it would have happened if the elder had been telling them the whole truth.

"Any word on Chef Daaé's last-known whereabouts?"

"The assistant on duty yesterday said he left the chef in the kitchen prepping for your date." Ford ruffled his hair. "Daaé's clan says the same, that he left for work on time but hasn't come home."

"I'll touch base with Hadley," Midas exhaled. "Let her know what we've learned."

"Remind her it's a two-way street." Ford pointed a finger at him. "Information flows both ways."

The OPA was more connected than the pack. They had contacts within every major faction in the city. But he didn't have to ask. If Hadley gleaned information critical to the pack's safety, she would tell him.

"Until we know for certain which of you was targeted," Ford continued, "we can't afford to assume your mate is the one wearing the bull's-eye."

"Knoxville is in town," Ares said quietly. "They're not the most stable pack."

Despite Claudia's belief she was being sized up as a potential mate for him, his mother's sole purpose for inviting the Knoxville pack for a visit was to evaluate the mental state of its new alpha and its dominants.

The pack was under new management as of nine months ago. Claudia had finally seen the writing on the wall, challenged her father, and put him down before he finished running the pack into an early grave.

"I doubt they're involved." Midas doubted they were that organized either. "They have nothing to gain by my death."

"Tisdale made it plain if they didn't clean house," Ford said, "she would send a maid to do it for them."

The maid would have been Midas, as second, and he would have challenged Claudia's father, killed him, and then forced the pack to choose a new alpha who was strong enough to hold the pack and weed out the bad seeds.

"Midas." Ares spelled it out for him. "She killed her old man to prevent anyone else from doing it."

"That's grudge material right there," Ford agreed. "All I'm saying is we need to keep eyes on her."

"Do it." Midas stared through the glass front entryway. "She's with Hadley." He turned. "Do it now."

"An eye for an eye is popular among gwyllgi," Ares allowed. "I'll go. I need to stay active to stay awake."

"Thanks." Midas tried to hide his relief. "Let me know when you're in position?"

"Sure thing." She hesitated. "I'll just grab more coffee from the break room before I go."

"You've been yawning since you met me upstairs." Midas studied her. "Why are you so tired?"

"We're babysitting Liz's nephew." She rubbed her red-rimmed eyes. "He's four months old."

Ford's eyebrows climbed into his hairline. "How did you manage that?"

"Liz's sister is having gallbladder surgery, and her husband is staying at the hospital with her. They needed someone to watch Baby Alex for a few days, and we volunteered for the practice." She smiled, but it didn't reach her eyes. They were too heavy. "He's adorable, oh so adorable, but he's also not thrilled both his parents are MIA. He never sleeps. *Never.* I swear. It's unnatural. He's always awake, and he cries unless you're carrying him. I really, really, *really* hope our kid isn't like this one."

"He'll settle down in a day or so," Ford assured her. "Little ones get ornery when their routines change."

"A day or so?" Ares deflated. "Jay is coming to pick him up tomorrow."

"In that case," Ford said on a laugh, "I hope you've got twenty-four more hours of sleeplessness in you."

Whimpering, Ares trudged off on her quest to load up on caffeine.

"I'll find a spare body to go with her," Ford offered. "She'll need sharp eyes to keep up with Hadley."

Two sets of eyes—and fangs—would make him more comfortable, as long as she didn't catch him at it.

"I appreciate it." Midas's gaze tagged the front door. "Do you think I should go?"

"Pretty sure the reason Claudia wanted to get Hadley alone was to talk about how good you are in bed."

A flash of heat singed his face and then drained away in a rush. "Are you serious?"

"What do you think girls talk about when they're alone?"

"I have no idea."

"You have dwelled in the dark for too long. I'm willing to bet they're talking measuring sticks right now."

Scrubbing his palms over his face, Midas wished he could hide behind his hands forever. "God."

"Come on." Ford slapped him on the back. "Post assignments now, die of shame later."

Later couldn't come fast enough for Midas.

FOUR

The bar Claudia selected had seen better days, probably, but not in my lifetime.

The soles of my new sneakers made sucking noises against the flaking laminate floor when I walked, and dingy stuffing burst from the stools and the booths in the corner. The counter gleamed in the low light, buffed to a polish by the bored young man with nothing better to do and no motivation for extending his efforts to the rest of the place.

"Shots for all my friends," Claudia announced. "Line 'em up and keep 'em coming."

Forty-five minutes later…

Gwyllgi can get drunk, for a few minutes, if they really dedicate themselves to the cause. Otherwise, the alcohol might as well be water. Me? I didn't have a fantastic metabolism, so I had to be careful what and how much I drank in unfamiliar company. Given what had happened last night, I was sipping Coke. Just Coke. That didn't stop Claudia from lining up shots for me too, but I had taken to nudging them her way.

The fact she didn't notice why her shot glass was bottomless said a lot about how deep she had climbed into the bottle. Under different circumstances, I might have been impressed with her single-minded dedication to chasing a buzz. Tonight, it worried me how desperate she was to escape her life, even for a few minutes.

"To the rotten son of a bitch who sired me." Claudia raised her glass. "May he burn in hell for eternity."

The others drank to that, but I didn't know her father from Adam, so I wasn't sure if I should sip or not.

"He's a waste of a shot," Ares murmured in my ear, causing me to jump. "He was a bastard."

"What are you doing here?" I set my Coke on the counter. "Babysitting me?"

"Did the diaper bag give it away?"

"I need to get to HQ." I hopped off my stool. "Be a pal and distract our hostess."

"I knew I should have stayed outside," she grumbled, clearly not a Claudia fan. "I have to pee. Can you wait that long?"

The stack of coffee cups in her hand earned her my sympathy. "Go on."

A vibration in my pocket gave me hope I was about to have an official reason to make my escape.

>>*I'm out of ABS.*

>*What?*

>>*Acrylonitrile Butadiene Styrene.*

>>*Plastic. For the 3D printer. I'm out.*

>*What do you expect me to do about it?*

>>*Bring a few spools to HQ with you?*

Heaving a sigh, I figured this was as close to divine intervention as I was likely to get.

>*Where do I get them?*

Bishop had the address ready to copy/paste in seconds, no surprise, and I promised to play fetch.

A 3D printer was all fun and games until enthusiasm outlasted the machine's ability to keep pace with Bishop's imagination.

"Midas?"

"Nah." I glanced up to find Claudia leaning over my shoulder for a glimpse at the screen. "Work."

"You're not so different from an alpha." She took another shot. "The city's not so different from a pack."

"You're right." The slight blurriness in her eyes concerned me. "I'm not, and it's not."

"No wonder Midas settled on you."

The word *settled* pricked my ego, but I told myself that my insecurities were tainting her intent.

For someone wanting to drill me about how to land a mate, she hadn't asked me a single question.

"I prefer to think I settled on Midas, but sure."

"Tisdale doesn't like me much." She claimed my empty seat. "I get why, I do, but...have you ever been so afraid of paying what you owe that your purse strings shrivel right up?"

"Yeah." An unexpected wave of kinship swept through me. "I have."

"I did have designs on Midas, but not for the reasons you might think."

A twist in my chest bumped my voice an octave. "Oh?"

"I wanted out," she explained. "He was my ticket to the good life."

Before I could tell her I didn't exactly regret him not punching her ticket, she had another drink in hand.

"I was a pack princess." She lifted her glass to the light. "I stood by and watched my father ruin us. When I was a kid, I had an excuse. I couldn't have taken him. You know how gwyllgi dominance fights go. They're brutal." Her lips trembled. "But I've been grown for a long time now and continued to do nothing."

"He was your father." I met her gaze, which startled her, then held it. "Family makes it complicated."

"Truer words." She set the still-full glass back on the counter. "I gave Midas a hard time earlier, it's what he expects from me, but I have to bring new blood into my pack, and he would never leave Atlanta." She flashed me a quick, almost shy grin. "Or you."

"Hey." I had an idea. "Explain this mating business to me. Both fated and chosen."

"You mean you don't know?" Her eyes widened. "He didn't tell you?"

"We've had our hands full lately." I grimaced. "I get the broad strokes, but I want the nitty-gritty."

Absorbing that, she tilted her head in thought. "You know how the whole soul mate thing works?"

"It's a wargs-only club for the most part, right?"

"Yes." She chewed her bottom lip. "There are a few gwyllgi with warg bloodlines only a few generations back who experience it, but it's rare. Incredibly rare. You'd know if you and Midas were one of the lucky ones."

Mood deflating, I had to ask, "How would I know?"

"It creates a bond, a magical tether, that joins your soul to his."

Jaw dropping, I debated marching back to the Faraday and smacking Midas for his secret-keeping.

Unless Claudia was wrong. Or lying. Either of those would make me happier than I was now.

Like everyone else, she had wanted Midas for reasons that had nothing to do with who *he* was but who his mother was, and that was all kinds of messed up in my opinion. He deserved better. I loved him, for himself and only for himself, but he deserved better than me too.

I had more baggage than Hartsfield-Jackson, and Atlanta's airport was the busiest in the world.

But he loved me.

And I...I was so far past ever letting him go.

"Otherwise, mating is marriage without the dress, rings, or cake."

Snorting out a laugh, I teased her, "None of the fun stuff?"

"Basically." She rolled her eyes in agreement. "I did see a guy go down on one knee once, but mostly the mating is assumed in more traditional packs. A couple sticks together long enough, and *bam*. Their scents entwine, their lives mingle, and the pack views them as a mated pair. End of story."

"Like a common-law marriage."

"The only exception to the rule is with alphas and future alphas. They're expected to put on a show."

"Oh joy."

The ringmaster of our show would be Tisdale, I had no doubts on that score.

Yet another tidbit Midas had neglected to share with me.

Probably out of fear I would suddenly catch the flu.

Again.

Frak.

"What did I miss?" Ares rejoined us. "Sorry it took so long. I fell asleep on the toilet."

"Thanks for sharing." I offered her the shot on the counter before me. "Maybe this will help?"

"Can't hurt." She tossed it back, and her eyes watered as she coughed out, "What the hell is that?"

"Paint thinner," Claudia told her with a wink for me. "You guys are heading out?"

"Yeah." I checked the time on my phone. "I have to get to work."

"Do you think...?" Claudia studied her hands. "Would you like to grab dinner one night?"

The ache in her voice, the dip in her chin, the fact she couldn't meet my eyes as she asked cemented an answer before I considered the ramifications. "Sure."

"We can make it a girls' night." Ares invited herself. "I'll need a day or two to catch up on sleep first."

"That would be great." Claudia jerked me into an impulsive hug. "Text me the time and place?"

"Sure." Passing over my phone, I let her enter her contact information. "See you later."

Once Ares and I cleared the bar and crossed the street, I gave her a bland look. "Girls' night?"

"Tisdale would murder me in my sleep if I left you alone with Claudia."

"She seems nice enough."

"Her dad was nice enough too, once upon a time."

"Sins of the father, really?"

"Claudia was his beta. A lot of the blood on his hands is on hers too."

I had no room to talk. I had done terrible things. I had blood on my hands that would never wash out.

But a wake-up call had saved me. My friends had saved me. When I least deserved their mercy.

Claudia and I weren't friends after a few drinks, but I could sympathize with her position. She struck me as a woman without many people to confide in, and she had chosen me. That didn't indebt me to her, but it did sway me enough to hope that I could become a positive influence while she was here.

We can't know until we glance behind us who or what will alter the course of our lives forever. A kind word, a hug, even *listening* worked miracles. For someone who lacked the support system I had, I could afford to lend that word, give that hug, or sit and let my ears do all the work.

"Who sent you to play I Spy?" I changed the topic. "Ford, Midas, or Tisdale?"

Chuckling, she stretched her arms over her head. "Why pick one when I can blame all three?"

"You're wiped." I shoved her, and she actually stumbled. "I'm going to work. You should go sleep."

"I can go home but..."

"The baby?"

"The baby," she agreed. "Cutest little torture device you've ever seen."

"I can give you the keys to our place. You can nap wherever."

Her lips parted, and a *yes* poised there, but she shook her head. "It wouldn't be fair."

"The offer stands, for either of you, if you need it."

"Thanks." She fell back a step. "I'm out."

Once she had turned to begin the walk back to the Faraday, I got out my phone and began texting the string of code back and forth to locate HQ's location for the day. As luck would have it, Bishop had set up shop across town from where I was, which meant I either had a lot of walking to do or a Swyft to call.

About to try my luck with the rideshare app, I hesitated when a glint caught my eye.

Having learned from past mistakes, I didn't chase after it. I texted Bishop, and *then* I chased after it.

Ambrose shot ahead of me, which was ten kinds of strange, as he was never one to volunteer for work, but he was invested in that glint too.

All of which told me whatever caused it was magical in nature and probably wasn't anything good.

For a second, I thought I was seeing the fading trail of a Martian Roach and cursed under my breath. We had busted our butts to get rid of them, but roaches being roaches, I figured there were still one or two we had missed. Upon closer inspection, the sparkles weren't quite right for that, thank the goddess.

About the time I got near enough to track the origin, Ambrose glanced over his shoulder.

Pivoting on my heel, I turned in time to watch the bar where I had left Claudia burst into flames.

The raw force of the explosion punched me backward and threw me sliding across the asphalt.

Once my ears stopped ringing, I rose on raw palms and abraded knees to survey the damage.

Ambrose hovered beside me, hands on his hips, his head angled where the glimmer had been.

"Thanks," I muttered. "You couldn't have helped?"

A shrug rolled through his shoulders.

"No chocolate for you," I grunted as I stood and tested to make sure nothing was broken. "Jerk."

Big surprise, the shadow wasn't paying attention to me. He had already returned his focus to where the glint had been, a distraction that might have saved my life. Any closer to the blast, and it would have roasted me like a marshmallow.

Others hadn't been so lucky, and I set off at a limping jog as I dialed Bishop. "I need you to—"

"Already done." Keys tapped in the background. "The fire department is on the way. Paramedics too."

"Midas?"

"He was my second call."

"Thanks." I had reached the epicenter, and the heat made my eyes water. "I have to go."

A string of impressive curses left his mouth before I ended the call, but they were in Faelic, or whatever obscure language he spoke, and I didn't understand more than the gist.

A wall of fire licked the sky, and the stench of black magic charred the air. The closer I inched, the higher the roaring flames burned until I retreated a safe distance to watch as the bar, and the bar alone, spouted plumes too thick for me to see more than a foot in front of me without retreating farther.

Phone in hand, I did what protocol demanded and called Tisdale. "We have a problem."

"Claudia?"

The immediate leap made my heart hurt for the untried alpha. "We went to a bar tonight."

"Oh, God." Tisdale lost her cool. "Is it still standing?"

"Not for much longer." I exhaled a ragged breath when the sirens reached my ears. "It's on fire."

"Is...?" She cleared her throat. "Is she...?"

"I don't know." I had the urge to rub my upper arms, but sweat beaded on my forehead. I was nowhere near cold, yet I was chilled to the bone. "When I left for work, she was still there with her pack. Ares and I chatted for a while out on the sidewalk, but then she headed home. I was leaving for HQ as the bar exploded."

"Exploded?"

"Yes," I confirmed. "This wasn't simple arson. This was a bomb."

Like the one that went off in my apartment.

"Like the one that went off in your apartment," she echoed my thoughts exactly.

"The fire department is here, so I need to go." I had other company too. "I just wanted to update you."

"Thanks, sweetheart."

With those words ringing in my ears, she ended the call. I was still staring at the screen, wondering if I misheard, when Midas yanked me into his arms and plastered me against his chest.

"You're all right," he breathed into my hair. "Thank God."

"Claudia and her pack were in there." I fisted his shirt. "I don't know if…"

"She's okay." He gave me enough slack to lean back and see around him. "One of her packmates got sick from the bar food they ordered, and she walked them back to their hotel. She must have left minutes after you."

Heady relief swirled through me, and I braced my forehead against his chest. "The others?"

"She came in with five." He stroked my head. "How many were with you?"

"Twice that." I hadn't counted them, but they had filled the bar. "Goddess."

A scream too big to fit a human throat belted out behind us as Claudia hit her knees on the pavement.

Shoving away from Midas, I ran to Claudia and dropped beside her, afraid to offer her comfort.

Alphas weren't supposed to show weakness. She might not have been alpha for long, but she had grown up under the direct rule of one. The tears in her eyes, the tremble in her body, the way she rocked back and forth, arms wrapped around her middle, might spell doom for her reign if her pack was as unstable as I had been led to believe.

A pack used to cruelty ought to find her grief a balm, but maybe not if they had no souls left to soothe.

"What happened?" Head bowed, too heavy to lift, she stared at nothing. "*How* did this happen?"

"A bomb." I might as well confess the rest. "A magical bomb."

"Who would do such a thing?" Voice a thready rasp, she asked the most damning question. "Why?"

Officially, the fire at Choco-Loco was still under investigation. The cleaners hadn't published their findings to their database, which meant all we had to go on was what Gray told us at the scene. It would be easy to omit that, to cast this incident in a better light, a less damning one, but word would get back to her. The line between what happened last night, and the pack's interest thanks to Midas's involvement, would get drawn quickly.

I had a choice to make, and a split-second to earn an ally or an enemy.

"A coven of witchborn fae have infiltrated our city." I gazed into the flames. "This...was meant for me."

Once she started nodding, she didn't stop, and when she finally did, the spark drained out of her.

"I'm so sorry for your loss."

"I want in." Sucking in a breath, she lifted her head and cleared her throat. "I want to help."

Right before my eyes, she transformed from a mourning, broken woman to a cold, determined alpha.

"This slight will not go unpunished," she growled, crimson rolling across her eyes as she stood.

Midas joined us then, and so did Ford, but her own people kept back, cringing away from her fury.

"We'll help you get vengeance," Midas vowed to Claudia, but his eyes were on me. "The coven has been a plague on Atlanta for too long."

"I'll walk you to your hotel," Ford offered, his voice polite, without a trace of the pity that might send her crashing back to her knees. "We'll provide transportation for your pack."

"Thank you." She nodded to him. "I can't..." She squared her shoulders. "I need to move."

That right there, the way Ford anticipated her needs and met them, made him an invaluable asset to the pack, and an excellent friend.

"I'll call Bishop," I volunteered. "He'll coordinate with Swyft and your hotel to get everyone there."

Swyft had stolen all the paranormal business in town, but the personal vehicle factor made renting a van or other large vehicle on short notice easier. Lots of soccer moms and dads, parents in general, had spun their hulking rides into moneymakers.

Bobbing her head, Claudia went to address the cluster of pack-mates that remained after tonight's fiasco. I couldn't tell if they took comfort from her words. No one would look at her. I couldn't decide if it was a fear response to her, to the situation, or to the shadow of the former alpha that loomed over their pack, but I didn't imagine their exhales of relief when Claudia strode off, Ford in her wake, her hands clenched into fists.

"This just got more complicated." I leaned into Midas. "Will this blow back onto the pack?"

"No." Midas snaked his arm around my shoulders. "Mother warned Claudia about the coven."

Not that I was pointing fingers, but I did wonder, "Why didn't Claudia postpone her trip?"

"Mom awards an annual scholarship, more or less, for new alphas who inherit packs in distress." His arm tightened, forcing us closer. "She takes one under her wing for a month, gives them a room at the den—not in the den, but in the house—and there's a considerable financial aid packet that goes along with it."

"I had no idea."

"No one outside the packs would have reason to know." He smiled down at me. "Now you do."

"Claudia was hoping to snag it," I realized. "She's asking for help to heal her pack the only way she knows how."

"That's my guess." He hesitated. "She has made advances in the past but—"

"I don't think she'll bother you again." I kissed his worried brow. "She was just yanking your chain."

I explained to him what she told me, that she would have taken an out if he had offered, but it was too late for that now, for either of them.

Fingers drumming my arm, he glanced down at me. "You two got along well."

"Yeah." I saw a lot of myself in her. "I guess we did."

"You didn't talk about...me...did you?"

Now it was my turn to frown. "Only in the abstract sense, why?"

"No reason." He pivoted as Gray trotted over to us. "Hey."

"Twice in one week?" He was out of breath, and his hair slicked to his scalp. "What the hell did you do?"

"Nothing I hadn't already done," I assured him. "Until now, the coven has been denned up, licking their wounds."

"A very gwyllgi turn of phrase for you," he rumbled, laughing.

"You know how it is with old mated couples." I smiled at him. "Finishing each other's sentences, wearing each other's clothes, stealing each other's food..."

"Stealing a predator's food?" Gray's eyebrows climbed. "It must be love."

"It is," Midas assured him. "Otherwise, she would have gnawed off my hands by now."

Laughter boomed out of Gray's deep chest, so at odds with the grim scene around us, and it felt good.

We all coped with grief in different ways, and laughter was the least self-destructive option.

"Aubrey has the fire under control." He wiped the amusement off his face. "He says it tastes the same. It's slightly off from what we encountered at the battle with the coven, but it's identical to last night's fire."

Part of me wished I could share the intel, use Aubrey as a source, but we had a promise to Gray to uphold. We would keep Aubrey's identity a secret for as long as possible. It was the only way to give the teen a taste of a normal life, considering what he was and what he was capable of.

But if he ever lost control, if the citizens ever paid for it, I would learn firsthand how Linus had felt during the past year when he took personal responsibility for me and my actions.

Second chances didn't come free, and they didn't come cheap. Someone always, *always* paid for them.

"The cleaners are on their way," he kept going. "I understand several of the individuals are gwyllgi?"

"From a visiting pack," I confirmed. "The alpha was lucky to escape with her life."

"We'll update you if we learn anything else." Gray bowed his head. "Let me know if we can help."

"I appreciate that."

Thinking back to how Claudia had pieced herself together in front of me, I doubted we would have to lean on Gray or his pride for help. Guilt must be eating her alive. She had known the risks, but she had accepted them. For their sake. And hers.

After what Midas told me, I couldn't blame her. The scholarship was nice and all, but I was willing to bet what she had been after was Tisdale's seal of approval. That would go further than a check or a few weeks' worth of lessons.

Alone again, Midas and I looked at one another, but I was the one to break the silence.

"There's already been too much collateral damage." I twisted one of the silver rings on my fingers, the one responsible for my Hadley persona. "Now my family is here."

"Don't go down that road."

"This could have been them. Addie and Boaz. They could have been in the lobby tonight, taken her offer, the same as me." I forced myself to leave the ring alone before my glamour flickered. "They could have stayed to grab a bite after I left." I swallowed hard. "They could be dead."

The night Addie and Boaz decided to drop in early was the first we had seen of the coven since the battle. Coincidence? Nah. I don't think so. More like a carefully executed strike against me, right to the heart. But why not blow up their hotel? Or their Swyft? Or the restaurant where they ate dinner?

They had gone after Midas and me and then Claudia and me. I was definitely the common denominator. Did that mean my family was safe as long as I wasn't with them? Or did it mean I had gone so far around the paranoia bend I ought to be crafting my own tinfoil hat right about now?

"Hadley."

"Our inner circle is feeding them information." I read the same pain in my heart in his eyes. "There's no other explanation."

Another packmate lost. No, lost wasn't the right word. *Stolen.* One with decent security clearance if they had ready access to Midas and me. We hadn't suspected a breach until now, so the coven mole or moles were a light touch, aided by wearing others' skins and partial, if not total, access to the hosts' memories.

A worse possibility slithered down my spine, that a member of my team might have been compromised. The information and resources available to OPA staff posed a much deadlier threat if they had been turned against me.

"I'm sorry." I touched his arm, echoing his grief while pulling him back from the ledge. "We'll find them, and we'll stop them."

Midas bobbed his head, and his breath came out harsh. He cut his eyes toward me then almost smiled.

Happy to distract him, I pressed for details. "What?"

"I believe you." He kissed my forehead. "You have never let me down."

"Give it time." I patted his chest. "You haven't known me very long."

The negative comment earned me a scowl, but he lost his chance to lecture me on self-worth when the screen lit on my phone. "Yeah?"

"You didn't call back," Bishop grumped. "What's happening over there?"

A snort escaped me. "Like you don't have eyes on me right now?"

"Smoke," he clipped out. "Makes it kind of hard to see out of overhead cameras."

Smarting from the well-deserved smackdown, I rattled off a quick report in my best potentate voice.

"Station Thirteen has the fire under control. Claudia is alive. A third of her pack left the bar when she did, so they're okay. The others…" I stared at the blaze. "She wants a piece of the coven for what they did to her people. We need to keep her in the loop, or she'll go vigilante on us."

Of that, I had no doubt. It's what I would do in her situation.

"Are you coming in tonight?"

"That was the plan, after the bar." I rubbed my forehead. "Addie and Boaz came in last night, which I'm sure you already know, you stalker. The rest of my guests must be here too, though I didn't think to ask."

A silence lingered during which I heard his teeth grinding.

Family? Or city? Which would I choose? Which was my priority?

Suddenly, this felt like a test I could fail, and if I did, he would lose respect for me.

Paranoia? Yeah. Probably. Maybe?

"Since it's pretty obvious I'm being targeted, that means we'll be moving my family from their hotel into the Faraday for the duration of their visit." The Faraday, despite its hiccups with me, still far outclassed any simple hotel on security. Even if it meant putting my mother underfoot for several days. "Can you coordinate that with them for me?"

"What will you be doing?"

"What do you think?"

As much as I wanted to rush to Boaz and Addie, they were both alive. *Safe.* We had time.

These people…

They had been guests in my city, and their time had run out.

On my clock.

At dawn, when I laid my head on my pillow, I would never fall asleep if I witnessed this then spent the night out at museums and nice restaurants like their deaths didn't matter, like the attack on my city, my people, to get to me, didn't matter.

"Put two in the field," I told him. "I'll check the burn sites, see if I can catch our firebug reminiscing, but I want eyes on me. I want to know if I'm being followed in a way I can't track."

"Milo and I will do the honors," he volunteered. "Sorry your reunion has gone bust."

"This is more important."

And a busy schedule also meant a valid reason for avoiding my mother.

Hello, silver lining.

"That glint I texted you about? Can you check surveillance in the area? See if you can isolate its origin?"

There was no guarantee it was connected to the explosion, but I wanted an answer.

"Already on it."

"I need to check in with Abbott too." I expected no miracles, but I could always hope. "Maybe he's made progress on a field test for rooting out who's been infected by any Martian Roaches we've missed or anyone whose skin is being worn by the coven."

The last two days made it more time critical than ever to ferret out any coven members in our midst. We had to act, but lips moved faster than we could mobilize. We had to plug the leaks before there was any hope of washing our hands clean of them.

"I can handle that," Midas volunteered. "I need to update Mom anyway."

"I called her earlier," I confessed. "I figured with it being pack related, she would want to know first."

"Thanks." A bright smile creased his face. "I appreciate that."

"Why are you goofy grinning at me?"

Bishop, who was still on the line, said, "He likes that you're getting close with his mom."

Annoyed with him being nosy, I ended the call without another word.

"I do like that you called her. It's a big improvement over the flu."

A flush threatened to burn my cheeks, but my face was already scalded. "Will I never live that down?"

"Gwyllgi have long memories, so no." He chuckled. "You won't."

"Crap," I muttered, half serious. "That means the same trick won't work twice."

"You'll think of something else, I'm sure."

"I can't decide if I appreciate your vote of confidence or if I'm insulted by it."

"Gray has this under control." He nudged me toward the sidewalk. "We should leave him to it."

A shiver of unease swept through me. "Where are you going?"

"With you." The way he looked at me called my sanity into question. "Where else?"

FIVE

The predator under Midas's skin didn't care that Hadley had survived a bomb. Make that *two* bombs. Or that she could survive another. He made his calls and sent his texts while keeping her in arm's reach. She humored him, though it must have annoyed her for him to hover. He couldn't help it with his instincts in his ears, roaring he must protect her at any cost, when she was more than capable of watching her own back.

The smoke from the bar fire had sunk into their clothes and hair, dulling his keen nose, but he still noticed the moment a fresh scent joined them on the street.

The shadow Hadley cast turned its head and paused while she kept walking, then it drifted back to her.

A Low Society necromancer must not pose much of a temptation if Ambrose dismissed him so quickly.

That, or he knew Boaz Pritchard was off-limits.

The punishing stride Hadley had maintained all night didn't falter. "What do you think you're doing?"

"I came to check on you," Boaz called, slightly out of breath from his jog. "What do you think?"

"You should be—"

"—where it's safe?" His winded laughter strained him. "I'm no potentate, but my job isn't a cakewalk."

A flash of insight into where she had learned the habit of talking over him blinded Midas.

"You need to go back to the Faraday." She didn't so much as turn her head. "This isn't your fight."

"I'm here." Boaz caught up with them. "And I'm good at taking hits."

That was the exact wrong thing to say to Hadley, and she stopped short, spun on her heel, and growled.

The slight widening of Boaz's eyes told Midas he hadn't seen Hadley in work mode often enough to grasp Amelie was gone. Hadley wasn't his little sister. She was more. So much more. And he had to accept that if he wanted a place in her life.

"People died tonight because of me, because they were in the wrong place at the wrong time."

"Goddess," he breathed, and his expression showed he was piecing it together. "You're the target?"

"There's a coven of witchborn fae in the city, and they're gunning for me."

Faint lines bracketed his mouth. "What do you want me to do?"

"Go back to the Faraday, to Addie. Keep her safe. Take our dad to see the art installation then go home." Hurt flashed across her face. "I can't lose you too. You're all…" She glanced at Midas, took his hand. "You were all I had left until I came here, but I'm not…" She bit down on the words. "I can't worry about you going off half-cocked and still do my job."

"All right." He scrubbed a palm over his scalp. "I'll do it on one condition."

An exaggerated eye roll, the familiar language of siblings, was her answer.

"Tell me you're happy." His jaw hardened. "And mean it."

A dull throb punched Midas behind his ribs, and Hadley must

have sensed how much the answer meant to him, because she tightened her fingers on his.

"I love my life here," she said, truth bright in every word. "I love my job, my friends, my purpose." She smiled up at Midas, and his heart turned over. "I love you too." Turning back to Boaz, she exhaled. "I make a difference here. I'm a different person here. I matter."

"You've always mattered—"

"—to you, yes. To our little brother, yes. But I was never myself in Savannah. I didn't know who I was there. I got lost, so lost, and I had no idea how far I had strayed from the path until it was too late to find my way back."

"I'm glad you've found what you were looking for," he rasped, "but I don't want you to lose you either."

"You never will," she promised, dropping Midas's hand. "I'll always be your annoying little sister." She walked into his arms, and he squeezed her until she squeaked. "Or I would be, if you would hurry up and marry Addie."

A low grunt rose up his throat. "I'm trying."

"Try harder."

From Hadley, Midas knew long engagements were common in the Society. Years could pass before either party got antsy about finalizing the paperwork. Gwyllgi tended to bond hard and fast, and mate within a year of meeting. Yet another deviation from the norm Hadley must have expected in a partner.

Releasing her, Boaz took a step back. "You would call if you needed me, right?"

"Nope." She patted his cheek. "I would most certainly not." She shoved him. "Now get."

"Take care of her." Boaz pointed a warning finger at Midas. "I would hate to make Lethe an only child."

"Lethe would eat your face." Hadley chuckled. "So would Tisdale." She waved. "Buh-bye."

Grumbling under his breath, Boaz crammed his hands into his pockets and started walking.

"I'll text Hank." Midas pulled out his phone. "That way we know Boaz did as he was told."

"There's a first time for everything."

"We're going to stop them." Midas tugged on one of her curls. "It's going to be all right."

The quick nod she gave him didn't convince him, but he understood her worry. Her family couldn't have picked a worse time to visit, but they were here now. The best she could hope for was they would view the art installation and go, as Hadley requested, before anyone got hurt.

THE SIGHT PROVED useless in identifying new hidden nooks or crannies where what remained of the coven might be holed up while they prepared to strike again. Midas suspected they had moved their operation outside the city, their base at least, and Atlanta's suburbs were a labyrinthine warren in comparison.

Bishop had shadowed Midas and Hadley all night, his texts were proof of that, but Midas hadn't sensed him once.

And Bishop, in turn, hadn't sensed anyone else following them.

That didn't mean much when anyone who blended in could hang out in the lobby and get a detailed rundown of almost everyone's schedule, social life developments, and horoscope sign reading for the night. Gwyllgi loved to gossip almost as much as they loved to eat.

An enforcer working out of the Faraday made the most sense as their firebug. The OPA was a possibility, but it fit that an enforcer overheard a rumor about their date night and set their plans in motion. An enforcer would also have known ahead of time when the Knoxville pack was in town, and how much chaos they brought with them. An enforcer could have made certain they were in the lobby, hidden in plain sight, to overhear any plans that were made. That could explain why the bar blew *after* Hadley left.

A bomb took time to place, set, and detonate. To get in and out again on the fly would prove difficult. To go undetected? Almost impossible. Unless you were a local the visitors had recognized and dismissed as a threat.

Had the Knoxville pack's arrival sparked this latest outbreak of violence? Or was the coven lashing out in response to Hadley's family visiting? Either way, the combination formed a perfect storm of distractions.

"What are you thinking so hard about?"

Midas glanced over at Hadley to discover they had circled back around to the Faraday. "Everything."

"I get that." She took his hand. "Are you up for visiting Abbott with me?"

"You just don't want to be alone with him."

"He's started harping on me taking vitamins," she grumbled. "How does that make me less flammable?"

"Maybe he wants you to live a long and healthy life, flame retardation aside?"

"Please?" She leaned in and fluttered her lashes at him. "I'll pay for your cooperation in hot wings."

Neither of them had felt up to eating on patrol, but a headache was settling in from the lack of calories.

"Only if you spring for extra ranch." He led her to the elevator. "Abbott is only pushy because he cares."

"He's worse than a mother hen." Her shoulders drooped. "Always pecking at me."

The doors slid open on Abbott, who stood waiting for them, and she greeted him with a low groan.

"How did you know?" She curled her lip at the pills on his palm. "It was Hank, wasn't it?"

Mumbling death threats, she picked up the red and purple children's chewable vitamins and ate them.

Midas kept his tone light. "Flintstones?"

"She won't swallow pills." Abbott held up a bottle. "This is the only brand she'll accept."

"Vitamins are horse pills," she complained. "Plus, they taste funny."

"Mom takes these individually wrapped cubes that resemble Snickers bars. Mybite, maybe?"

Hadley snapped her heads toward him. "What?"

"Hey." Hands up, Midas stepped back. "I would have mentioned it sooner if I had known."

"Find me that brand," she bargained with Abbott, "and I solemnly swear I will devour nougaty vitamins of my own free will."

"Done." He dug out his phone and sent a text. "I'll forward the information after Tisdale verifies."

"Thank you." She worked her mouth like the remaining grit bothered her. "Now, we have to talk."

Mood brighter, Abbott led them to his office. "Come on in."

Once Hadley and Midas sank into their respective chairs, Abbott shut them in and locked the door.

Leaning forward, Hadley asked, "Have you made any progress on field testing for hosts?"

"Yes and no." He sat on the edge of his desk. "We have a test that's accurate four out of five times."

"That sounds good."

"The problem is how the test is administered." He linked his hands on his lap. "Accuracy is dependent on a fresh blood sample akin to a diabetic pricking their finger to test their blood sugar levels."

"Not exactly inconspicuous," Midas said, reasoning it out. "The host and—whatever we're calling the skins being worn—would know they had screwed up and were under suspicion."

"Blood sugar testing takes seconds." Hadley frowned. "It would be harder for them to dodge us than if we had to send off samples for results."

"I doubt they would let it get that far." Midas crossed his ankle over his knee. "They would see the finger stick and bolt. Or attack."

A close cousin to amusement brightened her face. "That would make it even easier to spot them."

"Unless they suffer trypanophobia," Abbott explained at their blank expressions. "Fear of needles?"

"Okay," Hadley rallied, "so it's an imperfect solution."

"Right now, the kit consists of a lancing device, lancets, and a meter," Abbott explained. "I have one."

"One meter?" Hadley bounced her leg. "Or one to spare?"

"Both." Abbott rose to his feet. "You can use the prototype, should an opportunity present itself."

"I'm not sure how much good it will do." She held out her hand. "It can't hurt, though."

Actually, it would hurt. A lot. For such tiny needles, they inflicted a disproportionate amount of pain.

Abbott lifted a finger and left the room, and her arm dropped to her side as she waited for his return.

"Where is Superman and his X-ray vision when you need him?"

Midas ran a hand down her back. "I don't recall him spending much time in Atlanta."

Rising with a sigh, she rolled her shoulders to stretch them. "We need our own superhero."

"We have one."

The flicker of a smile was there and gone before he could savor it, but she plopped down on his lap, which was even better.

"Any ideas for my outfit?" She traced a finger over his lips. "I've watched crap-tons of science fiction and fantasy movies. Women end up draped in chains, cinched in leather, or poured into spandex. Which will it be?"

The hard clench in his gut was nothing new when it came to Hadley, but his desire still held the power to surprise him. It had been so long since he craved touch, since he had allowed himself to want, he tingled with need for her.

"It depends on if you plan on wearing this outfit in public or strictly when we're at home."

A throat cleared as Abbott rejoined them. "I hope I'm not interrupting."

"Not at all." Hadley kissed Midas's cheek. "You have the kit ready?"

"I do." Abbott reclaimed his perch. "Now." He clasped his hands. "Are you on any birth control?"

Hadley shot out of Midas's lap and was standing at the door as his arms closed over air.

"I'm not having this discussion." She slapped her hands over her ears, bolted, then called back, "Ever."

Midas chuckled until Abbott reached behind him, opened a drawer, and tossed him a box he fumbled twice.

"You are being careful?" Abbott folded his arms over his chest. "You're newly mated, and with the city in turmoil at the moment, I doubt either of you are ready to entertain the idea of pups."

Slow heat climbed from the base of Midas's neck up into his cheeks. "We've been careful."

More careful than the tatters of his male pride allowed him to confess, even to his healer and friend.

"That ought to last you a while." Abbott rose. "Call down, and I can have more sent up as needed."

The tips of Midas's ears flamed red when he noticed the box was full of condoms. Dozens of them.

"I should go check on Hadley." He shot to his feet then lifted the box. "Um, thanks."

"Not at all."

Halfway out the door, Abbott cleared his throat again. "The kit?"

"Yes." Midas threw on the brakes and pivoted toward him. "The kit." He took the pouch. "Thanks."

The healer's chuckles flowed into the hallway and chased Midas into the elevator.

"That man…" Hadley began, palms on her flushed cheeks. "He's so…so…"

"Yes," Midas agreed, torn between sharing his pain and hiding the evidence.

Sadly, the silver panels clued her into the presence of the box in his hand, and she started laughing.

"He didn't." She leaned around Midas. "He did *not*."

"Oh." Midas handed them over. "He did." He cringed. "He also offered to send up more as needed."

The doors opened on the top floor before she could answer, and she stepped out into the hall.

"I smell Boaz." Midas tipped his head to one side. "Addie too."

The hope in her voice almost trumped his embarrassment. "From last night?"

"From about an hour ago."

The door swung open, and Boaz stood on the threshold. "I thought I heard voices."

"I have to talk to Linus about letting randos into our home," she muttered at Midas. "Hello, Boaz."

"What do you have there?" He stole the box with glee. "Bonbons? Truffles? Cup…" he recoiled as if a snake sat on his open palm, "…cakes?"

"Give me those," Hadley hissed and snatched them back.

Addie popped her head out into the hall, and she beamed at Hadley and then at him.

"Hi, guys." She wiggled her fingers. "I made dinner. I hope you don't mind."

"Not at all," Hadley said stiffly. "Make yourselves at home."

"We haven't eaten tonight." Midas rested his palm against Hadley's lower back. "Thanks for cooking."

"That—" Boaz pointed, rediscovering his voice, "—is a box of condoms."

"Yes, dear." Addie wrapped her hand around his finger, led him inside, and mouthed, *"Sorry."*

When Hadley made no move to follow Addie into their apartment, Midas gave her a gentle shove.

"You need to eat," she said under her breath. "It's not good for you to go so long without food."

In reversing their roles, she found her feet, and he was happy to let her use him as her motivation.

"I hope you like Italian." Addie stood over the stove. "We've got chicken parm, cheesy baked ziti, garlic bread, bolognaise, and pappardelle that's a little thinner noodle than I meant for it to be."

"It smells fantastic." Midas's mouth watered. "You made all this?"

"It's cheaper to eat in than to go out." She set a stack of plates and a handful of silverware on the counter, indicating dinner would be served buffet-style. "Plus, we can talk here without fear of slipping up or being overheard."

"Hadley is learning to cook," Midas bragged. "She's very good."

"That's great, Hadley." Addie tossed a hand towel over her shoulder. "If you're not too busy, we can do this again tomorrow night." She beamed at her. "We can tag team dinner."

Hadley wasn't the only one more comfortable in the role of caretaker, and in Addie's case, he understood why she felt the need to fuss over Hadley. Her little sister had suffered from chronic fatigue syndrome and fibromyalgia. She had been housebound and often bedridden from the pain and exhaustion. Addie had been her caretaker, and just because this Hadley wasn't *her* Hadley, she couldn't seem to flip the switch of sisterly affection.

"I can try." Hadley thawed, unable to resist Addie's warmth. "You're more advanced than I am."

"You can set the menu," she offered. "I'll help you learn to cook whatever you like while I'm here."

"That would be amazing."

The sisters chatted while Midas and Boaz filled plates for them and then made their own. They moved to the dining room and settled in for a family dinner that reminded Midas of growing up in the den.

After his second helping, Midas sat back in his chair. "Are you comfortable in your temporary quarters?"

"The apartment is great." Addie pushed a tomato cube around her plate. "Four bedrooms, so plenty of space for everyone."

The reminder of who else had joined them shot tension into Hadley's shoulders. "How is...Dad?"

"Good." Her smile was more of a grimace. "Ready to see the art installation, but it opens tomorrow."

"He's butting heads with Mother." Boaz rolled his eyes. "They weren't thrilled with the original hotel choice. Now they're not thrilled with staying in a guest apartment. They've fought over food, luggage, and the choice of rental vehicle. I half expected them to start yelling 'his leg touched my leg' or 'she keeps looking at me' during that last half hour of the drive."

"They're both used to being top dog." Addie rubbed the spot between her eyes. "I'm with Boaz, though. I was ready to muzzle them halfway into the trip." She flinched. "No offense meant, Midas." She bit her lip. "Not that you are a dog, but I don't want you to think that I think that—"

"You're fine," he assured her. "You didn't offend me."

"So." Hadley crunched on garlic bread. "The real reason you keep inviting yourselves over is revealed."

Grimacing, Addie dropped her fork. "We're not imposing, are we?"

"No." Hadley reached across the table to her. "I'm teasing."

Fingers linking, she gave a playful tug. "Then you won't mind if we stay and watch a movie?"

"I don't want to say we're desperate." Boaz scratched his jaw. "But we're desperate."

Withdrawing to her side of the table, Hadley leaned into Midas and whispered, "Do you mind?"

Though he would rather spend the predawn hours cuddling her, alone, he said, "Not at all."

"The man of the house says you're welcome to stay."

Amused, Midas countered, "Only because the woman of the house asked so nicely."

A sour expression twisted Boaz's features, but Addie was all but clapping her hands with glee.

The Pritchards had disowned Amelie after her crimes and her bargain with Ambrose were exposed. For that reason alone, Midas understood why Hadley hadn't asked after her mother and why the others kept mentions of Matron Pritchard to a minimum. He couldn't shake the impression Hadley's silence stemmed from more than that one act of betrayal, but she would explain, when she was ready.

And if she never unburdened herself, he would accept that too. Just as she had accepted his past.

The four of them pitched in to make cleanup fast and painless, and they reclaimed their spots on the couch from the night before. They settled on an action flick to balance the scales after the romcom, but the movie didn't matter. The point was spending time together, and Midas wanted Hadley to soak up all the love she could get before Boaz and Addie returned home.

With Hadley using his shoulder as her pillow, Midas lowered his lashes to watch her observe her brother teasing Addie, who humored him with softness in her eyes. He knew she worried about them, but Midas saw the affection between them. Their marriage might have been arranged, but they were trying to make it work.

Midas wasn't sure when he fell asleep, only that he woke in an empty apartment with a note stuck to his forehead and a blanket pulled up to his chin.

A knock on the door provided him with the reason he was up earlier than usual, and he was tempted to pretend he didn't hear and go back to sleep.

After he removed the note, saving it for when his eyes were less blurry, he trudged to the door and found Ares waiting on him with blood smeared across one cheek.

Yeah.

Some nights it didn't pay to get out of bed.

SIX

As I sipped my second café mocha of the night, I listened to Reece's update, plucked straight from the cleaners' database, and regretted the sweet fullness curdling my stomach.

The wall in front of me was painted an unrelieved black, and the two rows of monitors anchored there blended in when not in use. The upper row held four monitors, each about thirty-four inches and filled with the shadowed outline of a teammate. We had a full house tonight, which was always nice. The lower row mirrored the one above it, but those were always on and flashing surveillance mooched off city cameras as well as our own private mounts.

"Station Thirteen retrieved fourteen bodies," he announced. "Eleven of those were gwyllgi, so it's safe to assume they're the Knoxville pack members Claudia reported missing. We'll have conclusive results in two weeks. The other patrons are unidentified, except for one regular whose wife called in to ask if her husband had been found since he, and I quote 'parked his ass on the same stool five nights a week and drank until he fell off it.'"

The cleaners would handle identifying the remains and notifying the families, so there wasn't much for me to do on that front but wait for the results and see what dots they connected for us later.

"We're almost through the list of Choco-Loco employees." Anca rustled papers on her desk. "All the alibis we've been given have checked out so far, but this changes things. Under the circumstances, I doubt we're dealing with an employee."

"Send me half of what's left." Lisbeth vanished from the screen then returned with a mug. "I can help."

"Thank you," Anca said warmly. "I appreciate it."

"Once we eliminate Choco-Loco's staff, we'll get started on the bar workers." Lisbeth shrugged. "Probably a waste of time, given the second location, but better safe than sorry, right?"

"Right." I sloshed my drink, which had gone cold. "You ladies have my thanks."

"What about the origins?" Milo drummed his fingers. "Any commonality there?"

"Both the fire and the bomb were set in the women's bathrooms."

"That doesn't mean we're dealing with a woman." Lisbeth hummed. "It's not like there are bathroom police, and the stalls are private."

"We can speculate the arsonist entered the ladies' room at Choco-Loco out of habit and at the bar out of necessity," Anca said, "but we can't afford to eliminate half our suspect pool based on conjecture."

"Neither establishment uploaded their security footage to a cloud," Reece added, annoyance in his tone. "They kept their backups on site. Needless to say, any evidence on the recordings was destroyed along with the equipment."

"Are we sure we're not dealing with two bombs?" Bishop rocked back, his chair squeaking on its wonky caster. "The first might have been a dud."

"I'm looking into it," Reece assured us. "The fact Choco-Loco was on fire prior to Hadley's arrival might indicate its timer was faulty. That could mean it failed to ignite as intended, but the result was the same thanks to its magical components."

"If that's so, I'm grateful the bomber is inept," Lisbeth tossed in then frowned at me. "We could have lost you."

"The ineptitude is what bothers me." Anca leaned forward, fingers in front of her mouth. "The coven is a ruthless and merciless enemy. They've proven they're well trained, organized, and intelligent. Why, then, are they fumbling now?"

Until she mentioned it, I hadn't framed it that way in my head. "You're right."

Milo leaned back in his chair. "Are we sure it's the coven?"

"The chemical and magical signatures are identical to the samples we gathered after Hadley's apartment was bombed." Reece clicked more keys to pull up a graph for us all to see. "Either the bomber is a coven member, or they had access to the coven's blueprints and materials."

"I don't trust this." I sloshed the cup in my hand, and it drew Ambrose's attention. "Any of it."

Twining around my ankles, the shadow hammed it up for a hit of sugar.

Careful to hide my actions from the others, I dropped the cup into the void to give him his treat.

"Remember this the next time I get thrown across the pavement," I muttered, but he ignored me.

"Ford mentioned you have family visiting," Lisbeth said shyly. "How do we keep them safe?"

That she offered without me asking meant a lot, but I had been wondering the same exact thing.

"They're here to view an art installation." I waved an absent hand. "Addie can tell us which one."

The reminder I didn't know, that I hadn't even asked, burned me with shame. Once Addie confirmed my mother's interest, some internal switch flipped in my head, and I ceased to care. It was callous and thoughtless to pin the outcome of the whole trip on Addie, and she deserved better from me.

Matron Pritchard was a stone around her neck, and I had to teach her how to swim before she drowned.

"A new Dale Chihuly at the botanical garden is my guess," Anca said. "It's the latest big draw."

"Can they do that safely?" I pulled on my bottom lip. "Or is it too risky?"

An outdoors location would provide them with some protection. The crowd and media coverage of an opening night would also go a long way toward insulating them. Then again, the coven had proven they were willing to take out innocent bystanders to hit their target. They might not mind if their efforts landed them on the news. But would they act if I wasn't in attendance? That was the real question.

After flicking a brief on the event on the screen for us, Reece declared, "The risk level is moderate."

"So far the coven is targeting you." Bishop rolled his neck. "They have eyes on you. Or ears. Or both."

"A compromised enforcer makes sense," Anca murmured. "Who else has that level of access to you?"

The thread of suspicion winding through my chest as she cast blame onto the pack made me ill. I hated what the coven was doing to us, making us doubt one another. They were tearing us apart from the inside, whether they had infiltrated us or not.

Leaving the kit with Bishop *after* I tested him ripped out my heart and stomped it flat as a pancake. I had trust issues aplenty. I didn't need the coven pouring more insidious whispers in my ears. I tasted acid in the back of my throat when I ordered him to test the others. Worse, I had the gall to be grateful Bishop had to handle it since I didn't know who they were or how to find them.

"Midas, Remy, and you guys are my social circle." I leaned against the wall. "Tisdale could find out what I have on my schedule through Midas, but the only danger there is her penciling in more family dinners." I thought about it. "That's about it. I don't get into the day-to-day with Boaz or Addie. I don't much talk to anyone else."

As far as social circles go, mine was small and slow to expand, but I trusted everyone in it. Or I had, before all this.

"We zeroed in on that glint you mentioned." Bishop tapped a few keys and shared a short burst of footage with us. "Looks almost like a flashbang on its lowest setting." He mashed his lips together. "The kind the pack uses."

"Greaaat."

Those tiny suckers, about the size of a scuppernong, were made for the pack by local witches. They were more flash than bang, unless you were gwyllgi. The high-pitched wail emitted upon detonation was outside of necromantic hearing, which explained why I had focused on the sight and not the sound it made. That would also explain the way Ambrose reacted to it. The magical burst had piqued his interest or appetite.

Urgent vibrations in my pocket reminded me I had muted my phone before our meeting.

The number belonged to Midas, and I ducked into the kitchen to answer. "Sorry I left without—"

"Claudia was killed last night."

The words landed like bricks between us, and I smarted from the impact. *"What?"*

The outburst drew the team's attention, and I tucked myself deeper into a corner to avoid their eyes and ears.

"A challenger took advantage of her grief. They fought, and she lost. Cameras caught all of it."

"Two-thirds of their pack gets incinerated," I snarled, "and they blame her?"

"Hadley—"

"*I* was the target." I punched the nearest wall. "This was *my* fault. It wasn't hers. How could they...?"

"The challenger was a supporter of her father's," Midas said gently. "He was biding his time, and he took the first opening she gave him. The others were too stunned to intervene. They were reeling, and he took advantage of that too."

I almost asked him how we could fix this, but there was no repairing this.

Claudia was dead.

Dead.

A vibrant, ambitious young alpha with a heart big enough to make the tough calls, and she was gone.

Fingers curled into a fist at my side, I already regretted punching the wall. *Ouch.* "What can we do?"

"Mom has asked the Knoxville pack to leave." Heaviness settled into his voice. "It's not right, but it was a witnessed challenge. There's nothing we can do but let them go."

"Get them out of Atlanta before they start making messes, you mean?"

"Yes," he gritted out, and I heard his disapproval loud and clear.

"Okay." I steadied my nerves. "What do you need from me?"

"I wanted you to be aware of the situation, but what you're doing is more important."

"I don't mean workwise." I was almost done at HQ. "Are *you* okay?"

"Violence is a part of who we are," he said quietly. "We're predators, and weakness can be tantalizing."

The distance he put between the emotion simmering in the words coming out of his mouth told me what he thought of the line he was feeding me. One he must have choked on a time or two as well.

"That doesn't answer my question."

"I'll make peace with it. In time."

A warm handed landed on my shoulder, and Bishop raised his eyebrows to ask if I was square.

A nod was all I could spare without drawing him into our conversation, but he stayed put afterward.

"I'll touch base with you soon." I curled my fingers around my phone. "I love you."

"I love you too."

Midas ended the call before I dragged it out more, which was good and bad. "You heard?"

"Enough," Bishop said, but what he meant was *every last bit.* "Gwyllgi aren't necromancers."

"Gwyllgi aren't so different from necromancers." I pocketed my phone. "We take down rivals, end reigns and lives, stage coups. Less blood is spilled, sure, but the political and financial consequences can prove more ruinous for the families left behind than for the person who earned the hit."

"You can't reform the pack." He searched her face. "You get that, right?"

Chagrin at being caught having those exact thoughts swept through me. "Am I that transparent?"

"Beneath the wrapping, Midas's gift is no different. Don't fool yourself into thinking it is. That he is."

"I accept him for who and what he is, Bish."

And miracle of miracles, he returned the favor.

"And the pack? Their laws? Their customs? Their traditions?"

"It's a work in progress." I twisted my lips. "I can't and won't stomp on their beliefs because they're not mine. I can't ask them to change a fundamental part of who they are for my comfort. I get that. All of that. I'm struggling to move my line in the sand a little farther out than it used to go."

"Then you're on the right path." He dropped his arm. "I would worry if you said it was easy."

"Nothing in my life is ever that." I laughed under my breath. "Are you coming out with me tonight?"

"Do you really have to ask?" He glanced over his shoulder toward the command center. "Milo is going to shadow us, see if he picks up anything I missed." He led the way out of HQ. "I don't expect him to find anything."

"Because you're that good?"

"Because there's nothing to find." He locked up behind us. "The bomber is acting on intel they overhear at the Faraday, not what they glean from tailing you. That's my working theory. They know you'd spot them, or that Midas would scent them. It would be risky, and the coven has proven they're risk averse."

I didn't call Bishop out for glossing over possible OPA involvement. It was nice to pretend with him, for a few hours anyway, that our team was untouchable. That the people under our protection were safe.

"Their numbers are dwindling. That could make them reckless."

"True." He led the way out of the parking garage and down to the street. "Or it might make them think."

"Thinking is bad for us." I hated smart enemies. "Thinking means they're a step ahead of us."

"They've been that since Choco-Loco burned. Before then, really. This puts them two or three ahead."

"Oddly enough, that doesn't make me feel any better."

"I like having you around, kid." He ruffled my hair. "And not only because of your questionable judgment when it comes to the OPA's expense account. It's my job to tell you the hard truths."

"Mmm-hmm."

"Have you seen your dad yet?"

"Nope."

"Are you going to visit with him?"

"We have to make an appearance together at some point." I bet he was looking forward to it as much as me. "Even if it's in the lobby."

For a nice change, Bishop let the topic drop before I ripped it out of his hands and stomped on it.

"Do you sense that?" He kept his head forward and his stride even. "It's like…"

Skin crawling up my spine, I sensed the presence a heartbeat later. "We're being watched."

"Milo isn't responding." Bishop checked his phone. "He may be laying low."

Even a dimmed screen doubled as a beacon for trouble on a dark street. He might not be able to answer without giving away his location.

"Maybe." It was a better alternative. "We'll give him five minutes, but then we're hunting him down."

"Deal." Bishop shook his head with a grin. "Before long, the team will be meeting at HQ face-to-face."

"I don't want to violate their privacy." I chewed on my bottom lip. "I hope they understand that."

"We have precautions in place," he reminded me. "At the end of the day, they know what they signed up for, and they're aware the OPA will take any measures necessary to protect them, even at the cost of their anonymity."

As it happened, we didn't need the five minutes. Within three, the sensation evolved into the familiar *click-clack* of claws on asphalt. I let myself believe, for a second or two, that it was Midas come to check up on me. But he had never given me the heebie-jeebies, even there at the start, when I was convinced he would kill me the second he learned my true identity.

The phone in Bishop's hand buzzed like an angry wasp, and Milo's name flashed onscreen, but Bishop couldn't afford to divide his attention with a threat closing in on us.

"Hadley Whitaker," a male voice boomed. "Beta of the Atlanta Gwyllgi Pack."

A knot formed in the vicinity of my stomach and clenched until my abs trembled. "That's me."

A man stepped into the streetlight, flanked by two others and a mangy, underfed gwyllgi on all fours.

"I'm Lon Burke, Alpha of the Knoxville gwyllgi pack."

Of average height, the man was wide and thick with muscle. Salt-and-pepper hair hung to his shoulders, and his neat beard had been trimmed close. He wore jeans, a Henley, and a pair of boots.

The guy had seriously gotten himself all done up to do this. He wasn't even wearing fighting clothes.

"I challenge you for the rank of beta in the Atlanta gwyllgi pack."

The cadence of his speech told me this was formal, and he had brought his own witnesses.

Under my breath, careful not to take my eyes off the guy, I asked Bishop, "Can he do this?"

"It's highly unorthodox, but you are Midas's mate. The pack will honor the outcome."

"Frakking hell."

"Will you fight?" The challenger shoved his hands into his pockets. "Or will you forfeit?"

"Midas is going to kick your ass for this later," I warned him. "Then Tisdale will stomp on what's left."

"I'll take my chances," he said in a friendly voice. "They're an honorable bunch. They won't be happy for me to step into the prince's role, but they'll have to crown me all the same."

There was no literal crown, and if there was, Tisdale would beat him to death with it first.

"Hurry this along." Bishop took a healthy step back. "Kick his ass, kid, then we need to get back to work."

"We're trying to figure out who blew up two-thirds of your pack, not that you seem to care."

"What pack?" Lon angled his head to one side. "There are a dozen left, maybe, here and at home."

"And what happens to them if you win?"

An easy shrug rolled through his shoulders. "They go their way, and I go mine."

"Why kill Claudia if her position was only a steppingstone to the one you actually wanted?"

"We had old scores to settle." A smile kicked up one side of his mouth. "I'll make this quick."

No regret. No grief. No...nothing.

Even if Midas had never taken me to the den, even if I had never met his pack, never met Samzilla, I would gnaw off my own arm before I let this guy spread his corruption through a healthy, vibrant pack.

Hands in my pockets, mocking his posture, I asked, "Rules?"

"No weapons, only natural talents."

"Your natural talent is a weapon."

He spread his hands wide in answer, and I didn't argue. Why would I, when he had stacked the deck in my favor as well as his?

Hope you don't get papercut when your house of cards falls down.

Okay, okay.

That was a lie.

Deep down, I hoped he got decapitated by the Queen of Hearts.

Angling my head toward Bishop, I flicked my gaze skyward. "Can you make sure we get this on film?"

"Reece has been recording since we hit the streets," he assured me. "There will be a record of this."

That both simplified and complicated things. Ambrose wasn't a natural talent, more like *un*natural, but he was a part of me, so I figured that counted. Which meant using him could bite me on the butt when the footage was reviewed, and it definitely would be. I just didn't have much choice in the matter.

"Okay then." I spread my arms. "Ready when you are."

Credit where credit was due. The guy was *fast*. He charged me while the change took him, and the beast in him burst free in a crimson wave that threatened to crest over my head and crush me beneath him.

Whirling aside with seconds to spare, I laughed at the near miss to rile him. I was determined to win this without laying a finger on Lon. More than defeating him, I wanted to humiliate him. *Ruin* him. Destroy his credibility as a fighter and prove he had no right to call himself an alpha.

Petty? Yes. But so was killing Claudia for the crime of having a heart within hours of it being broken.

Bon appétit, I thought at Ambrose. *Make it convincing.*

Ambrose wove in and out of Lon, gulping chunks of his innate magic with each violent strike, forcing him to struggle to hold his form. For my part, I spun aside, almost dancing and still avoiding his clumsy lunges by miles. The crowd was enthralled. Or terrified. Or some combination of the two. Their eyes were wide, their lips parted, and they shivered and shook as if a taste of violence had made them hungry for it too.

A sour tang hit the back of my throat, and I gagged as Ambrose shuddered against the disgusting flavor.

Shifters weren't to his tastes, but I hadn't fed him since the battle, so he wasn't passing up free food.

A low growl poured from Lon, the biggest threat he could muster, as crimson magic dripped from his fur.

Lurching toward me, Lon gathered his strength to pounce. I side-stepped his graceless jump then booped him on the nose with the tip of my finger. That perked him up, and he snarled, throwing more weight behind his next wobbly attack. I hopped to the left to avoid his teeth, and Bishop cackled with delight.

The urge to mime waving a flag while shouting *Toro* almost overcame me, for which I blamed all the cartoons I watched as a kid, but I behaved for the cameras.

Pity for Lon, Ambrose enjoyed his job. Too much at times. This was one of them.

Lon landed wrong on his next leap, turning an ankle, and he fell onto the asphalt, his sides heaving.

"I can do this all night," I warned him. "Are we done here?"

Rather than answer, Lon closed his eyes and let rip a snore of epic proportions.

"I don't understand." One of the two witnesses inched closer. "He's...asleep?"

"No, he's an asshole." I shrugged. "But yes, an unconscious one."

The second glanced at me then hit his knees and bowed his head. "Alpha."

Others I hadn't noticed stepped into the light and joined in the chorus.

"Alpha."

"Alpha."

"Alpha."

"Whoa." I bent down to restrain Lon's wrists with a sigil. "I'm *not* your alpha."

"You defeated him," the first to speak reminded me. "You won his position."

"Goddess," I breathed. "Just give me a minute, okay?" I turned to Bishop. "Milo?"

"Safe," he assured me. "He's splitting off to patrol now that we have this under control."

Walking away from the pack, I pulled out my phone and called Tisdale, who was less likely to yell at me.

"Why do I expect the worst every time your number flashes on my screen?"

"You're smart?"

Amusement laced her voice. "What's happened now?"

"The asshat who murdered Claudia last night jumped me on the street and challenged me for beta."

A string of curses blistered my ear before Tisdale regained control of herself. "Are you all right?"

"I won," I assured her. "Midas is still beta."

"Don't make me drive all the way into town to throttle you," she growled. "Are *you* all right?"

Motherly concern was just plain weird. "Yes?"

"Yes or no." She snapped her fingers. "Well?"

Checking myself over, I confirmed what I already suspected. "I don't have a scratch on me."

"You almost gave me a heart attack." Metal jingled in the background. "I'm on my way."

"I said I was fine." I shot Bishop a pleading glance. "You don't have to—"

"Call my son and tell him what you told me."

Kicking a rock, I mumbled, "Do I have to?"

"You really don't want me to do it for you, sweetheart."

Taking her at her word, I ended the call and prepared to take my medicine, dialing before I lost my courage.

"Lon challenged me," I blurted after Midas answered. "I won, I'm fine, and you're still the beta. Your mom is on her way, and I'm not sure, but she sounded mad. The Knoxville pack keeps calling me alpha, and it's freaking me the frak out." I sucked in a breath and blasted out, "I need you. Please come save me."

For long moments, Midas didn't say a word, but then he sighed. "I'll be right there."

He ended the call, which hurt, and I would have gnawed on my thumbnail if my hands weren't gunky.

"A minor scuffle, and you're coming unglued." Bishop stepped up beside me. "This isn't like you."

"I know, I know." I pocketed my cell and started popping my knuckles. "Tisdale is coming."

"Wait." He laughed. "Are you *scared* of her?"

"Um..."

"Technically, she's your mother-in-law."

"And?"

"That means she's family, and she's not going to bite you."

"Family?" A breath stuttered out of me into a shaky laugh. "Seriously?"

Bishop waited for me to explain my tone or my words or my panic, but I didn't talk about this.

Ever.

To anyone.

You could share blood, a last name, or an address your whole life with the person or persons who brought you home from the hospital and it—*you*—mean nothing to them.

It's not like I expected Tisdale to love me, or even like me, because I was mated to her son. She was nice to me, but we hadn't known each other long enough for me to guess how she reacted when members of her family disappointed her.

Midas adored her, but then again, Boaz had loved our mother too.

Until she, and Dad, disowned me.

But it was the kind of falling out that might fall in again when he finally married Addie or they had kids. It wasn't that he would forgive her what she had done to me so much as he had a big heart and holding a grudge was harder for him than most. I could picture him deciding one day that I had healed, that I was okay, and start to work mending what was broken in our family.

In my humble opinion, there wasn't enough super glue in the world.

But how long would he hold out unless I gave him a good reason?

I had plenty of them, but call me greedy, I didn't want to share.

A soft whine in the throat of the stringy gwyllgi on four knobby legs brought my head around as Midas turned onto the street where we waited and prowled toward me. He didn't spare them a glance, and that dismissal left them cowering, huddled together and panting the way dogs did when they got nervous.

Each step he took forward tempted me to take one back, but I couldn't say why exactly. He would never hurt me. I wasn't afraid of him. But...yeah. I had to force my feet from itching to turn and run.

"Congratulations." He swept his gaze over my face then down my body. "You're all right?"

Spinning in a quick circle, I proved I didn't have guts hanging out my spine or anything. "I'm...weird."

One of my favorites from his arsenal of smiles kicked up the right corner of his mouth. "I'm aware."

"Jerk." I shoved a palm against his chest. "This whole thing was..."

"...weird."

"Anyone who doesn't know Hadley will think she's the weak link." Bishop invited himself to join us. "Anyone who's wanted to take a shot at Tisdale, or the Atlanta pack, will aim for her too." He tagged Lon with his gaze. "Unless she gives a demonstration of why that's a bad idea."

"This was enough." Though Claudia deserved to be avenged, I

shook my head. "I'm not killing him."

"They'll target you even harder if they think you're a bleeding heart *and* the weak link." Bishop flattened his lips into a hard line. "Look where compassion got Claudia. Her own people killed her."

"You're not going to goad me into lopping off his head while he's asleep." I tucked a wayward curl behind my ear. "Midas, you're the expert here. What do we do with him? With them?"

"Lon is outcast. He can no longer belong to the Knoxville pack. That's the price of an alpha's defeat."

Curious what that meant for Midas and Tisdale down the road, I decided the rules for an alpha stepping down must be different than an alpha defeated in a challenge. He would never boot his mother out of her home or ask her to live apart from the others.

That was one helping off my plate. "And the others?"

"We appoint a new alpha or consider integrating them into the Atlanta pack."

The way he said *we* gave me hope. "You're alpha too, right?"

"Yes." He pinched the bridge of his nose. "I am."

Hands linked at my spine to keep from touching him, I rocked back on my heels. "Are you mad at me?"

A chuckle was all the backup Bishop provided before making himself scarce.

"Why would I be?" Midas dropped his arm. "Nothing that happened here is your fault."

"You didn't sound all that happy on the phone, and you look ready to spit nails now."

"I want to shift and rip Lon open from throat to groin."

"Oh," I said quietly. "You didn't sound too happy with me earlier either."

And I had left him a love note promising him medium rare burgers with Old Bay fries for dinner too. That was simple enough to cook, even for me, and the classic meat and potatoes combo ought to suit everyone.

"I only just introduced you to the pack." He brushed his fingertips along my cheek until his hand slid behind my head to fist in my hair. "I worried Claudia's death might change how you saw them, how you see me." His fingers tightened but not painfully. "This doesn't help with that."

"For two people who talk as often as we do, we don't communicate well, do we?"

"We need to work on it." He drew me close. "Assuming you're going to stick around?"

"A whole bottle of acetone couldn't dissolve the adhesive where I'm stuck to you at this point."

"Good." He brought his head down to mine. "If glue hadn't worked, I would have invested in chains."

I didn't notice he wasn't laughing at the joke with me until his mouth crushed mine in a bruising kiss that left me in real danger of drifting right off the pavement into the sky like an untethered balloon, and then I didn't notice anything at all as his fingertips dug into my hips.

"No wonder Abbott sent you home with a wholesale box of condoms."

A bucket of ice water in Bishop's hands wouldn't have been half as effective in shattering the moment.

"How do you know about that?" I whisper-screamed. "Are you stalking me in the Faraday?"

"You say stalk, I say surveil…" Mischief glinted in his eyes as he winked at me. "Don't get your panties in a twist. I came by earlier to drop off a package from Reece for Abbott, and we got to talking. I was in the lab. I saw you in his office."

"You saw us, or you listened in and cackled gleefully to yourself?"

"Hmm." He pretended to give it real consideration. "I was holding it in until I saw you leave with enough rubber to retread half the tires in Atlanta."

Unable to look Midas in the eye, I pivoted on my heel and left him to handle the gwyllgi problem.

Sadly, Bishop followed me, chuckling all the way.

SEVEN

Our worst suspicions were gaining meat on the bone by the time Bishop walked me back to the Faraday, pretending he had to pick up a bucket of extra crispy from nearby Ben's Fried Chicken. We had managed to go a night without an explosion, but that could only be because I hadn't had any particular destination or plans in mind.

An idea forming, I glanced over at Bishop. "How do you feel about traps?"

"I'm against walking into them."

Eyes rolling, I slowed to a halt several yards from Hank and the front door. "I meant setting one."

"I do enjoy a good game of Mouse Trap."

"I'm guessing that's a game played in ye olden times."

"Kids these days," he muttered. "Who are we trapping?"

So many enemies, so little time. "The bomber."

"That would lead us to the coven." Staring off into traffic, he mused, "How do you see it going down?"

"Think about Choco-Loco." I turned the idea over in my head. "Midas and I would have been alone with Chef Daaé. Another intimate setting would minimalize casualties. Why not recreate that atmosphere?"

Due to their magical nature, the fires had struck true. Only targeted buildings had been consumed. That meant we didn't have to rely on isolation to keep down the property damage. We just had to hope the pattern held and have Station Thirteen, as well as Aubrey, on standby if things went south.

Bishop looked unconvinced. "Do you think they would fall for it twice?"

"We can fuel the gossip for a day or so, really play up the idea of a makeup date night. The pack loves to gossip, especially about Midas and me. We'll keep the details and the location to ourselves until the day of to limit the amount of time the bomber has to scope out the place."

"Advance warning means we can get cameras in place to catch what we miss," he said, more convinced. "We can pull in backup from a few different sources so we're set for whatever the coven hits us with next."

Whoever the bomber was wearing to soak up gossip might not be who they wore when they committed the crime, and that skin could be swapped out just as fast for one capable of spitting the magical fire we now knew could kill me and Ambrose both. The coven was *not* making this easy on us.

"I'll put out feelers," Bishop said, taking a healthy step back, "see if I can find a place."

"Sounds good." I frowned at his expression. "Let me know when you're finished testing the team."

"Will do."

"Where are you…?"

Easing into the shadows, he was gone before I finished asking the question.

"Hadley."

Slowly, I turned my head toward the Faraday and spotted Tisdale striding down the sidewalk toward me.

"Oh, hi." I waved like an idiot. "How's it going?"

"Better now that I've seen you for myself." Her strong, thin arms encircled me in a hug I expected to be ten levels of awkward but was actually kind of...nice. "Are you sure you're not hurt?"

"I handled it." I withdrew from her embrace, spotted her scowl, and blurted, "And I'm A-okay. Not a scratch on me."

"We'll see." She took my hand and tucked it against her side, tugging me after her. "Abbott can be the judge of that."

"That's okay. Really. I saw him yesterday." I yanked, but she dragged me. "You know what they say. Absence makes the heart grow fonder."

"You're worse than Lethe was as a girl." Tisdale nodded to Hank, who smirked at me with his smirky face that needed punching for always having salt ready to apply to any open wound. "She would dream up any excuse to avoid the healer."

"I can't imagine why." I stumbled into the lobby. "Healers are so kind and gentle."

We drew stares as she hauled me into the elevator and mashed the down button.

"We're lucky to have someone as skilled as Abbott. He truly has a gift."

As often as he had patched me up, I could hardly argue with her there.

"Did something happen to you when you were a child?"

Whipping my head toward her, I had to search to find my voice. "What do you mean?"

"To make you hate going to the doctor."

Sweet relief sluiced through me, and I missed whatever else she said over the roaring in my ears.

Mother had refused to take me after the age of six or seven. I had too many scars, too many bruises, too many secrets. I took over-the-counter medication and prayed it did the job. Otherwise...well...I doubt the outcome would have bothered her too much. Especially after Macon was born.

Fear kept me alive more than any gel capsule. Fear she would develop an interest in him. Fear she would age me out and decide there was an easier target under her roof.

There was a reason why I stayed home to attend college, and plenty of reasons, aside from my own horror and heartbreak, that the disownment had terrified me.

That one decision kicked me out of the Pritchard household for good.

And since I had never told anyone *anything,* no one grasped why that was the worst-possible outcome.

Clearing my throat, I kept my voice light. "Midas didn't mention my childhood?"

"Hadley," she exhaled. "There is more to you than meets the eye." She wrapped a lean arm around my shoulders. "More to your past and your present than you've told me."

"Midas knows" was what I said, but even he hadn't seen the whole picture.

"I don't doubt that." She rubbed my upper arm. "What I hope is that one day, you'll confide in me too."

"There are things I haven't told anyone."

"We all have those things, sweetheart, and for the most part a secret or two doesn't hurt anyone." She gave me a gentle squeeze. "Just remember, a secret loses its power when more people learn it."

For the barest moment, I rested my head on her shoulder and breathed in the scents of earth and sugar.

I would have liked having a mom who smelled like her, like growing things and sprinkle cookies.

"Thanks."

She kissed the side of my head. "Tell me that again after Abbott is through with you."

Groaning, I let her march me into his office. I ducked my head to look extra pitiful, but also so she wouldn't see the silly grin tickling the edge of my mouth as she mothered me better than mine ever had.

ONLY AFTER ABBOTT pronounced me hale and hearty did Tisdale escort me to the lobby where my stomach dropped into the soles of my feet as if the elevator car had plummeted down the shaft with us in it. The wobble in my knees sent her into a tizzy, and she would have hauled me back to the infirmary if I hadn't lied about tripping over the threshold.

She was standing in the lobby dressed in a nice pantsuit.

My mother.

Annabeth Pritchard.

Matron Pritchard.

A sour expression puckered her lips, and her sharp eyes missed nothing. Including my stumble and the attention it drew to Tisdale and me. A quick assessment dismissed me as anyone of importance, and that was...relief...rushing through me to tingle in my fingertips.

Part of me had always expected her to pierce my glamour with that cold stare upon our first meeting, to see down to the Amelie buried deep within the Hadley, and I had braced for her worst. But that was the little girl in me who wanted to cower behind Tisdale and hope I blended into the potted plants to avoid Mother's notice. The future potentate couldn't afford to show weakness, not in front of a predator.

"Let me tell my babysitters where I'm going," Tisdale said, "and then I'm taking you to your apartment."

"Yes, ma'am."

As I stood there, next to the elevators and sweet escape, Addie came around the bend with her father on her arm. No, that wasn't right. *Our* father.

Goddess, having two lives and two families got confusing when my past and present collided in person.

"Hadley." Addie's bright greeting made me smile. "What are you doing down here?"

Our father, who hadn't recognized me, jolted at the sound of my name and spun toward me.

A flash of hope that almost blinded me filled his hazy eyes, but then he saw me, and all that vanished.

"I need a drink," he murmured. "I'll meet you at Michelle's."

An upscale restaurant for a simple family dinner, but it was Society owned, and I bet half Mother's enjoyment came from knowing Boaz, therefore *she*, had to foot the exorbitant bill in front of their peers.

No wonder Addie was so keen on cooking. I would hit the grocer to skip the spectacle of shame too.

Addie watched him go, her shoulders tight, and Mother pounced on that show of weakness.

"Honestly, I don't understand why you booked him a room." Her lips curved in the mockery of a smile. "He never leaves the bar. You might as well have booked him a stool."

Hurt and embarrassment colored Addie's cheeks, and she was the last person who deserved the barbed tip of my mother's tongue lashing her.

Crossing to them, I took Addie's hand. "You're heading out to dinner?"

Our sister-bonding time flew out the window as she nodded, her gaze tagging my mother as if to explain the change in plans, but I was okay with a quiet night at home with Midas.

"We're just waiting on Boaz." She pulled herself taller. "He's always the last one ready."

"Why does he need so much gel when he barely has any hair?"

Addie snickered and held on tight, but Mother's shoulders snapped back on my periphery.

"How are you familiar with my son's dressing habits?" Her lips twisted. "Or do I want to know?"

"This is Hadley Whitaker," Addie said coolly. "My little sister."

A spark of interest kindled in her gaze. "The potentate."

"Apprentice," I said, my heart booming in my ears, my spine wilting by slow degrees, "but yes."

"An unorthodox appointment for a woman," she said, but not unkindly. "What drew you here?"

Since it would have outed me to say *I came to escape from you*, I opted for a more diplomatic response. "I wanted to make a difference."

More polite than made me comfortable, she inclined her head slightly. "Are you joining us for dinner?"

Grateful for a valid excuse to pass, I reassured myself it wasn't cowardice but prudence to decline.

"Hadley is going to her room," Tisdale informed them as she joined us. "She needs to rest."

Gwyllgi hearing being what it was, I figured she had followed our conversation from across the room.

"This is Tisdale Kinase." I handled the introduction. "Alpha of the Atlanta gwyllgi pack."

"Kinase." Mother's features hardened. "Your daughter is a neighbor of mine."

A swell of pride in her daughter swept across Tisdale's face. "Yes, I believe so."

"Her pack makes an unholy racket. Like small dogs barking." She tightened her scowl when she noticed her gaze kept sliding down Tisdale's face, unable to hold her stare. "Do you know how grating that is on the nerves? I try to garden, but what they get up to gives me a headache."

Staring right at her, Tisdale admitted, "I have experienced grating on the nerves, yes."

I almost laughed, and it was as if Mother sensed it. She flipped her gaze to mine, and I coughed loudly.

"Perhaps you could mention to her that her neighbors would appreciate some peace." Mother mashed her lips flat. "I would hate to get the Society involved."

"I'll mention your concerns to Linus," Tisdale returned smoothly.

"He and Grier live between you and my daughter's pack. If there is a noise problem, I'm sure he's noticed it too. He can bring it up to his mother the next time they chat."

The veiled threat put color in Mother's cheeks. She was out of favor with the Grande Dame, and she knew it. She had no intention of making a case against Lethe and her pack for that very reason. She just wanted to throw Tisdale's daughter's imperfections in her face.

Huh.

I was definitely sensing a theme here.

"That won't be necessary," Mother clipped out. "Adelaide, I'll wait for you outside. This lobby does nothing for my allergies."

Eyes on me, she snapped out her hand, and I flinched away from it.

Flinched?

More like I fell over myself avoiding the blow.

Except she hadn't tried to hit me. She wanted to shake my hand.

Crimson flecks ignited in the depths of Tisdale's eyes as she read my body language.

"I was in a fight earlier tonight," I babbled in explanation. "I'm still jittery with adrenaline."

Withdrawing her hand, Mother edged away from me. "I hope you can join us for a tour of the museum."

There went the hope they were here for a garden art party. A museum, with various exhibits and private spaces, would be much harder to secure. Maybe impossible. I would definitely talk to Addie about nixing the viewing. Our parents would be total brats about it, of that I had no doubt, but they would be alive to kick their feet and roll across the floor. No art was worth paying your life as admission.

"I'll see what I can do," I lied through my teeth. "Enjoy your dinner."

Purpose in her stride and phone to her ear, she exited the building and disappeared from view.

Tisdale's pointed stare burned a hole through my right ear, straight to my brain, but she didn't ask me if I was okay or all right, and I was glad. I didn't want to lie to her. Pretty sure with her keen senses, she heard my knees knocking the whole time I spoke to my mother.

"Why do people think dog jokes are hurtful to gwyllgi?" Tisdale deftly smoothed over the awkwardness. "I love dogs. I hope she is allergic to them. No animal deserves the treatment she would give it."

Lips parting to agree, I shut them just as fast to avoid inviting more conversation.

Addie swooped in, her head bowed and her fingers twisting in a knot. "I am *so* sorry."

"You're Hadley's big sister." Tisdale patted Addie's tangled hands. "I'm so glad to meet you."

"She's not that..." Addie mashed her lips together. "Okay, she is that bad."

"It's all right," Tisdale assured her, but her knowing gaze met mine. "I don't hold children responsible for the words or actions of their parents."

Dread twisted through my chest, a corkscrew to the heart.

She knew.

Tisdale *knew*.

Or she suspected.

Frak, frak, frak.

No. I was being paranoid. That was all. Tisdale didn't know I was a Pritchard by birth. I was projecting. Yeah. Projecting. That was it.

Where's a teleporter when I need one?

Had I not already given my heart to Midas, I would have offered it up on a silver platter just then. He strode across the lobby, aiming straight for me. He didn't stop until we stood toe to toe, and he engulfed me in a hug that lifted me off my feet and left them swinging the way Boaz sometimes did when we hadn't seen one another in months. But I had seen Midas hours ago.

"I've come to rescue you," he whispered in my ear. "Twice in one night."

Forget being independent. Forget being strong. Forget self-respect. "Yes, please."

"Mom." Midas turned me loose then kissed her cheeks. "I'm taking the invalid to bed."

Turning her head, Addie coughed into her fist and made a strategic retreat toward the front door.

"You can call me if you ever want to talk." Tisdale clasped my hands. "You don't have to wait for disaster to strike to use my number."

"Yes, ma'am." I peeked up at her. "I'll remember that."

"Come on." Midas looped an arm around my waist. "Let's get you down for a nap."

"Make sure you feed her." Tisdale pointed at him. "She needs to keep up her strength."

Smile on his lips, he bobbed his head and echoed me. "Yes, ma'am."

Mashing my face into his side, I let him guide me into the elevator blind. "Thanks for the save."

"Mom worries about you." A shrug moved through him. "She can be worse than Abbott at times."

"No one is worse than Abbott," I grumped, and told him about my trip to the infirmary.

Ready to shower, eat, and spend quality time *alone* with Midas for the first time in days, I stepped into the hall but pulled up short when I noticed the box in front of our door.

"Are you serious?" I nudged it with my toe. "Another one?"

"Don't touch it." Midas hauled me back. "What if it's another bomb?"

After taking a healthy step back, I palmed my phone and dialed Abbott. "Did you leave us a gift?"

"Oh. Yes. The box. I got your note."

More suspicious than ever, I asked, "What note?"

"A note was taped to the infirmary door, in your handwriting, so I had a nurse drop the condoms off at your door. I would have mentioned it while you were here earlier, but I didn't want your perfectly healthy sexual appetite to embarrass you in front of your mother-in-law."

"Which nurse?"

"Your friend, Lisbeth."

"Thanks." I ended the call before he picked up on my worry and dialed Lisbeth. "Hey."

"There was enough rubber in that box, it would have bounced if I dropped it."

"Well, that answers that question." I slumped against the wall. "You did bring up the box?"

"Yes." She hesitated, her quick mind filling in the blanks. "Unless someone tampered with it, it's legit."

"No one else has been up here since we left," Midas said, reading off his screen. "Only Lisbeth."

The security crew must have fed him an update, maybe even a slice of surveillance from our hallway.

"I think we're good." I caved to the awkwardness and blurted, "Bye."

Her laughter rang in my ears as the call ended.

"Someone pranked us." I let us into the apartment. "But who?"

Dollars to donuts Bishop was the culprit. Lisbeth was likely in on it too. And Remy. Oh, yes. Remy. Little miss *let me forge your signature* had clearly been practicing more than signing my name.

Traitors.

"The possibilities are endless." Midas picked up the box and set it inside the door. "Does it bother you?"

"Everyone in this building is so invested in our personal lives they're donating condoms to the cause."

"Welcome to the pack." He kicked off his shoes. "Where our business is everyone's business and everyone's business is everyone else's business."

Awkward as it was to ask, I was on a roll tonight. "Can they tell we haven't...?"

The scarlet flush that raced from his chin to his hairline gave me my answer. "Does it bother you?"

"That they can smell our business, or that we don't have business to smell?"

There. Nice and vague and right to the point. Middle schoolers were probably more descriptive.

"Both."

"We're moving at our own pace." I led him to the couch and shoved him down so I could plop across his lap. "I don't care what the others think they know." I linked my arms behind his head. "I care that you're here, I'm here, and we have a few hours alone together before I start snoring and drooling." I scratched his scalp with my fingernails, and his eyes rolled closed. "You know, really driving home how lucky you are to have me sleeping next to you."

"I am lucky." He nuzzled my cheek. "I don't mind the snoring or the drooling."

What a pretty little liar. "I've woken up to find you wearing earplugs."

"I did wake up that one time convinced I'd fallen asleep in the forest during a lumberjack convention—"

Fisting the pillow beside him, I smacked him in the face with it. "Meanie."

Midas took the hit but caught my wrist and yanked me forward until I fell against him. Tossing the pillow onto the floor, he trapped my wrists between our chests then coiled his arms around my back to keep me from escaping.

Amusement sparkled in his eyes, heat too, but it was the soft laughter that convinced me he needed kissing.

Wriggling to get higher, which caused all sorts of interesting things to happen in his lap, I pressed my lips to his. He kissed me back, and I took us deeper with a nip of my teeth that gained me access to his mouth. The slow glide of my tongue along his coaxed him to moan, and I smiled against him.

"You'll only encourage bad behavior if you reward it like this."

He tucked his face in my neck and breathed me in. "You always smell so good."

"It's a patented combination of sweat, deodorant, and whatever I've killed recently."

"It works for you." His breath warmed my throat. "It works for me too."

Curling my fingers into the soft fabric covering his chest, I asked, "How do you feel about removing your shirt?"

"Like it's a trap." He locked me tighter against him. "You'll wait until I'm preoccupied then bolt."

A snort of laughter escaped me. "I'm not a bolter."

"You're not a great liar, Hadley."

Fluttering my lashes, I gazed adoringly up at him. "What if I promise not to budge?"

"Your promises have more loopholes than fae contracts."

"Ouch." I reared back. "That actually hurt."

"Want me to kiss it better?"

"Hmph."

Angling my head away, I showed him what I thought of his offer, which is to say I made it super easy for him to nibble on my throat until my toes curled and I was squirming on his lap. I almost fell off the couch in shock when he smoothed his thumb over the button of my jeans then traced the zipper's teeth to the apex of my thighs.

"Midas," I whispered, hands now free to dig my nails into his shoulders.

"You don't know how long I've wanted to do this." He stared at me, crimson flecks dancing in his eyes. "I want you, Hadley."

While I worked on unsticking my tongue from the roof of my mouth, he began making tiny circles that caused smoke to pour from my ears.

"Me too." I trembled. "I mean, I want you. Not me. That would be weird."

"You are so...you." He increased the pressure. "I love that about you."

"I'm a weirdo," I panted. "Just say it." I rocked against him. "I am at peace with my geekiness and my—"

The orgasm exploded through me like a bottle rocket, and my breath punched from my lungs. I shivered and shook, whimpering as he lightened his touch but kept his skilled hand right where it was.

Muscles turned to liquid, I slumped over him, my face mashed into his shoulder.

Linking his arms at my spine to keep me from spilling onto the floor, he murmured, "Now we're even."

"You didn't have to pay me back." Shirt got in my mouth, but I couldn't lift my head. "No one is keeping score."

Rubbing his hands up and down my back, he confessed, "I didn't want you to think it would always be..."

"I have to stop you right there." I finally got my neck to cooperate and turned my head toward him. "This is a relationship, not a performance exam. Neither of us have been intimate with anyone in years, right?"

Hand closing over my nape, he held me down like I could possibly rise. "Years about covers it."

As in, he hadn't had sex in longer than I had been alive.

"Neither of us lasted five seconds. Who cares?" I managed to scooch close enough to kiss his throat. "I like that we're both rusty. It puts less pressure on both of us to get everything right on the first try. Or the second. Or the third." He swallowed hard, and I nipped his ear to be extra helpful. "See where I'm going with this? We'll practice. We'll get better. Together."

"I already need a cold shower every time you look at me like you love me."

"I must do that a lot, you know, since I love you, and I have trouble keeping my eyes off you."

His hesitant smile mingled fragile hope with shining happiness into the most perfect expression, and just like that, it became my new life's mission to keep that look on his face.

"Seriously," I reassured him. "You have nothing to prove to me, in bed or out of it."

"I can't help but feel *graded* on everything I do." He referred back to my exam comment. "Every aspect of my life is witnessed and evaluated by the pack, by rivals, by outsiders, even by my mother."

"Please don't bring your mom into this."

He chuckled at the joke, but then he sobered. This was a sore spot for him, and I had to tread softly.

"I want to get an A plus," he murmured, "but I would settle for a C minus."

"I'm not grading you on sexual performance. That's..." I discarded several options before I settled on. "That's not healthy. For either of us."

"I want to please you."

"The fact you're mine-all-mine pleases me."

Hello, double standards.

"I want to pleasure you."

"You just did."

"I want—"

"—me to film us so you can evaluate your own performance?"

"No."

A horrible idea occurred to me, but it was so great I had to put it out there.

"I can see it now." I rallied my strength and sat upright. *"Attack of the Gwyllgi Prince with Love on His Mind and a Roll of Quarters in his Front Pocket."* I laughed so hard, I worried I might have peed a little. "I would *so* watch that."

"How about *The Necromancer Gets Bitten by a Gwyllgi and Runs Screaming.*"

"Depends." I choke-laughed. "Are we talking about the same gwyllgi? Like is that the sequel? And has he run out of quarters yet?"

The bone-rattling growl that pumped through his chest only made it more hilarious.

To me.

"You are not funny," he said, doing his best to keep a straight face.

"And yet, you laugh." I thumped his nipple. "You're only encouraging me."

About to fist the hem of his shirt and yank it over his head so I could enjoy the view, I froze at a knock on the door. Beneath me, Midas did the same.

"Are you expecting anyone?" I slid off his lap onto the couch. "It's almost dawn."

"No." He rose, bent to kiss me tenderly, then crossed the apartment and greeted our guest. "Ares?"

An acrid stench that had become too familiar to me filled the room when she entered uninvited.

"Hadley." A tear tracked down her cheek, slicing through soot and grime. "Your sister…"

"No." I was on my feet before I knew it. *"No."*

"Ares." Midas stood beside me, his hand on my back. "What happened?"

"Matron Pritchard and Mr. Whitaker got into a fight in the lobby yesterday. They were arguing about the service and food at the restaurant Mr. Whitaker chose. Matron Pritchard made it plain she was eating at Michelle's tonight, and he could starve if he chose not to join her." More tears fell, carving grooves down her face. "I warned Addie to mix it up, just in case, but she must have caved under the pressure."

And the mole overheard and made their plans, likely believing I would go out with my family to dinner.

No, no, no.

A clamp snapped shut around my lungs, and oxygen whistled through my teeth. "Who told you this?"

Whoever it was, they were wrong. *Wrong.* There was no other explanation.

"I saw it for myself." She bowed her head. "I went to Michelle's before I came here."

"You followed them," I realized, my voice sounding distant in my ears.

"They're your family," Midas explained for her. "I had them watched."

Since the OPA was doing the same on my end, I could hardly blame him, but why hadn't Bishop…?

Pivoting on my heel, I jogged into the kitchen and located my phone, which I had left on silent.

Bishop had texted me twenty-three times.

Lisbeth thirteen.

Even Anca, Milo, and Reece had touched base with me.

And I had been too busy riding Midas's hand to keep in contact with my team during a time of crisis.

"This isn't your fault." Midas trapped my back against his chest, his hands clasped at my navel. "The bomber has only targeted you. You had no reason to think they would go after your family."

But we had both known, deep down, it was a possibility. Otherwise we wouldn't have each assigned them guards to watch over them whenever they left the Faraday. We wouldn't have moved them to the Faraday in the first place if we hadn't had concerns.

I had chosen my city over my family, and I had failed them both.

Not enough, not enough, not enough.

No matter what I did, it was never enough.

"I need to go." I broke free of him. "I need to be there."

I fell to my knees when I tried to pull on my shoes, and I almost couldn't get back up, but I had to move.

It wasn't like Addie would have been alone. Boaz would have been right there with her.

The one person who had loved me unconditionally, who had never hurt me, never hated me, was gone.

Part of me withered and died on the spot. I might not be a Pritchard anymore, but Boaz was my brother.

My brother was dead.

EIGHT

Midas held Hadley's hand to leash her, but she tugged against him, blind in her grief and rage. She made it onto the sidewalk before elbowing him, twisting free of his hold, and running straight for the plume of smoke on the pink-and-orange horizon. He allowed her to maintain the lead, but he kept close enough to watch her back.

He wasn't surprised when Bishop jogged from an alley wreathed in shadows to join him.

"This is going to get ugly fast." He cut Midas a look. "Can you restrain her?"

His feral half took orders from her, which meant she could free herself, but that abuse of power sat wrong with her. Usually. "Yes."

"Good." Bishop frowned at the back of her head. "Poor kid can't catch a break."

Hadley was a fighter, but even the strongest could get knocked down until they could no longer rise.

"Will Linus come?" Midas wondered. "Does he know yet?"

"He's already on his way." Bishop slowed his pace. "He and Boaz had issues, but he's worried for Hadley. He doesn't want her to face this alone." He came to a stop as they reached the scorched restaurant. "Grier is with him."

"That means Lethe will come too."

Grier's power made her unique, but it also made her a target. Lethe would never allow her best friend to leave Savannah without a guard. Despite their troubled histories, Grier had grown up next door to Hadley and Boaz. She had loved him for most of her life, and she would mourn him. Deeply.

Hadley would need Grier to help make sense of this shared loss. And Addie... Midas wasn't sure how Hadley would process the loss of the woman who had welcomed her into sisterhood with open arms.

The deaths of Mr. Whitaker and Matron Pritchard left Midas uncertain as to their impacts. Hadley hadn't been close to her "father," but she liked him. The woman who had birthed her and then thrown her away rather than deal with the scandal fueled by her crimes was another matter.

It didn't mean Hadley wouldn't grieve her, but he had no expectations as to how her sorrow might manifest.

The smoke burned Midas's sinuses and made him cough as he fought through it to reach Hadley.

As wind teased the edges of the black plumes, Midas understood why she hadn't rushed the fire.

The restaurant was ash. Nothing but ash. The magical fire had devoured it whole.

Once that registered, Hadley hit her knees, but she didn't scream as Claudia had done, and there was no sense of defeat about her. No one could see her and not understand she was mourning, but no one would dare engage her with that murderous wrath twisting her face either.

There were no words to make this better, no magic to bring them back, no miracle waiting in the wings.

All Midas could do was kneel beside her as her fists clenched and her jaw ground with white-hot rage.

Ambrose whirled in a circle over her head, a funnel of dark

intent, and Midas swore the shadow cast him a worried glance as if he too were concerned for her. But that couldn't be right. If she was close to breaking, Ambrose ought to be rejoicing.

"You don't need to be here for this." Bishop crouched on her other side. "Let Midas take you home."

Voice distant, eyes vacant, she stared ahead, seeing nothing. "This is exactly where I need to be."

"I was afraid you'd say that." Bishop reached in his pocket and, moving faster than Midas credited him for, stabbed her in the upper arm with a hypodermic needle. "Midas, you might want to catch her."

A red haze blinded him, and his teeth ached to clamp shut over Bishop's throat, but Hadley's spine curved as she began to collapse. Midas made his choice, the only choice, and grabbed her shoulders before she kissed the pavement. "What the hell do you think you're doing?"

Above them, Ambrose popped like a balloon after a pin pierced its surface and vanished from sight.

"You want to go next?" He produced a second, larger needle. "I came loaded for bear, which in this case means gwyllgi. I put you down, and you're not getting up for forty-eight hours."

"Try it," Midas growled, his entire body vibrating.

"Settle down." Bishop spread his hands. "I'm faster than you think, Goldilocks."

"Explain yourself..." water pooled in his mouth, his fangs itching his gums, "...or I will kill you."

"Still mad about me blowing her up, huh?" He checked the streets from left to right. "Not here, and not now."

"I'm not moving an inch, and neither are you, until you give me a reason."

Bishop stared at him, in the eye, which not many people dared to do if they wanted to keep breathing. A heartbeat passed, then two, and the beast under his skin turned restless, eager, quivering in his gut.

"Linus made the call, and he was right to," Bishop said at last. "He couldn't predict how she would react, how bad it would get, and he wanted her neutralized until he got here." He studied the sidewalk. "It could have been worse. It could still get worse. You know their deal."

Midas did know their deal, and it sickened him to his core to think Linus would ever raise a hand to her.

But he would, if he had no other choice.

And Midas...he wasn't sure he could let that happen anymore.

Hadley wasn't an unthinking, unfeeling monster. She was more, she was better, she was *his*.

"Dial it down," Bishop warned. "You're going to leave me without a choice, and that would suck."

With Hadley unconscious, there was no harm in asking, "Have they found the bodies?"

"No." Bishop scanned the wreckage. "This building was all wood. It was over as soon as it started."

"Let me know when they're recovered." Midas stood and brought Hadley with him. "And don't visit until I tell you I'm ready to see your face again without gnawing it off then picking it from my teeth."

"That's what I like about you gwyllgi." Bishop eased a few steps away. "So visual."

Unease rippling down his spine, Midas turned from Bishop and carried Hadley to their home.

HADLEY SLEPT the entire day and well past dusk on the futon in the loft of their apartment. The height and the wall at his back settled his other half, and he appreciated how the narrow staircase meant no one could sneak up on them.

Linus might come through the front door, or he might use the fire escape, but there was only one way he would gain access to the loft. Through Midas.

A commotion in the hall perked his ears, and he leaned forward, ready to pit himself against anyone who dared harm his mate in her weakened state.

The knock on the door was unexpected, but their guests didn't wait for him to give permission.

"Midas?" a familiar voice called as the door swung open. "Are you here?"

Grier Woolworth entered the loft with her long, dark hair in a ponytail high on her head. She stared up at him through the thick fringe of her bangs, her eyes ice-blue in color but warm when she spotted him. She had known Lethe long enough to guess he would have chosen the high ground to make his stand.

"Bishop warned us guests might not be welcome." She didn't come closer. "Are you okay with this?"

"Yes," he growled down at her, his voice unrecognizable.

"We're here to help." Grier flashed her empty palms. "We're not going to hurt her."

Heart pounding, lungs burning, he crouched at the head of the staircase. "I can't risk that."

"She hasn't done anything wrong."

"*Yet.*" His lips peeled from his teeth. "That's what you mean."

"We're here to make sure she doesn't escalate." She inched forward. "We care about her too."

Years of friendship with Grier clashed with his primal instincts concerning his mate.

Grier was pack, *family*, but she was just as capable of sinking a blade through Hadley's heart if it kept her former best friend from embracing her darker half again.

"Stay where you are, Grier." Fur brushed the underside of his skin. "I don't want to hurt you."

"Then don't." Linus strolled through the door, hands in his pockets. "Hadley would never forgive you."

The wraith usually at his side was absent, thanks to the ward barring his kind entrance to the building, but Linus was no less dangerous without Cletus.

Fingernails lengthening into claws, Midas widened his stance. "But she would be alive to hold a grudge."

"I give you my word, I won't harm Hadley unless she becomes a danger to others."

Already shaking his head, Midas couldn't trust him. "She's my mate."

"I'm aware." Linus stopped beside Grier, shielding her with his body, which earned him an eye roll from her as she allowed it. "Even if she wasn't, I would do everything in my power to save her from herself."

A third figure entered the living room, her bright-blue hair kissing the tops of her shoulders.

"Hey, little bro." Lethe edged past Linus and Grier, stopping with one foot on the stairs. "May I?"

Though it pained him to deny her anything, he couldn't stop his instinctive denial. "No."

"You don't trust me?"

"With Hadley?" He exhaled. "No."

"I'm not going to murder your mate. I'm not a monster."

Midas slid his gaze to Linus, regretting how her comment had wiped all expression from his friend's face.

Grier leaned into Linus, comforting him with a hand on his arm. "Can we get anyone for you?"

As tempted as he was to huff and puff and blow them out of the apartment, he caved. "Mom."

"She's downstairs." Lethe backed up a few steps. "I'll let her know you're ready for her."

Hurt from his rejection tightened her features, but Hadley hadn't woken up, and he couldn't settle.

The elevator chimed, and footsteps announced another visitor Midas wished he could toss out.

"Lisbeth called." Ford ambled in like he was here for one of his usual visits. "I brought food and drinks."

Not so long ago, Midas would have shed his human skin and attacked Ford on sight for having the gall to invite himself in. It shamed Midas to remember how fast his obsession with Hadley, his jealousy over the infatuation he helped create, nearly ruined their decades-long friendship.

"Just burgers and fries." He hit the steps and paused where Midas blocked the landing. "You mind?"

Throat tight, Midas stepped aside and let Ford sit beside him, dangling his long legs over the edge.

"I brought Hadley an apple pie, the rectangular kind, but I figured better safe than sorry."

When Ford offered him a burger, he accepted it. When he offered him fries, he took those too. When he handed over a drink, and Midas sipped to wet his parched throat, he spat it on the stairs and coughed so hard he saw stars.

"Oops." Ford snatched the cup and gave Midas a different one. "That's Granny's moonshine."

Once the burn down his gullet eased, Midas rasped, "How can you drink that?"

"I don't drink it." His laughter rang out in the silence. "I use it as an all-purpose cleaner."

Willing to admit he wasn't at his brightest, Midas wiped his mouth. "Then why...?"

"Hadley might decide she wants something stronger than a Coke when it really hits her." He glanced over his shoulder to where she rested. "This is guaranteed to wipe her memory for hours at a time."

"Thanks."

"I should go." Ford rose and left the bag of food behind. "Your mom will be here soon."

"Yeah" was all he could think to say, and it cost him to get that out.

"Call me if you need anything." Ford paused on the stairs. "Food, alcohol, revenge, manly hugs, hairstyling tips. I'm here for all of it."

"Thanks," he said again, his brain and tongue getting tangled with the effort to be social.

No sooner had Ford hit the bottom than Tisdale swept into the apartment with her guards.

"Sweetheart," she exhaled, motioning the pair of gwyllgi to wait in the hall. "My poor sweetheart."

Despite it all, warmth unfurled in his chest at the sight of his mother running up the stairs toward him. But she didn't stop when she reached him. She kept going until she sat on the futon with Hadley, her hands fluttering over Hadley's still form.

The presence of his mother soothed, but the nearness of his alpha stabilized him, allowed him to think clearly for the first time since Bishop depressed the syringe into Hadley's upper arm.

A soft moan parted Hadley's lips, and Midas rushed to her side, falling on his knees.

"She responded to you," he rasped, confused by her instant alertness. "Why?"

"My sweet boy." Mom cupped his cheek. "I'm her alpha too. I can call her, and she has no choice but to come. She is bound to you in soul and bone, and you are my soul and bone. We're kin. That's why. She trusted you to protect her, to let her rest, to find her strength and her calm."

"Her family..."

There was another brother, a little brother. Macon. And Mr. Pritchard. But they didn't belong to Hadley. He supposed, thanks to the disownment, they didn't belong to Amelie either, but they still had to be notified.

"She has you, and she has me. She has her friends and the pack. She will survive this."

Aware his voice came out sounding lost and too young for his years, he whispered, "Linus."

Rising gracefully, she walked to the edge of the loft and stared down. "Mr. Lawson."

From where he knelt, Midas saw Linus tip back his head. "Yes?"

"Harm this child, and I will split you open from neck to navel and feast on your entrails."

"I gave her my word I would stop her if no one else had the strength," he said softly. "I'm not a liar."

"She doesn't know," Grier murmured, hand on his arm. "She can't know."

"I'm a dybbuk," Hadley croaked, her head tilting toward Tisdale. "Do you know what that is?"

Expression thoughtful, his mother folded her arms across her chest. "That explains...many things."

Grinding the heels of her palms into her eyes, Hadley rubbed away her disorientation.

"There's only one dybbuk who's been named and lived." His mother touched her lips. "You're Amelie."

"Amelie Madison née Pritchard," Midas confirmed when Hadley left her hands over her eyes.

"That was the secret you've been keeping," his mother mused. "I expected it to be spectacular, but I find myself impressed despite all expectations."

From between her fingers, Hadley asked, "You're not mad I lied to you?"

"None of us are who we were born. We evolve from the day we enter the world until the day we leave it. That's life." She flicked a glance at the ceiling as if searching for the right words. "Most of us retain our birth names so that we can be recognized no matter how much we change, but some of us discard those too." She shrugged a shoulder. "Names are labels, they have power, but they can be peeled off or written over."

Still hiding in the dark, Hadley dared another question. "What are you saying?"

"I don't care who you were in your previous incarnations. I care who you are now."

"What if that changes again?" Her fingers slipped lower. "What if *I* change again?"

"Change is inevitable, sweetheart, and all any of us can do is hope that the skin we choose to shed is less than the new one we have decided to wear."

Dropping her hands to her sides, Hadley stared at the ceiling like it might provide her with guidance.

"I need Linus to keep his word." She pushed herself upright. "I need him to act when others hesitate."

"I understand." His mother angled her head toward Linus. "Apologies, Mr. Lawson."

"Accepted," he said with ease. "Can we see her now?"

"I'll come down." Hadley swung her legs over the edge of the futon. "There's no room for a party up here."

Midas wished he took more comfort from her words, which sounded almost right, but her tone was flat and her eyes empty.

"I'll do the honors." He scooped her up and carried her toward the stairs. "I don't mind."

Hadley leaned her head against his chest, placed her hand over his heart, and shuddered just once.

Midas hit the bottom, his mother behind him, but he struggled to close the distance to Linus and Grier.

"You didn't have to drive all the way here." Hadley struggled weakly until he set her on her feet. "I'm—"

"Don't say you're fine," Grier warned. "You're not. I'm not. No one in this room is okay right now."

"What do you want me to say?" Hadley folded her arms across her stomach. "He was my *brother*."

"And he loved you more than anything in the world."

"And Addie..." Hadley hunched over like she might be sick. "She's...gone. I never told her..."

Unable to witness more of Hadley's pain, Grier rushed her, and

Midas gritted his teeth to keep from snapping at her. Grier yanked Hadley against her and squeezed until sobs burst from them both.

Slowly, so as not to provoke Midas, Linus joined them, stroking the curved line of Grier's spine.

The elevator chimed, and it carried through the apartment's open door.

Remy ran across the hall and skidded to a stop before colliding with Grier, Linus, and Hadley.

"There were no bodies," she shouted, fist pumping the sky. *"No bodies."*

Grier closed her eyes as if it might erase the past few hours if she screwed them shut tight enough, but Hadley broke from the huddle to clasp Remy by her wrists in a bruising grip.

"What are you talking about?" Her voice wavered. "How do you know?"

"Do you think I wasn't here with you because I didn't want to be?" She made a dismissive noise. "Unlike these losers, who came to you empty-handed, *I* brought news."

Hope draining from her expression, Hadley shook her head. "The heat…"

"Me, myself, and five other *I*s spent the day sifting through the debris after the cleaners left." She held up her blistered hands, which were angry from the intense heat she had shoved them into over and over while she panned for clues. "There are no bone fragments. No teeth. No nothing."

"The average house fire burns at one to two thousand degrees," Bishop said from the hallway. "Your average practitioner would be lucky to pack that much heat, and it's doubtful they could do it without help from a coven or an artifact." He paused to let that sink in. "There were remains at the bar. There were none at Michelle's."

A tremble started in Hadley's calves and climbed up her body until she vibrated with the stirrings of dangerous hope.

"For comparison," Bishop continued without entering, "a crematorium burns bodies at fourteen to eighteen hundred degrees. There are always bits left. Always. Splintered bone, melted dental amalgam, jewelry, phones, other electronics people keep on their person at all times."

"You're saying none of those things were found," Hadley said slowly, staring at the damage to Remy's hands. "Does that mean...?" She swallowed hard. "Why was no one there?"

What Hadley was saying finally struck Midas through his protective haze, and he should have gotten it sooner. The restaurant had staff. Cooks, waitstaff, a hostess, among others. Yet no remains were found?

"We don't know that yet, kid."

Appearing to digest that, she stared toward the door. "Why are you still in the hallway?"

"Your man threatened to eat my face earlier, so I figured better safe than dinner."

She cranked her head toward him. "Midas?"

"Last week, he blew you up," he reasoned. "Last night, he tranquilized you."

"You're lucky Midas didn't rip out your throat," his mother said from behind him. "I would have."

"Midas." Hadley gentled her voice. "You can't murder everyone who hurts me."

Eyebrows climbing, he kept his mouth shut because she was wrong, but he didn't want to tell her so.

Releasing Remy, she walked into his arms and mashed her face into his chest. "I can hear you thinking murder thoughts."

"I'll try to think quieter."

A laugh huffed into his shirt, and her fingers tightened around him. "What does this mean?"

The weight of what she asked pressed down on him until he ought to have sunk through their floor into the lobby.

"I don't want you to get your hopes up and then get hurt all over again." He buried his face in her hair. "But I don't want you to lose all hope either."

"That's a fine line to walk." She tipped her head back, her chin on his chest. "I'll see what I can do."

"We're here to help." Linus eased forward. "We'll do whatever we can to locate those responsible."

As protective as Hadley was of her city and her role in it, Midas expected her to pass on the offer.

"Okay." She turned a grateful expression on Linus. "I think..." She glanced at Grier. "I would like that."

"You're in charge." Linus returned his hands to his pockets. "What do you want us to do?"

Pulling away from Midas, Hadley wrapped herself in the mantle of potentate and summarized the past few days for everyone. The longer she spoke, the further she distanced herself from the role of grieving sister. It worried Midas, how well she compartmentalized, but there would be time to mourn later. He would make sure of it. Nothing good would come from letting wounds like this fester.

"Do you have any idea who the inside man might be?" Grier chewed on her thumbnail. "Or woman?"

"None." Hadley took Midas's hand and held on tight. "An enforcer makes the most sense, but we don't have concrete evidence pointing toward any one person."

"The OPA is clear," Bishop added gently. "I tested each person myself. The leak isn't at our office."

"I'm sorry." Showing none of the relief she must have felt at having her team cleared, Hadley turned her head toward his mother. "This means the coven has taken another pack member."

"We all knew it was possible," she said tiredly. "We've suspected it before, and here we are again."

"I don't grasp the finer nuances of the alpha/pack bond," Linus admitted to Tisdale, "but can you sense anything through your connection to the others?"

"I would have hunted them down myself," she replied on a gusted breath, "if that were possible."

"Their scent might give them away." Midas thought of Krista, the teen girl the coven had taken from their pack to lure the others away with the drug Faete. "Fresh skins smell like black magic."

"Old skins have no scent at all," his mother countered. "And I suspect that's what we're facing."

"I hate to agree with her," Bishop called, still in the hall, "but she's right. This person must have been embedded before the shit hit the fan. Otherwise, we would have noticed the wrongness, or smelled it."

"The practitioner must have sworn off magic for the duration of the operation to avoid a gwyllgi nose outing them," Linus agreed. "That level of discipline would require a master of the art, or the flip-side of the coin. A neophyte without an established magical signature who embraced abstinence to ensure they read as clean."

"A newbie would explain the sloppy bombs." Bishop grunted. "The longer you avoid using your magic, the weaker it grows."

"Inexperience could be the mitigating factor," Linus added in support of their working theory. "A newbie isn't as likely to get complex magics right on the first try. As Bishop said, it would explain why the first bomb failed to detonate."

Luck was all that had spared Hadley, and it terrified Midas to know hers could run out at any moment.

"Our trap won't work now." Hadley stared toward the door. "No one would believe it after this."

"Trap?" Midas rumbled. "What trap?"

"Bishop and I were tossing around the idea of setting up another date night to lure out the bomber."

Grinding his molars, Midas kept from stomping out and stran-gling Bishop with his own tongue.

"Murder thoughts," Hadley singsonged. "He was right to stay in the hall."

"The date idea won't fly," Grier cut in, "but a wake might work."

"That would put others in danger." Hadley sliced her hand through the air. "The whole date angle was so the bomber wouldn't think it was odd if only Midas and I showed."

"Not many people in Atlanta know Boaz, Addie, or their parents well. We could pick and choose who got invites." Grier drummed her fingers on her arm. "We could keep the gathering small to limit the risks."

"We can't protect them." Hadley shook her head. "I won't endanger more people."

"Let me handle that." Grier and Linus shared a glance that spoke volumes. "I can keep them safe."

"You're sure?" Hadley bit her lip. "Of course you're sure."

"You're fine." Grier lifted a shoulder. "We haven't spent much time together since...everything happened...so you're right to ask. If we were in my city, talking these stakes with my people, I would do the same."

Drawing him back into the conversation, Hadley rubbed Midas's arm. "What do you think?"

"It's a good idea." Though he hated admitting it. "It could work."

"You're not on board." She read him too easily. "We're going to have to trust Grier can deliver."

"She can," Linus promised, draping an arm across her shoulders. "She wouldn't offer otherwise."

"I'm not doing this without you." Hadley fisted Midas's shirt. "We can find another way."

"I trust them." He exhaled through his teeth. "It's hard where you're concerned, but I do."

"Before we get into specifics, we're going to need to test each of you." Hadley broke away from him. "Bishop, do you still have the kit?"

"Yup." He stepped into the doorway, tossed her a bag, then retreated. "Lancets are in the side pouch."

"I must have missed a memo." Grier glanced from her to Midas. "What are we testing for?"

"Abbott and Reece, with help from Doughty," Hadley informed them, "developed a rudimentary test to determine if a person has become a host to a Martian Roach or if their skin is being worn by the coven."

Blinking at Hadley, who tossed the bag to Midas, Grier cleared her throat. "A what now?"

"The parasitic roaches I mentioned," Linus murmured. "Hadley nicknamed them Martian Roaches."

"Why am I not surprised?" Grier smothered a grin. "As in *The Martian Roaches Who Invaded Atlanta*?"

The dip in Hadley's chin at the gentle teasing kicked Midas's protective instincts up a notch.

Hadley was so...*Hadley*. She was more comfortable in her own skin than anyone he knew, and he hated how the collision of her past with her present rattled her, diminished her, made her think twice before speaking or acting when one of the things he loved most about her was her spirit.

"I'll administer the tests," his mother offered. "You look like you would enjoy pricking them too much."

Since Midas didn't disagree, he stepped back to give her room and volunteered as her first victim. "Where are Hood and Eva?"

"Lethe left them at home." She used an alcohol wipe to clean his fingertip. "Their pack is too young to run smoothly without either of their alphas present, so Hood stayed behind. Neither of them wanted Eva involved in this mess, and I can't say I blame them. Even if I do regret missing a chance to visit with my granddaughter."

His mother qualified as a field medic, and she had some formal education in medicine. The skills weren't necessary for an alpha, but they didn't hurt. Neither did the stab of the lancet into his fingertip, the way she massaged his finger to coax a few drops to form before he healed, or how she wiped those on a thin paper strip she fed the machine.

"Congratulations," she announced five minutes later. "You're not infected."

After disposing of the materials, he waited on Hadley to get tested and be cleared before they sat on the couch and watched the others go through the motions.

Grier, Linus, Remy, Bishop, and finally his mother—all tested negative.

"This is good news." His mom passed the kit to Remy. "Be a dear and test my shadows, will you?"

Half listening, Midas tensed when he thought she was calling out Ambrose, but she meant her guards.

Gleefully, Remy pressed the button on the lancing device, popping the needle in and out. "Sure thing."

"Everyone present is who we think they are, and that does my old heart good."

Whenever his mother played up her age or her health, he knew she was posturing for outsiders.

"Hadley and Grier can plan the wake," she carried on, "as the two closest to the deceased."

The *deceased* caused Hadley's breath to freeze, her heart to skip, but she exhaled and sank against him.

"Bishop—" His mother caught herself and pivoted toward Hadley. "I slid into mother mode, didn't I?"

"I was thinking alpha mode." She had recovered enough to smile. "I get it, though."

"We're all alphas of a sort," she agreed. "I didn't mean to take over, so I'll blame habit."

Remy reappeared and made a beeline for the kitchen with her medical waste. "They're both clear."

"Excellent." His mother accepted the kit and set about sterilizing it. "I'll call your sister, get her here for testing." She repacked it. "Are we missing anyone else?"

"Ford," Midas and Hadley said together, and then she added, "Ares too."

"Remy?" His mother repackaged the kit. "Would you mind doing the honors?"

"Drop the kit off with Lisbeth when you're done with Lethe and

Ares." Hadley tilted her head. "She can test Ford and bring the kit back to HQ."

"And me?" Tisdale arched her brows. "How can I help?"

"I wouldn't presume to give you orders." Hadley held his mother's stare with ease. "I would appreciate it if you could mingle with the enforcers, though. See if you pick up any weird vibes. You know them better than anyone."

"I can arrange for refreshments to be delivered for them the night of the wake. You're pack, and you lost your sister. They won't find it odd." She touched Hadley's arm. "I'll work the party, get them talking."

"Thank you."

"You wouldn't have been strong enough, you know."

Confusion pinched Hadley's face. "For what?"

"My son." His mother drew in a shuddering breath then pushed it out. "He's suffered, and he's come out the other side of his tribulations stronger, but his trials have left their mark on him."

Midas's fingers itched to comfort her. "Mom…"

"Midas couldn't have loved anyone who didn't understand pain." Expression tight, she kept going. "And they couldn't have understood him." She kissed Hadley's cheek. "You couldn't have understood each other." She withdrew. "I can't hold your past or your mistakes against you when fighting so hard to correct them has made you the incredible woman you are, and the perfect match for my son."

Surprising the room, Hadley embraced his mother without prompting. "You're a good mom."

"I consider you my daughter, Hadley. You're free to call me *Mom* when or if you're ever ready."

"I might take you up on that after…" Hadley withdrew. "I have things to get right in my head first."

Nodding her understanding, his mother let Hadley retreat without another word and turned to him.

"I must return to the den." She kissed his cheek. "Keep me updated on the wake, and I'll make my plans from there." She tapped his shoulder. "Just so you know, I'm taking Lethe with me. I need all the help I can get smoothing over the Knoxville incident with our neighbors and deciding what to do with the survivors."

"Thank you." He stole the hug he missed out on earlier. "For everything."

"Silly boy." She patted his cheek. "That's what mothers are for."

She spoke the words to him, but he got the feeling they were meant for Hadley.

NINE

Bishop mumbled a goodbye to me, hightailed it out of the hall, and rode down to the lobby with Tisdale.

Now that she knew my secrets, I could imagine how that conversation would go.

Lots of threats, on both sides. Promises of retribution, on both sides. And then an uneasy truce.

Or so I hoped.

"How soon do you want to schedule the wake?"

Jerking my attention back to Grier, I replayed the chunk of conversation I had spaced out on, but my brain was spinning its wheels, worried about Bishop and Tisdale alone in an elevator. How much damage could they do to one another during a sixty-second drop?

Never mind.

I didn't want to know.

Locking those worries away for later, I forced myself to focus on Grier for real this time, but it was hard. I had trouble adjusting to our dynamic. She was here, in the loft where she had spent so many nights with Linus, as a guest. As *my* guest. This had been their space for a year and change. Arguably, Grier belonged here more than me. The imbalance left me feeling like I ought to ask her permission before I got a bottle of water out of my own fridge.

Awkward as it might be to have her in my space, I had to remind myself she wasn't here for me.

I had lost my brother, and she had lost her first love, and a friend. She had come to pay her respects.

That was it. That was all. It had to be.

There were no bodies. There were no bodies. There were no bodies.

The endless loop of Remy's words wasn't helping matters. With my brain fried extra crispy, I couldn't get it to stop hopping from thought to thought like frog legs avoiding a pan of hot grease. "Tomorrow."

"That's...quick." She checked with Linus. "Are you sure you don't want to take another day?"

I could tell then that she was viewing this wake as a genuine farewell to our lost loved ones.

And I could also tell, I hadn't given up on my brother or Addie or the others.

Hope is both a misery and a miracle.

"No one knew them here," I reasoned. "They'll expect the formalities to be observed in Savannah."

An itch between my shoulders had me searching out Linus, and sure enough, he was watching me.

Chills skated down my spine, but I hadn't lied to Tisdale. Linus didn't require my consent, but he had it. It would hurt him, deeply, to clean up my mess, but he would do it. He was a good man, and a good friend.

While I respected his concern, I didn't plan on embracing the dark side because of my loss.

Then again, I was obviously in denial. I could tell. I knew the signs. I couldn't trust myself. Not yet.

I had to believe he would know if or when I made a wrong turn and correct it before taking extreme, but necessary, measures.

"Okay." Grier hovered on my periphery. "I can handle this if you have somewhere else to be."

She was giving me an out. A pass. An escape route.

A way to pretend, for a while longer, that the wake was window dressing.

Coward that I was, I took it. With both hands. And I ran with it.

"I would appreciate that." I flashed her a wobbly smile. "Midas?"

With his hand pressed to my lower back, ready to guide me out, he said, "I'm with you."

We made our exit without explanations or excuses. I didn't want to lie to them, so I didn't, but I couldn't be here anymore. I needed open air, a purpose. I needed to make progress and not regress. I couldn't waste another minute curled up in bed while the coven picked off everyone close to me.

No sooner had we hit the streets than Remy called me. "Did you find everyone?"

"Yeah, Lethe is clear. She left with Tisdale. Ares is good too, but *yikes*. I had to test her out in the hall just to hear myself think. That kid they're watching has a set of lungs on him. I thought I might do a twofer and test Liz while I was there, but she was at work."

"Wait." I held up a finger. "They still have the baby?"

"There were complications with the sister-in-law's surgery. She and Liz are on baby duty until the grandparents arrive to take over." She caught her breath then finished her recitation. "Lisbeth was with Ford. They were staring longingly into one another's eyes. I pried them apart long enough to test them. Both are clear. She's got the kit, and she'll bring it to HQ tomorrow."

All good news. Thank the goddess. "Are you still at the Faraday?"

"About to walk out the door, why?"

"Head downstairs to see Abbott about your hands. All of your hands. All of you...and their hands? Whatever. You know what I mean." I gestured Midas forward. "I should have made that a priority. My head wasn't in the right place earlier. I'm sorry."

"Fine," she said gruffly. "Only if it'll make you feel better."

"It would." A smile tugged at my mouth. "Much better."

Grumbling under her breath, she ended the call to, I hope, seek medical treatment.

Abbott knew who and what she was, and he was the only person I trusted with her secrets and her care.

After putting up my phone, I checked with Midas. "Did you catch all that?"

"I did." He cut his eyes toward me. "You're a good alpha to your people."

The praise caused heat to rise in my cheeks, and I ducked my head until they cooled.

Without a destination in mind, I fell into the old habits of walking my familiar patrol routes. I wish there had been a disturbance, a physical outlet for my helpless anger and anxiety, but the city remained quiet, as if she mourned with me. Which was ridiculous since she was still bonded to Linus.

And Linus wouldn't regret never seeing Boaz again, would he?

Surprising no one, least of all myself, I circled back to the restaurant. I wasn't sure how long I stood there before I noticed a peculiar gleam among the debris or when I decided to pursue it. Midas didn't stop me when I picked my way through the wreckage to reach it, but he followed to keep me from stumbling or collapsing, one or the other.

Nestled in a pile of ash, a ring winked up at me. The thick gold band was familiar, as was the glass stone.

Once upon a time, I had begged Boaz to let me wear his class ring. Other girls had worn their boyfriends' rings, and it made me jealous. I didn't date much in high school. Most of my friends ended up having sex junior or senior year, which I also envied, but not enough to get naked with a guy I would have to see for the rest of school, who would ask questions about my scars.

Fear tasted metallic in the back of my throat when it hit me Midas would see them too.

Suddenly, his choice to see me as I truly was as opposed to the glamour I wore made me twitchy.

"Gold wouldn't have survived this without warping or the glass cracking."

Startled from my thoughts, I glanced over at Midas. "It's pristine."

Well, as pristine as any piece of jewelry that had survived daily wear since his teenage years could be.

"Do you want me to get it for you?"

The words hung in my throat, so I nodded, which came easier.

Midas crouched and raked his fingers through the crumbling flakes, collected the ring, then cleaned it on his shirt before handing it to me. "What does this mean?"

Along the inside of the band, Boaz's stamped initials had faded with wear, but I could still read them.

"This means..." I slid the ring onto my finger, "...my brother is alive."

That was the obvious conclusion.

What does this mean?

A direct link to my brother rather than my sister hinted that the coven knew my true identity.

What does this mean?

I didn't have a frakking clue.

"Boaz's ring was planted. They meant for you to find it." He crouched again and ran his hand through the ash one last time. "The Remys and Bishop wouldn't have missed it. It's too big."

"Who planted it?" I rubbed my thumb over the stone then slid the ring off my finger and put it in my pocket. "The bomber? Boaz? The coven?"

"Boaz would have called or made contact if he was able, so that leaves the coven or their agents."

"Why haven't they reached out? If they took hostages, why not name the terms for their release?"

"I don't know."

But we both had a good idea why they might have kept them, what they might have done to them.

If my brother or Addie, or their—*our*—parents, had miraculously survived, I would have no choice but to greet them with a finger stick and not a hug.

That really, really sucked. It made my head throb and my heart ache. But I had to be smart about this.

Until I reached for him, I hadn't noticed Ambrose's absence, which unsettled my stomach. Usually, I kept a closer eye on him. Now was not the time to relax my vigilance, no matter how well-behaved my darker half had been acting lately. Key word *acting*. More than likely, he had been hiding from the crowd in the loft he suspected might lynch us. Normally, I would applaud the performance, but just now I needed his help.

"Can you sense anything?" I reached into my pocket, impressed by how well I had trained myself to stuff them full of chocolates without thinking about it. "I know you taste magic on a person, but what about a place? Can you try?"

I paid a modest toll of three white chocolate truffles rolled in crushed pecans for his cooperation.

Midas watched, more curious than anything about Ambrose's quirks. "Do you think he'll find anything?"

"I'm not holding my breath." I walked the rest of the site but knew better than to expect another clue. "I should have asked him sooner, but it didn't cross my mind. He's attuned to energy sources that will fill his tank, not residual magic that's less than a mouthful."

I got my answer when Ambrose swirled to a stop before me and bounced his shoulders in a shrug.

Disappointed when I should have known better, I asked, "Would sampling the other sites help?"

Quick to stick out his hand, he waited for me to toss him more chocolate to buy his opinion.

"I'm guessing that's a yes, but also that it will cost me."

The shadow bobbed its head and curled its fingers in a *gimme* motion.

"I'll pay up once we get there. Otherwise, you'll act like I tricked you into working for free and pout until I waste premium chocolates on one of your tantrums."

Ambrose, who was quick to laugh at me, did, miming a fit of hilarity that bordered on slapstick.

"Midas?" I checked with him to see if Ambrose freaked him out as much as he disturbed Bishop. "Do you mind two more stops?"

"I'm game for whatever you think will help." Curiosity brightened his eyes. "Can I…feed him?"

On his best behavior, Ambrose walked over to Midas, bent at the waist, and stuck out his hand.

"Don't fall for it. You can't touch him." I shooed the shadow away. "He's just sucking up to you."

"Does that mean I shouldn't feed him?"

"Now that you can see him, and you've expressed an interest, I expect he'll start begging you for scraps."

We started walking back to the site of the first fire, Choco-Loco, which was closer to our position.

"What can he eat?" Midas laced our fingers. "Is there anything I shouldn't give him?"

All of a sudden, I felt like a pet parent giving instructions to a gullible pet sitter.

"Never tell him it's okay to feed on anyone or anything. He needs my permission for that." Though, after watching him skim from random people on the street, I had my doubts that was as true as it used to be. "With you and I bonded now too, I'm not sure how it will work going forward. It might be like my ability to issue you orders. You might be able to do the same to him with a direct command."

"I hadn't thought of that." Midas angled his head toward me. "We'll need to figure it out, eventually."

"Yeah, we will." I glared at the shadow tucked within Midas's shadow. "Or else accidents might happen."

Hand tightening around mine, Midas took my meaning, and he set his jaw.

One wrong word from him might damn me as easily as I could damn myself. How terrifying was that?

At least as terrifying as it must be for him to know that I could wrest control of his beast away from him.

"Are we soul mates? Fated mates? Cosmic partners in a predestined love?"

Based on Claudia's explanation, and Ambrose vouching for our bond, the answer was a resounding *yes*. Such a connection would explain the influence we each held over our other halves, but it felt weird bringing it up to him instead of the other way around.

"We're...complicated." He rubbed his jaw. "The truth?"

Tugging on his arm, I leaned against him. "That would be nice."

"I don't know."

"Explain."

"At first, I thought so, yes. Now I'm not so sure." He was quiet for a moment. "There is a bond. We know that much. We can both sense it."

"But?"

"It doesn't function how it was explained to me." He slanted me a searching look. "Each pair is different, but usually not this divergent. We don't pick up on each other's thoughts or emotions. We're connected, but I'm not sure how. A link has been established, but it's almost like it hasn't been activated yet."

How the heck did you activate it? Add batteries? Pull out the plastic tab? Dial an 800 number?

"You're telling me we have a wonky bond?"

Finding a soul mate was like hitting the lottery when you were a warg. Gwyllgi hybrids like Midas, with their half-warg and half-gwyllgi lineage, didn't often experience the same bone-deep connection to their partner. They had too much fae in them, and fae were much, um, *freer* in their affections.

"I haven't brought it up," he admitted, "because we have so much else on our plates right now."

Aside from the real danger we might pose to one another if we didn't hash out how much influence we each wielded over the other, I couldn't blame him for shelving it for later. Until this extra stress hit, it could have waited. Now, not so much. We needed to talk it out at the very least to make sure it wasn't another type of bomb about to explode.

"Do you think it's okay?" I placed a hand over my heart. "Will it break?"

"I don't think so." A deep groove bisected his forehead. "We'll figure it out."

"It doesn't bother you?" I rubbed my chest. "That we're in mating limbo?"

Midas stopped in his tracks and used our joined hands to haul me against his hard chest.

"I'm not in limbo." He lowered his head, his warm breath skating across my mouth before his lips touched mine. "I'm right here, with you, where I'll always be."

"I didn't mean to derail us." I tightened my grip on him. "It just hit me, when you mentioned how we can each probably exert control over the other."

We hadn't tested his theory on my end, but it was on the to-do list now, and I had a hunch about the outcome.

"I'm happy to answer any questions you have to the best of my ability." He kissed me again, quick and soft. "I want you to know that I don't need the bond to tell me you're—"

"—my own person?"

"*Mine.*" He smiled against my lips when he stole another kiss. "All mine."

Spluttering laughter, I let him get away with it. "Am I going to wake up with a tattoo branding me one day?"

Heat flashed in his eyes, and he slid his gaze down my body. "How many do you have, anyway?"

"It's a surprise."

The fact we could laugh together and tease one another meant the world to me on a good day. That we could talk about our future, uncertain as it might be, without missing a beat... Yeah. It meant everything.

Our reprieve lasted long enough for me to remember how to breathe again, but then we were at Choco-Loco, and Ambrose was zooming off to explore. His recon didn't take long. Within a minute, he skidded to a stop before us and reported by spreading his hands wide.

"Here." I handed Midas three more truffles. "Toss them in, wrapper and all. He doesn't care either way."

Shadow morphing into the outline of an eager dog, it thumped its silent tail and lolled its tongue.

"He can assume any form?" Midas flung them one at a time. "Anyone's form?"

"He can mimic any shadow he's encountered from what I can tell, but he can only manifest one face."

Midas dusted his hands then flashed his empty palms, like Ambrose really was a dog who required proof he was out of treats. "Linus's, right?"

"More or less, yes. He took artistic license, but from a distance, we could pass for him."

Mouth tight, he watched the shadow reshape to match my outline. "Can he manifest now?"

"This is it." I caught the flicker of annoyance through my bond with Ambrose. "Unless I lose control."

"You're so much stronger than I ever knew." Midas fisted his hand in my hair. "I had no idea."

"I don't deserve all the credit. Those tattoos you're so interested in counting? Linus designed them. They help me control and contain Ambrose. Day to day, they do the heavy lifting." And they looked good doing it. Linus truly was an artist. "They give me space to think and act beyond obsessing over whether a snap in my temper is me having a bad day or Ambrose nudging me toward a bad decision."

While absorbing that, Midas turned his gaze skyward, toward the lightening horizon. "We have time to hit the last site if you want."

"Yeah." I had to go if there was even a slight chance of discovering another clue. "Might as well."

I was dragging by the time we arrived. The ring in my pocket must have weighed a thousand pounds.

"Ambrose." I tossed him three more treats as I stood where the bar used to be. "Do your thing."

Straining my eyes for the telltale gleam of another clue, I was reminded of the glint that saved my life.

"The night the bar was bombed, I was standing outside on my phone when I saw this glint. I was going to check it out when the place exploded."

Ambrose was fast, but one day he wouldn't be fast enough. That was simple math and plain truth.

"Bishop reviewed the footage from that night. He said it resembled a flashbang. The kind the pack uses." I bit the inside of my cheek. "I should have told you sooner, but there was Claudia and then the challenge and then…"

The news about Boaz and Addie had been my true breaking point.

"We're all under a lot of stress." He scrubbed a hand down his face. "Things are going to slip through the cracks." He reached for his phone. "Every enforcer is required to sign out their gear at the start of a shift and must account for it before they go home."

"Our mole won't be that careless."

They would steal a replacement from another enforcer or from the supply room to stay under the radar.

"It won't hurt to check."

"Every clue leads us that much closer," I agreed. "That extra bit of distance probably saved my life."

"You think they lured you away." He searched my face. "You think someone was protecting you."

I think I was desperate to connect dots, to forge connections, to make this nightmare make sense.

"It has to mean something." I flashed Boaz's ring. "*This* has to mean something."

Or else it meant nothing, and I was unraveling faster than a ball of yarn in a roomful of kittens.

"The same person protecting you might have also protected your family."

His tone came out questioning. He was asking me if that's what I thought...what I *hoped*...had happened.

"I don't know." I raked my fingers through my hair. "Maybe?"

Ambrose reported in and shook his head. Then he coiled around Midas's shoulders like a mink stole.

Midas had the good grace not to shudder, as Bishop would have, but then again, he was curious about the other man in my life. Maybe he really didn't mind cozying up with Ambrose for my sake.

"We need to identify the bomber." Midas led me with light fingers on my elbow to the corner where he called us a Swyft for the ride home. "It's the only way we're going to get our answers."

"You're right." I leaned against his side. "Ares left a handful of seconds before I saw the glint at the bar." I wrestled my phone from my pocket and shot her a text. "I need to ask if she noticed anything unusual."

Yet another ball I had dropped while juggling so many, each its own mini ticking time bomb.

"Do you want to eat before we go home?" Midas glanced at me. "Ford did bring us burgers."

"We can eat those later." I recalled our guests. "Let's pick up something hot for Linus and Grier too."

"Does he eat?"

"Only when she makes him." I snorted. "Mostly she eats his food too, except for a bite or two."

"One of the many reasons she gets along so well with Lethe."

Once our Swyft driver arrived, we gave him the Faraday's address, and I ordered pizzas online.

With dinner handled, I texted Ares to ask if she had noticed anything peculiar at the bar that night.

She replied with a disappointing *no*, but she had been farther away than me from the explosion.

Bad news must travel fast, because Hank didn't so much as squint at me funny when we passed him.

"I'm sorry for your loss," he murmured as the door shut behind me, but I heard him.

Midas and I waited for our order in the lobby, and I was glad no one was around to push condolences on me. I was too afraid in my current mood that I would push them back, and no good little potentate went around instigating shoving matches.

When the food arrived, I tipped the delivery girl then asked her to bring the extra meat pizza on top out to Hank. Poor guy never left his post these days. The least I could do was feed him in thanks for his efforts to keep the residents safe.

And no, I wasn't going soft because he was decent to me one whole time.

Back up in the loft, we found Linus standing before the windows, a phone pressed to his ear. Grier sat on the couch with pages of notes splayed around her. Lethe sat on the floor near her with a greasy bag on her lap, and crumpled burger and fry wrappers littered the floor.

So much for leftovers. All the food Ford brought was gone. Even, and it hurt to see it, my apple pie.

"Good thing we brought food," I muttered to Midas. "I hope there's enough."

"Not my fault your hostess skills are rusty." Lethe stuck a fry in her mouth. "I was starving to death."

Grier nudged Lethe in the shoulder with her bare foot. "No, you were not."

"You're supposed to be on my side." Lethe flung a second fry at Grier's head. "Traitor."

Grier caught the fry and wrinkled her nose. "Do you want this back?"

"Yes." Lethe held out her hand. "Duh."

"We brought pizza." Midas held the boxes high. "You don't have to fight over cold fries."

"But I like cold fries." Lethe polished off the remaining ones to prove her point. "Hot pizza works too."

"The wake plans are done." Grier shuffled her papers. "I waited to finalize the bookings in case you wanted to take a look first."

"I trust you." I twisted the clunky ring that had somehow made its way back onto my finger. "You know them almost as well as I do."

"We settled on a rustic steakhouse owned by a former colleague of Linus's," she continued, ignoring my use of present tense, "a professor from Strophalos University." She flashed me a photo on her phone. "He's Society, and he's excited about renting it out. He even volunteered to help in exchange for an introduction. Apparently, he's a big fan of yours. He mentioned a fight with a chupacabra?" Her eyebrows rose. "The catch is, we pay all damages."

That was the purpose of insurance, his and ours, and we both knew it. The OPA was liable for any damage caused by its agents. His butt was covered either way. What she had agreed to pay was a hefty bribe, a premium I would reimburse. Not that I blamed the guy for being greedy when his business had a wrecking ball aimed at it.

"He was *very* concerned for his employees," she said with a snort. "So *very* concerned he felt the volunteers for our event ought to receive hazard pay. With an administration fee tacked on, of course."

"Goddess what a headache." I rubbed my forehead in sympathy. "Thanks for making the arrangements."

"Catch me up to speed." Lethe cleaned up her mess, tossed it in the trash, then got a drink. "You ditched your sisterly duties and then what?"

"Lethe," Grier warned her in a low voice. "I volunteered to handle it."

"That's because you're a sucker." She cut her gaze toward me. "Well?" She waited. "Impress me."

"Hadley doesn't owe you an explanation." Midas stepped up to Lethe. "You need to watch your tone."

"Baby brother, she hasn't heard my tone yet." She honed her glower on him. "Neither have you."

"As hard as it is for you to believe," he said, sounding tired, "this isn't about you."

"This is about Amelie—I mean, *Hadley*—doing what she always does."

Lips gone numb, I still asked, I was curious. "And what is that?"

"You stir up a shitstorm and then duck before any of the muck splatters you."

"You didn't like Boaz." Midas stepped closer to her. "You barely knew Addie. Why do you care?"

"You know who else gets splattered when this happens?" Lethe jerked her chin toward Grier. "Who always gets splattered around *Hadley*?"

The urge to defend myself never manifested, and I didn't look too hard at why. "You're right."

"No." Grier squared off with Lethe. "She means well, but she's wrong."

A growl poured out of Lethe's mouth, and her hands curled into fists down at her sides.

"You're my best friend," Grier said quietly. "I get you want to protect me, but Hadley isn't an enemy. She made mistakes. Guess what? We all have. None of us have clean hands. There's blood on all of ours. The life she's carved out for herself here impresses the heck out of me, and I won't let you diminish it in my name." She shot her friend a knowing glance. "If you've got a beef with Midas, take it up with him. Don't take it out on her."

"Fine." A snarl curled her lip as she stared down Midas. "Let's take this outside."

Guilt hit me hard that I had come between Midas and Lethe. "Your problem is with me."

"Pin a rose on your nose," Lethe sneered, shrugging off Grier's attempts to rein her in.

"Leave Midas out of this." I spread my hands. "Let's handle this between ourselves."

"Hadley, you don't have to humor her." Midas touched my shoulder. "I can—"

"You shouldn't have to defend your choices to her." I slid my gaze to hers. "He's sacrificed enough, don't you think?" Pallor swept through her, and her mouth fell open in shock that he had told me. "He's always made the hard choice, always put himself second to those he loves, and I'm over it. You might let him do it for you, but he's not doing it for me."

Wide palms landed on my shoulders, and Midas turned me to face him. "How did we get here?"

"You made a lot of questionable life choices." I rolled a shoulder. "And you laughed at my jokes."

"They were pity chuckles, and that's not what I meant."

"I love you." I clasped his wrists. "I'm willing to beat up your big sister to prove it."

Lethe strutted over, and I let him go with a wink that promised I would be okay, but she didn't leave.

"Let's eat." Lethe crouched as she lifted the boxes from the floor where Midas had tossed them to play referee. "I'm hungry."

Turning her back on me, she carried the stack to the dining room and placed them on the table.

"I'm confused." I pivoted on my heel to keep her in sight. "What happened to taking this outside?"

"You called me out on being an asshole, and I decided you were right."

"Just like that?"

"Amelie was selfish, and I didn't like her much. She hurt people I love, and I take issue with that." She let out a breath. "She was also Grier's best friend, and I admit I was jealous of their shared history too." She flipped open a random lid and helped herself to a slice. "I expected Hadley to be Amelie 2.0, a shiny new label slapped on the same old product." Her forehead creased as she chewed. "Grier has a marshmallow heart, and I figured she was giving you a pass when she bragged on you. Linus's views tend to fall in line with hers, so I didn't give either of them much credit." She set aside the thin crust and flicked a glance at her brother. "I didn't give you much credit either." Her gaze wandered back to mine. "I gave you none at all, and I was wrong to write you off without meeting the new you first."

"Today is a day for the history books." Midas brushed his fingertips down my spine. "Today is the day Lethe Kinase admitted she was *wrong*."

"I didn't say I was wrong." She selected another piece. "I was just less right than usual."

"You literally said *I was wrong*," Grier chimed in. "We all heard you."

Cocking her arm, she flung the crust at Grier and hit her between the eyes. "Shut up."

"Make me." Grier stuck out her tongue. "I dare you."

"I have a better idea." Lethe scooped up six more pieces. "I'm going to eat your share."

Jaw dropping, Grier pointed at her. "You *monster*."

"I might be a monster, but I'm the monster with all the cheesy pepperoni pizza." She cackled and bit into her stack like it was a sandwich. "Suck pineapple and ham, Grier."

Mouth gaping, Grier kicked off her shoes. "Why don't you suck my big toe instead?"

"Ladies," Linus intoned, pocketing his cell and stepping between them. "There's plenty for everyone."

Both of them turned to him, and he let one side of his mouth quirk in the tiniest of smiles.

"I placed an order the moment Lethe picked up the boxes."

"I love you." Grier bounced over to him. "You are the absolute best."

"You are no fun," Lethe grumped in his direction. "None."

Wading into the fray, mildly afraid of getting between them, I did what I should have done first and announced, "Boaz and the others are alive."

That shut them up.

Sure, they were looking at me like I was crazy, and maybe I was, but I had their attention.

Now to redirect it before blood—or more food—started flying.

TEN

A slim black dress swirled around Hadley's knees, and Midas kept getting caught with his eyes roving her legs. The stilettos were new, and they did interesting things to her calves. He couldn't tear himself away.

"You might want to dial it down a few notches," Grier cautioned beside him. "This is a wake, not a rave."

"She's beautiful." He hadn't meant to say it, but he didn't regret it either. "I can't seem to help myself."

"I respect that." She twirled untouched wine in a glass. "I have the same trouble around Linus."

"But this isn't the time or the place."

"We have one chance to sell this."

Her own pale eyes were dark with what he would have mistaken for grief if he didn't know it for worry. The room was filling with people come to pay their respects. Most were here for Hadley's sake. The rest were part of their team. The mixture of the oblivious and the undercover kept his teeth on edge.

Women's room is clear.

Men's room is clear.

Parking lot is clear.

Kitchen is clear.

Alley is clear.

Voices whispered through his earpiece as the enforcers, all tested and cleared, made their rounds.

Drawn to her like a magnet, Linus's gaze found Grier, and he inclined his head toward the door.

Behind him, his wraith, Cletus, hovered above the crowd in his tattered cloak, his cowl hiding the void of his face, as he searched for unseen dangers.

"I have to return to my post." Grier lifted her glass in acknowledgment. "More guests are arriving."

As people entered, Grier drew an impervious sigil on each of them, playing the gesture off as a necromantic rite of mourning. The sigil was an invention of hers, a close secret kept by her inner circle. It worked as advertised, making those who wore it impervious to harm.

Between Linus and Grier, Hadley and himself, they had taken every precaution. From the sigils to the location, the trap was set with as much control of the outcome as they could manage between them.

Hadley ended her most recent circuit of the room beside him. "I got nothing."

"I haven't noticed any peculiar behavior either." A heavy sadness filled him. "We know everyone here."

"We expected the bomber to be one of us." She rested her hand on his forearm. "It sucks to have it confirmed."

"It's not confirmed yet," he reminded her then checked his phone. "Mom says the party is in full swing."

"I can't see them targeting the Faraday a second time." She kept her head down to hide her expression, but the words were spoken as more of a prayer than a certainty. "They know we're on to them now."

"I don't mean to intrude," a willowy teen all but whispered. "May I have a word, Midas?"

"Go." Hadley nudged him toward the young gwyllgi. "I'll be right here."

Suspicion bloomed when the girl led him to a quiet corner, and he resented the coven that much more for making him doubt the young among his own people. "How can I help you, Amber?"

"I had an appointment with Doc Liz at the infirmary, but she didn't show."

"There must have been an emergency at the hospital."

Liz was a surgeon who worked at the local human hospital, but she pitched in when Abbott needed a hand, usually with young females in the pack.

"That's what I thought too, but she's not returning my calls to reschedule."

"When was your appointment?"

"The night Choco-Loco burned." She rested her small palms over her flat stomach. "That's why I gave it a few days. I didn't know about the fire until after she missed our appointment, but I figured if she wasn't working over at the hospital, then she must be helping people hurt in the other bombings. I didn't want to take her away from that."

Midas hadn't seen Liz in a week, maybe two. Their paths didn't cross all that often, but he didn't want to admit that and worry the girl. "I'll call Ares. She can get a message to Liz for you."

Using Ares to reach Liz set a bad precedent and might leave her feeling like a receptionist for her wife. That was conflict he didn't want to invite into their home. But the girl was worried, and his inner beast picked up on her nerves and wouldn't settle until he took action.

Keeping his voice low, Midas asked, "Can Abbott help?"

"It's personal," she whispered back. "I would rather talk to another woman about it."

"I understand." That is to say, he understood her situation was beyond his ken. "There's a healer in Buckhead—Briony Timms. She's a friend of Abbott's. She can see you if it's an urgent matter."

"I'll wait for Doc Liz," she mumbled, cheeks pink. "I—I'll take the number though. Just in case."

Once he got her squared away, he returned to Hadley, who had been half listening to their conversation if her frown was any indication. Unable to resist, Midas traced the scooped neckline that exposed several inches of her back.

"You're distracting me." She bounced her shoulders. "Behave."

"You're distracting me." He relished the chills rising on her skin. "You should have worn a burlap sack."

"I was fresh out," she demurred. "All I had in the pantry was cling wrap, and that felt risqué for a wake."

A mental picture of Hadley bound in clear plastic unspooled into his head and stuck there.

"You're growling." She backed against him until her shoulders hit his chest. "Loudly."

Suddenly, he was grateful she hid the front of his pants. "You paint a vivid picture."

"Can you two fake it a while longer, or do I need to separate you?"

Midas clenched his fists when he noticed Bishop standing beside them.

"I get we're all happy there's evidence to support Boaz and company might be alive, but you shouldn't be *that* kind of happy in public, let alone here and now. Think with the head on your shoulders, not the one in your pants."

As much as Midas wanted to snarl and snap, mostly Bishop's neck, Bishop was right to call him out on his behavior. There were myriad ways this could still go wrong, and Midas wasn't doing Hadley any favors if he let her hope sweep him away too.

If the coven had her family, they might be torturing them for information on her weaknesses.

If the coven had her family, since they hadn't asked for a ransom, their skins might be payment.

If the coven had her family, they might already be dead and their remains kept from their eternal peace.

If, if, if.

None of the outcomes at this point were favorable, and it was dangerous letting her pretend everything would be all right if she believed it hard enough. That was setting herself up to fail, to blame herself even more, and he couldn't encourage it any longer.

She might not survive it.

"Thank you," Midas mostly said without growling. "I forgot myself."

"No problem." Bishop tensed like he expected more or worse from him. "We all want the same thing."

"We'll behave." Hadley rested her hand on Bishop's arm. "Thanks for checking us when we needed it."

Shrugging like they had made him uncomfortable, Bishop ambled back to his corner.

"I'm doing that thing I do where I pretend everything is normal and okay even when I know it isn't." She pulled away from Midas. "I'm great at compartmentalizing. Fantastic, really. I can turn off messy emotions like a pro."

From the first time she flinched away from him, he'd known she had been abused at some point in her life. He spent enough time around children of all ages who had rebounded from horrors that would shatter an adult to recognize the signs. He had also learned no good came from pressuring someone to share their past who wasn't ready to give it voice, give it life.

The past changed how people viewed a person in the present, no matter how many promises were made beforehand, and the last thing people who had survived trauma wanted to see was their pain reflected in the eyes of their friends or loved ones.

"Everyone grieves differently." He linked their hands. "No one will judge you."

"When this is over..." She let the sentence die a slow death. "I have things to tell you."

It was as if she had pulled his thoughts straight from his head, and he went very still.

"I can't face it right now. Not with everything up in the air. I just..." She dug her nails into her palms. "I owe you my story. You told me yours, and I haven't shared mine."

"You don't owe me anything. Ever."

"I didn't mean it like that." She gave his fingers a reassuring squeeze. "I want to fill in the blanks instead of leaving you to do it for yourself. I want you to have the facts about me and not have to guess at them. I want you to know everything so that nothing ever surprises you. I want... I want one person in the whole world to know my story, and I want to be the one to tell it. To you."

Drawing her against him, Midas rested his chin on top of her head and breathed her in. "Thank you."

"Sorry I'm late."

Twisting aside, he spotted Ares dressed in black fatigues. "Glad you could make it."

Several of the others had shown up in their uniforms, dropping in as their work schedules allowed.

"What kind of friend do you think I am?" Her breath smelled strongly of coffee. "I wouldn't miss this."

Dark circles smudged the skin beneath her eyes, which were bloodshot. Her lips were cracked, and a line was worn in the skin of her brow from the frown she hadn't shaken since the last time he saw her. Sleep continued to elude her, if the caffeinated twitch in her eyelid was any indication, but the yawns kept coming.

"I'm sorry, Hadley." Ares clasped hands with her. "So sorry for your loss."

"Thank you." Hadley hugged her. "I'm glad you came."

Midas noticed her wife hadn't joined her, but he could understand why. Liz must have stayed home with the baby to prevent him from melting down in public when Hadley was already stressed to the max. Too bad the timing hadn't worked in his favor. Now he would have to put Ares on the spot about Amber.

"One of Liz's patients was here earlier." He infused apology into his voice. "Liz missed their appointment and isn't returning her phone calls." He hesitated. "How is Liz? The pregnancy is going well?"

"There have been recent complications, nothing too serious, but Liz took some time off work." Ares kept bouncing her gaze from face to face, scanning the room as if counting heads. "With Baby Alex giving us a nightmare introduction to Parenting 101, she must have forgotten to cancel." She returned her focus to his chin, as high as she dared look. "She never answers work calls when she's on vacation. They all go to her answering service. I'll let her know the calls aren't being forwarded so she can put in a tech support ticket."

The phone in Midas's pocket vibrated, and he checked the display. "I need to take this."

"I'm going to find the coffee." She shooed him on. "Then I'm going to start a caffeine IV."

"We got problems," Ford said into his ear. "We're missing a lot more than a single flashbang."

After catching Hadley's eye, he paced to a quiet corner of the room. "What do you mean?"

"The vault is short. I'm sending over the list so far. See if anything jumps out at you." An old country tune played in the background, and horns blared. "There's no telling who's been skimming unless we get lucky and spot them on the security camera."

The vault held surplus from the armory, which meant it got inventoried monthly versus nightly.

"Anyone with access to the vault has access to the surveillance room too."

"That's what I was thinking too." Ford sighed. "Hey, is Ares there yet?"

"Yeah." He rubbed his jaw. "She looks ready to fall over. Need me to hold her until you get here?"

"Nah." He paused. "I probably ought to keep my nose in my own business."

As much as the pack loved gossip, Ford was more restrained than most. "What's wrong?"

"I walked out with her, and Hank asked when Liz was coming home." He sounded uncomfortable sharing what was meant to be a private conversation. "Last I heard, Liz was home with the baby, but Hank made it sound like Liz had been gone for a while. Any idea what's going on there?"

A warning prickle slid down his spine. "What did she tell him?"

"She acted like she didn't hear. Breezed right past him. I figure he hit a sore spot, and she didn't want to answer in front of an audience." The noisy truck engine fell silent. "I didn't get to follow up with her. She got in a Swyft, and I headed to the garage."

"You're here now?"

"Just parked."

"See you inside."

Eyes sweeping the room, Hadley sidled up to him. "What's wrong?"

"Ares is lying." He put away his phone. "We need to keep an eye on her."

Pain flashed in her eyes, alongside determination, as he filled her in. "Do you think...?"

"I can't tell." He stared after Ares. "She reads the same as always to me, except..."

Hadley turned her face up to his, waiting. "Trust your instincts."

"If Hank is right, and Liz hasn't been home for some time, then she can't be babysitting now."

Abbott cautioned the test was accurate four times out of five. That Ares might prove to be the exception left a sour taste in his mouth. He couldn't picture her betraying the pack, the true Ares wouldn't, but the coven were masters of unimaginable horrors.

A grim certainty darkened her eyes. "We need to check her apartment before she gets back."

Midas had been about to suggest the same, but there was a problem. "You'll be missed."

"As much as I hate being left behind, I agree." She let wariness show. "Update me when you can."

"Keep her busy." He bent and kissed her, soft and quick. "Call or text me if she leaves."

"I will." She clung to him a moment longer. "Be extra careful."

"I'll be back as soon as I'm done."

Entering the hall at the rear of the restaurant, he faked the need for a bathroom break and bumped into Ford. "Watch over Hadley for me."

"You're leaving?" His eyebrows climbed. "You've got a lead."

"I'll touch base when I know more."

"All right." He pointed behind Midas. "There's an exit through the kitchen."

Midas took Ford's directions and cut through the bustling cooks hunched over their workstations while a man dressed all in white walked the line and barked orders that injected steel into the workers' spines.

"What are you doing back here?" The head chef flicked his wrist. "The kitchen is for staff only."

Ignoring the man, which caused his face to mottle, Midas located the door and left.

Had there been time, he would have engaged the man to soothe his ego and ensure his silence, but there was none.

Midas had the Swyft app open and a ride booked before he hit the sidewalk.

The driver pulled up as he began to pace, and he climbed in before the car rolled to a complete stop. Leg bouncing, he counted the seconds as if it would make the recalcitrant Atlanta traffic move faster. This time of night, he had a better chance of reaching the Faraday quicker by car than by foot. But he wished he had opted to run to burn off the nervous energy gnawing on him.

Ares might have been compromised, but it gutted him to question her loyalty.

Using his time wisely, he texted Abbott for a light interrogation on Liz.

>*Has Liz been in the clinic lately?*

>>*Looks like the last time she signed in was five days ago.*

>*Has she missed any appointments since then?*

>>*Not that I'm aware of, but I can ask Lisbeth to check.*

>*Do that.*

>>*What's wrong?*

>*Maybe nothing.*

Maybe everything.

With that done, he touched base with his mom to avoid bumping into her in the lobby and wasting precious time on explanations.

>*I'm on my way to the Faraday.*

>>*That was fast. Where's Hadley?*

>*At the wake. We have a lead.*

>>*Do you need backup?*

>*This is recon. I can handle it.*

>>*Text if that changes.*

>*I will.*

The temptation to text Hadley an update twitched in his fingers, but he had no news, only worries.

"Have a nice rest of your night."

Midas flicked his gaze out the windshield and noticed they had reached the Faraday.

"You too."

He slid out of the car, set his phone to vibrate, and tucked it into his pocket.

"You're back early," Hank said from his spot by the door. "And without Hadley."

Hank was far more perceptive than many gave him credit for, which was one of the reasons Midas had put him on doorman detail. Tonight, he wished Hank was slightly less observant. Then again, if he was right about Liz, he might have inadvertently given them their first real lead on a potential mole.

"I forgot something upstairs." Midas didn't owe him an answer, but it was polite, and it alibied him if anyone else saw him hit the elevators and wondered. "Then it's back to the wake."

Expression carefully neutral, Hank nodded and opened the door for him.

Voices and laughter reached him when he entered the lobby. The gwyllgi enforcers hadn't known Boaz or Addie, and without Hadley around, they had turned their wake into a giant pizza party.

The path to the elevators was clear, and he walked it briskly to discourage anyone from interfering with his ground-eating stride. He got lucky. There were no witnesses when he mashed the button for Ares's floor, and no one stopped the car during its ascent.

The arrival chime sent a shiver of anticipation down his spine, and his inner predator roused to wakefulness as he strode down the hall to the familiar door. He stood there a moment, listening, but heard nothing. He raised his hand to knock, hoping a frazzled Liz would answer with bags under her eyes and spit up on her shirt, but no one came.

The code to enter the apartment was already on his mind, and he mashed it into the keypad.

The light flashed green, the lock turned, and still no one moved on the other side.

Bracing himself for the worst, he eased the door open and began clearing the rooms, one by one.

Liz wasn't home.

There were no signs of a baby having ever been there.

But there was a laptop that woke at his touch, and its screen flickered to life. No password or pin required. Lazy security for an enforcer, but Ares might have wanted instant access or simply not cared if it was for home or shared use. He cursed at the highlighted video she had watched last on YouTube, a synthesized baby's cries on an eight-hour loop.

What the hell?

The empty apartment offered him no insights, but Hadley might see more than him. He took out his phone and recorded every inch of the space, aware Ares would smell him in her den and know it had been violated. This was his one and only chance to document how she had been living before she hid or destroyed any evidence he might find.

Part of him hoped the truth was simpler. That Liz had left Ares, and Ares had invented the baby story to give herself time to grieve and cope in private before having to answer hard questions. And the pack, being nosy as ever, would be full of them. But this felt bigger than a domestic situation.

Aware time was short, he made quick work of his task and exited the apartment. He hesitated in the hall, tempted to knock on her neighbors' doors to ask if they had scented or heard anything peculiar, as well as when they last saw Liz. But that would spread damaging rumors if this all turned out to be one big misunderstanding, and Midas didn't want that for Ares or Liz.

The ride down to the lobby gave him a moment to process, but he still wasn't sure what he saw meant.

As he stepped out onto the sidewalk, a car with a Swyft sticker on the windshield appeared, and Ares climbed out of it.

His heart gave one solid thump, but it couldn't catch its normal rhythm.

Hadley hadn't called him. He tried her and got punted to voicemail. He tried Linus. Grier. Same result.

A growl rose in his throat when Ares spotted him, eyes wide, and the beast in him lunged for her throat.

ELEVEN

I woke staring at the ceiling, which was weird. I had been standing a second ago, with a glass of wine I had no intentions of drinking in my hand. I didn't hurt, but I didn't *not* hurt. I was sore, maybe. Muffled. It was a weird sensation I had trouble naming, but I was experiencing it in full force.

Warm fingers brushed my outstretched arm, delicate but strong, and I struggled to turn my head.

Grier joined our hands, her smile a hesitant thing, and mouthed the words, *"You're okay."*

Or maybe she had asked if I was okay.

I sucked at lipreading.

Her eyes flicked past me, and I fought to roll my head in that direction.

Linus lay on my other side, his hands laced at his navel, his legs crossed at the ankles.

The wraith rode on unfelt air currents, its fingerbones clacking, clearly agitated as it drifted in this void.

I must be dreaming.

This was too frakking bizarre to be reality.

A pinch in my chest twisted into a full-blown ache, but I had no injuries I could see. Though the black fabric of my dress could be hiding an ugly secret. I might be bleeding. Or maybe it was Ambrose rousing.

That I couldn't tell was not a great indicator of my present state of being.

Unable to do more than twitch my limbs, I resumed staring at the ceiling, which was starting to blacken.

Goddess.

The building was an inferno, burning down around us, ash sprinkling us like rain without hitting our skin.

An explosion?

Had a bomb gone off?

Was that why it was so quiet?

I hoped it hadn't burst my eardrums, then I decided it was better than the alternative. That I was dead, which would also explain why I couldn't hear a frakking thing.

About to come unglued, I began fighting whatever compulsion held me down until Grier hauled herself closer, flung her body over mine, and pinned me.

The girl had definitely been eating churros on the regular since the last time she body-slammed me. I was in greater danger of her bony elbows puncturing one of my lungs than her weight suffocating me, but still.

Ouch.

A sense of timelessness swamped me, and I started drifting off again. I might have taken a nap if I hadn't heard my name bellowed from a great distance. I knew in my bones it was Midas, but I couldn't budge to comfort him. I couldn't so much as twitch with Grier starfished above me.

An eternity later, my ears popped, and smoke clogged my lungs. Sirens wailed, and water filled my nose. I shot upright, knocking her off me, and choked until the deluge from the firehose became a sprinkle. And still I heard that raw and ruined voice screaming my name. Over and over and over.

"Midas," I rasped, gaining my feet. *"Midas."*

Our collision would have knocked me onto my butt if he hadn't caught me before I fell.

"You didn't call." He crushed me against him. "You didn't call."

"Shh." I pressed my hands to his cheeks. "I'm okay."

I stroked his face, his throat, his chest, reassuring myself he was here, that I was alive.

Around us, the others began stirring, and it was as if they were waking from a dream too.

"The circle held." Linus helped Grier to her feet. "You are remarkable."

"You're just trying to butter my biscuits."

"I'm not sure what that means," he confessed, "but I suspect the answer is...yes."

"I'll explain later." Beaming, she kissed Linus hard. "Let's evacuate the others."

"What happened?" I didn't have the heart to tell Midas I couldn't breathe past his hold. "A bomb?"

"Oh yeah." Grier dusted off her palms. "It smacked us all around like pinballs."

Uncertainty mingled with confusion, but everyone looked okay. "Did the sigil work?"

"You wouldn't know if it didn't," Linus said darkly. "You would be ash."

"Good to know." Swallowing hard, I focused on the devastation. "I don't get it. The pinball analogy."

Maybe my brain was still too rattled to make all the dots connect. No, wait, I couldn't even find the dots.

"I used a sigil on each individual person," she explained patiently. "Think of it as a bulletproof bodysuit."

The impervious design, the one no one was supposed to know

existed because in the wrong hands, para or human, invulnerability could prove world-ending.

"I've never tested it under these conditions," she admitted. "It seemed prudent to add another layer of protection."

Had I been able to move my arms, I might have smacked her for not telling me that in the first place.

Linus must have read my mind or noticed the clench of my jaw, because he cut me a warning look.

"The problem is, the explosion was so intense, it tripped the wards I set. Well, that's not the problem." A sigh moved through her. "The actual problem is, the wards activated a second after the initial blast, allowing the momentum to knock us off our feet and into the ward that sealed around us." She checked with Linus, who nodded, then kept going. "The ward was solid, and usually people are... squishy...but we were all impervious at the time, so we kind of flounced around and knocked into each other."

"Like pinballs in a machine," I finished for her.

"Well, Teach?" Grier ribbed Linus. "Did I ace the test?"

Smiling at her in a way I hadn't known he could, with his whole face, sparkling eyes included, he promised, "I'll let you know once my brain stops bouncing in my skull."

"Meanie." She elbowed him harder. "It kept us alive, didn't it?"

"It would appear so," he allowed, "but that might be the brain damage talking."

Fighting her own smile, Grier gestured to him. "Do you see what I have to put up with?"

"I'm not sure this is the same Linus." I wouldn't have recognized him. "He's so..."

"Handsome?" Grier supplied. "Sexy? Brilliant? Clever?"

It was interesting to watch Linus's usually pale face cycle through so many shades of red. I hadn't known he could blush, let alone so spectacularly. I was pretty impressed. It was almost like watching a laser light show cast over his features.

"I was thinking *happy*, or maybe *relaxed*, which is weird considering a bomb just went off."

"Grier yanks the stick out of his butt." Bishop picked his way closer. "That's what you're seeing."

"He's not that bad." Grier slid her arms around Linus's narrow waist. "For the record, I like his butt."

"He's my boss." I found somewhere else to look. "I don't want to know about his butt."

"Can we please stop talking about my butt?" Linus sounded pained. "And myself in general?"

"The restaurant is clear," Bishop announced. "The staff and guests are out on the street, safe and sound. Ford is corralling them until the EMTs arrive."

"Good." An exhale shuddered through me. "We need to debrief them and send them home."

"EMTs," Grier said thoughtfully. "We can pass the kit over to them and let them BS their way to getting us blood samples to test everyone who was in attendance."

"Except for Ares." I fisted my hands in Midas's shirt. "Tell me she didn't walk in on you."

"Let's get you home, and then I'll show you what I found."

"But Ares—"

"—got away." Midas rubbed my arms. "I couldn't reach her before she ducked back into her Swyft and vanished into traffic, and honestly, I wasn't worried about her just then. All I could think about was you."

"Hey, I don't get blown up that often," I protested. "Hardly at all, really, if you divide the total number of times into my age."

"Hadley." He spoke my name as if it weighed fifty pounds and he was afraid of dropping it on his foot.

"Fine." I looped my arms behind his head. "You may carry me home." I hopped and locked my legs around his waist. "Well?" I snapped my fingers. "You are the slowest manservant I've ever ridden."

Midas cupped my cheeks in his palms, and yes, I mean *those* cheeks. The fact he did it beneath the dress had highly inappropriate chills dappling my arms. He stared down at me for a long moment then shook his head. "You're still not funny."

"And yet your abs ripple."

His lips parted and then mashed shut and then flattened into an impenetrable line.

"You were going to say it's strain from holding me." I hammered his shoulders with my fists. "Put me down."

He only held on tighter, which caused me to flush, given where he was holding, and started walking.

It was a long, hot march back to the Faraday.

TWELVE

Back at the apartment, we spread out to refresh, regroup, and reassure family and friends we survived. I was the only one with idle hands, given that most everyone I cared about had been involved. A few even had front row seats for the big boom.

In another life, that might have depressed me.

In this one, I was happy with quality over quantity.

"Would you do the honors?" I passed Bishop Midas's phone. "I need to change."

Bishop nodded and set to work syncing it with the new ginormous television we had mounted last week.

Linus had, of course, not bought one during his tenure as potentate. He was all books, all the time. Me? Not so much. The recent addition made him pale as though pained to see technology creeping into what had once been his private haven of art and literature.

Good thing he hadn't noticed I turned his bookcases under the stairs into VHS and DVD storage.

I mean, I didn't want to see a grown man cry.

Ducking into the bedroom, I changed into bleach-splattered

jeans, a tee with faded bloodstains, and new sneakers. I scooped up my hair to get it out of the way then washed my face and brushed my teeth, all to avoid what Midas had to show us for a few seconds longer.

Eventually, short of showering, I had run out of personal hygiene excuses and rejoined the others.

Everyone turned to stare when I entered the living room. I wasn't sure how long I had kept them waiting while I delayed the inevitable, but it was clear they had started to worry.

Bishop handed over Midas's phone so that I could control the flow of the video. "Just hit play."

"Here we go." I went to stand with Midas. "Walk us through what we're seeing."

"This is footage of the apartment Ares shares with her human mate," he began, breaking it down so that Linus and Grier could keep up with the names in play. "Ares told us she and Liz were babysitting their nephew while his mother had gallbladder surgery, but I saw no signs an infant had been in the apartment. There was also no sign of Liz."

The footage, and his narration, was circumstantial evidence at best. But he hadn't heard my side yet.

After he finished, he gestured to me. "Your turn."

"I was keeping an eye on Ares at the memorial." I started pacing. "She was drinking a lot—coffee, not wine—but she had this look. Hyperaware, even though she could barely keep her eyes open. Like she expected something to happen." I chewed the inside of my cheek. "I don't know what she saw, but she freaked. She dove for me, like she was going to tackle me, but I couldn't risk waiting to find out if she was protecting me or attacking me. I used her momentum against her and threw her into the wall."

"Then she knew the gig was up." Bishop scowled at the screen. "She got her legs working and bolted."

"The way she took off, I don't think she was running from us. She looked like she was chasing someone."

"It all happened so fast." Grier shook her head. "From my perspective, I couldn't tell either way."

"I didn't notice Ares until she attacked," Linus said. "I was too late to see more than her swift exit."

"Get Reece on it," I told Bishop. "Maybe his shiny new cameras captured who—or what—we missed."

Goddess knows the invoice I signed off on, for essentially disposable cameras given they wouldn't survive the blast, had caused me heart palpitations. They owed me more than their brief lives, they owed me answers, and I expected them to pay up.

Next on the list was another ugly possibility. "Midas, we need to locate Liz."

Odds were good that if Ares was compromised, she would have eliminated Liz to maintain her cover.

"I'll start making calls." He stepped into the kitchen, dialing as he went. "This is Midas Kinase…"

Blocking out his low conversation, I watched the video from the beginning, with my nose almost mashed to the screen like it would help me see what I had missed the first time. Like where she was keeping Boaz. Or Addie. Or their parents. *Their* because *our* made me all the more confused as to how I felt about either of them surviving…or dying.

My mother wasn't my mother, but she never had been really.

My father wasn't my father, but he never had been either.

My twisted family tree gave me a headache.

When I came up empty, I watched it again, and again, and again.

Until Linus pried the phone from my hand and set it aside, forcing me to either step back or stand kissing close to him. He correctly guessed which option I would choose and shifted to farther block my view of the screen. "Have you heard from Ford?"

"No." I checked my pocket. "Wait." I had been so zoned-in on the video, I had missed his text. "Yes."

The silent setting saved lives in my line of work, but it also caused a lot of calls and texts to languish until I remembered to check my phone. Someone ought to develop an app that sensed when the user was in mortal peril, muted all notifications, then flipped the switch again once the coast was clear.

Hmm.

Now I knew what to ask Reece for at Christmas.

"He says everyone in attendance tested negative." I read it out loud. "They've all been sent home."

"I'm sorry." Grier leaned into Linus, but her eyes sought mine. "I know Ares was your friend."

Big difference between *was* and *is*, and grief slammed into me in a merciless wave.

"I don't see anything that points to Boaz or Addie," I said quietly. "I thought when we found the bomber, we would find them. I let myself believe it was going to be okay, but that was silly, wasn't it?" I trusted Linus to tell me the hard truths, always. "It's not going to be okay, is it?"

"It's not silly." Linus rested a cool hand on my shoulder. "One way or another, we'll find them."

What he meant but didn't say was dead or alive. I could read it in the grim set of his jaw.

"They couldn't keep hostages in an apartment in the Faraday," Grier reasoned. "The doorman would have noticed and told someone."

"Unless they used the fire escape," Bishop offered. "Hadley isn't the only one enamored with them."

"I didn't expect the bomber—" I couldn't call Ares by name, "—to have put them in a box and tucked them under the bed." I tapped my foot to burn nervous energy. "I don't see anything that indicates she's purchased more food, water, or other supplies necessary to keep them alive. I don't see anything that points to another location. I don't see *anything* period."

"That's a good idea." Grier snapped her fingers. "She wouldn't have to have supplies delivered here. Think about it. There are apps for everything these days. I use the one for groceries all the time."

"We need her laptop." Linus stared at it onscreen. "It woke without a password when Midas touched it." A careless thing for a security expert, unless it wasn't. "We can access any of her linked accounts through it."

"I'll head down and grab it." I wanted to move, and this would give me purpose. "I'll be right back."

Midas caught me on the way out with a hand on my arm. "I'll have Ford bring it up in a minute."

"He's already there," I guessed. "You posted guards at the apartment."

"We need to know if Liz, or anyone else, attempts to access it."

"Have you had any luck?" I gestured to his phone. "Locating Liz?"

"The hospital confirmed she's on leave, but according to them it's been over a month and counting."

Recalling what Bishop said, I told him, "She was still seeing patients in the infirmary until last week."

"Why break from one job and not the other? And then flake on those patients without a word?"

An uneasy sensation twisted my gut into intricate knots. "Liz may be compromised too."

For a couple as close as Liz and Ares, it would have been all or nothing with them.

"Call Ford." I touched his arm. "I need to chat with Hank."

Easing away from him to prevent our calls from overlapping, I dialed the front door and waited. "Hank."

"Hadley."

"Can you tell me when you last saw Liz?"

There was zero hesitation in his answer, but he sounded wary. "Five days ago."

Since the night she missed her appointment with the gwyllgi teen.

"Are you sure?" I hated to press him for details when it must seem he was about to get in trouble for his earlier line of questions. "Ares told me she's home on vacation."

"It was my little brother's birthday, and my relief was late. I was thinking how our dads were going to kill me if I showed up without the ice cream cake when Liz approached me. I called her a cab, but I didn't catch where she told him to go. Five minutes later, my relief arrived. I handed him the keys, called a Swyft, and left. I haven't seen her since." He must have decided it was better to ask now than get blindsided later. "I asked Ares about this earlier, but she blew me off. Am I in trouble? With Ares?"

"No," I rushed to assure him. "You did nothing wrong."

His usual frustration with me shone through, reassuring me Hank was himself. "Then why—?"

"I can't talk right now, but we'll brief you later." I ended the call and returned to Midas, who stood waiting for me. "You heard?"

"That means Liz left under her own power."

"Ares could have invited her out to get rid of her away from the Faraday." I tapped my cell against my chin. "Do we know if Liz has family we can call?"

The nonexistent baby had me doubting she even had siblings, but I didn't know Liz as well as Ares.

As well as I *thought* I knew her, anyway.

If it came down to it, Reece could dig up the answers for me, but first things first.

A knock on the door announced Ford's arrival before he let himself in with a bag slung over his shoulder.

"Howdy, y'all." He lifted a hand. "Good to see you again."

Ford playing the *aww shucks* card on Linus and Grier made me feel like I was a member of a special club, one who maybe had a secret decoder ring. It was pretty cool being on the inside while they were on the outside for a change, but we were all friends here, so I shot Ford a stare that clearly said to knock it off.

"I'm not sure you should be eyeballing me like that," he drawled. "I have a girlfriend."

Okay, so maybe I needed to work on my warning looks if they screamed *come hither*.

"I was very intimidated." Midas smothered a grin. "I shook in my boots."

"With laughter," Ford muttered out of the side of his mouth.

"You two think you're so cute." I walked over, relieved Ford of the bag, and headed to the dining table to lay out what he brought for us. "Bishop, the laptop's yours."

"Cool." He settled into a chair in front of it. "I needed a new one of these."

"Not to keep." I growled at him. "To interrogate."

Snickering ensued from Ford's general direction, and I suspected Midas was laughing on the inside.

Lip curling, I announced, "I hate you all."

"You can always come home with us," Grier offered, "to Savannah."

The offhand comment floored me, and I dropped the bag with a clunk. "What?"

"If they keep being mean to you," she said clearly, "we'll take you home with us."

This time, the growl in the room wasn't mine.

"As much as I appreciate the offer—" even if she was joking, "—Savannah isn't big enough for two potentates." I slid my gaze to Linus. "Or is that three? Two point five, maybe?"

"I'm almost retired." His lips curved at that. "I would prefer not to re-up, but I will if called upon."

Fine hairs lifted down my nape as the growl changed pitch.

Leaning a hip against the tabletop, I angled toward Midas. "I've worked too hard to stop now."

"I agree," Linus said, pride warming his voice.

"And I guess I like a couple of people who live here." I shrugged. "Like one or two."

"Don't poke the gwyllgi," Bishop said absently, fingers clicking over the keys. "It won't end well."

Chin high, I corrected him, "The gwyllgi shouldn't poke me."

Actually, I wouldn't mind if one particular gwyllgi poked me, but that wasn't for public consumption.

"Before this escalates further," Ford drawled, "I would like to apologize for my bad behavior."

"Suck-up," Bishop muttered. "You're not one of the two."

Hand to his heart, Ford demanded, "How do you know?"

"I bring her café mochas every night before shift." He grinned. "What have you done for her lately?"

"I started dating her friend," he said defensively.

"You make it sound like you're dating her as a favor to Hadley." Grier whistled. "Ouch."

"That's not what I meant." Ford groaned. "I like Lisbeth. Not because Hadley told me either."

"This is embarrassing me, and it has nothing to do with me." Bishop angled the laptop toward me. "This is the household account for grocery delivery. There are two addresses. One at the Faraday and one in a bad part of town."

"That's good news." I leaned over the table. "Pull the address up on a map."

The top search result was for Women's Medical Center. He clicked on the most popular image, and a red cinderblock building with fading blue trim appeared onscreen. Sun-bleached flyers in the window touted everything from free birth control to onsite GED classes. I could picture Liz volunteering there with ease. Hiding kidnap victims? Not so much.

"Well, that's a bust." I slumped with disappointment. "We'll still need to clear it, though."

"Maybe not a bust." He switched to the previous screen. "Looks like the center closed a month ago."

"Okay." I chewed on my thumbnail. "I can see why."

"Ares had groceries delivered there yesterday."

"What?" I dropped my arm. "Bring up the list."

A mix of shelf-stable foods, mostly protein bars and junk food, bottled water, and toilet paper topped it.

"How far is this?" Grier spoke from behind me. "Can we check it out tonight?"

"Not far." I calculated the distance in my head. "Let's hope we're not too late."

The wake accomplished one thing. Ares knew Midas was onto her. She wouldn't have rabbited otherwise. And if she started erasing their trail, she might burn the evidence. All four witnesses included.

"Midas and Ford, you're with me." I patted Bishop on the shoulder. "Get me eyes on that building."

"I'll head back to HQ." He stood and took the laptop with him. "I'll put Reece on surveillance."

"Sounds good." I hesitated over Linus and Grier. "Usually, this is the part where I run out of orders to give and people to give them to, so I'm drawing a blank."

"We can handle patrol," she offered. "That way your team can focus on you, and we can make sure your raid doesn't flush out more rats." She grinned, and we were two teenagers again. "Or Martian Roaches."

"That would be great." I experienced a twinge at handing over the reins to my city, even for a night, even in part to the man who still held her. "Thanks." Facing the others, I wiped my damp palms on my pants. "Let's go."

The fate of my world rested on the outcome of this trip, and that was as exhilarating as it was terrifying.

We could be *this* close to finding them. *This* close to setting things back to rights. *This* close to...

...the truth.

However much it might hurt.

THIRTEEN

Midas texted his mother an update. The operation belonged, officially, to the Office of the Potentate. He doubted his mother would protest the pack ceding that right, given his mating to Hadley, but there was little he could do in any case. The bomber had targeted her, and then her family. The case fell under her jurisdiction, even if the person responsible was gwyllgi. Or wore the skin of one.

Meting out punishment, however, might get sticky.

Traditionally, the OPA handed gwyllgi offenders over to the alpha for a trial and sentencing. That might not be an option in this instance. No confrontation with witchborn fae, or hosts, had ended in anything less than bloodshed. But the pack would be on edge if the future potentate put down one of their own.

All the more reason to do as his mother suggested and make his union official in the eyes of the pack.

"Almost there," Hadley said under her breath, sensing his unease.

Midas had forgotten Linus used the Society's car service when Hadley accepted his polite offer of a lift to the clinic. That might have been a willful choice. He hated riding in these branded sedans with their haughty disdain for their passengers. Or maybe that was just him feeling out of place in their world, so different from pack life or fae mores, making the ease with which Hadley had integrated into his all the more impressive.

The interior of the car was as red as a mouth opened on a scream. Old blood and crushed herbs perfumed the air, and with the AC blasting, it was as cold as the grave. He couldn't wait to escape. Ford looked primed to bolt with or without the car stopping first, but the pomp didn't bother Hadley.

Plus, he couldn't argue with Linus's reasoning. The Swyft database had been hacked in the past. They couldn't risk it, or a cab company, giving away their location. Ford's truck, while convenient, was hardly inconspicuous. Better to use an untraceable mode of transportation than to announce their plans.

The crimson sedan rolled to a stop, and the driver peered through his pristine windshield at the derelict surroundings with faint concern.

"Master Lawson requested I drop you here," the driver said in a wooden tone. "Does that suit Madam?"

"This is fine." Hadley offered him a polite smile. "We can walk from here."

The driver exited the car, circled the trunk, and opened her door.

"Thank you," she murmured, tucking a folded bill into his front jacket pocket.

That brightened his mood considerably, and he dipped his chin. "You're most welcome."

Midas ducked out onto the sidewalk behind her and filled his lungs with fresh night air.

"Move it." Ford shoved him in the spine. "I want out too."

Joining Hadley on the sidewalk, he gave Ford enough room to soothe his twitchy inner beast.

The driver sniffed at them, bowed to Hadley, then got in the car and left.

Ford growled at the receding taillights. "He wouldn't even look at us."

"Trust me, you're in good company." Wry amusement kicked up Hadley's lips. "He wouldn't have looked at me either if he had a clue I'm not High Society."

"You're the potentate's apprentice," Ford argued. "I figured that's why he was deferential."

"Uh, no." She chuckled and started walking toward their final destination. "Linus told him I was a friend, which is how we got the car service in the first place. The driver made the assumption that Linus would only have High Society friends, and we didn't bother correcting him."

"That's ten kinds of messed up, darlin'."

"That's the Society for you." Her smile spread. "Whenever I get good and offended by the disparagement, I fantasize about the Low Society rising up against their High Society overlords." She laughed. "But that will never happen. They have magic, and we don't. It wouldn't be a fair fight. More like a slaughter."

"You might want to keep that fantasy under your hat when you're around Linus."

"Linus and Grier are well aware of the inequalities of the system we were born into, and they thwart it at every opportunity with their progressivism, but they only get away with being eccentric because they're both stupid powerful and filthy rich."

"I haven't noticed a status gap as much in Atlanta." Midas frowned. "Is that your doing?"

Shifters adored her for treating them like people, with thoughts, dreams, feelings. He could picture the Low Society embracing a woman who broke through the glass ceiling with gusto too.

"As much as I would love to take credit for it, Atlanta isn't as deep in the Society's pocket as Savannah. They're old school there. Makes sense, with the Lyceum downtown and all. Atlanta is more of a melting pot, and it allows those class lines to blur."

A peculiar tang in the air hit the back of Midas's throat, and he motioned for the others to slow.

Glancing at Ford, he asked, "Do you smell that?"

The comment perked Ambrose's ears, and Hadley's shadow crept across the pavement before them.

"No." Ford shook his head. "I'll have to get closer."

"Don't leave me hanging." Hadley closed her hand over Midas's upper arm. "What is it?"

"Blood." He flared his nostrils, but the scent didn't fade. "And black magic."

Her nails dug in, almost piercing his skin. "That's not unexpected, right?"

The question she asked wasn't the one she wanted answered, and he came up empty on platitudes.

"The coven leaves behind a stain wherever they go," Ford said, sparing him. "That's a fact."

"They also leave wards behind." She stared ahead. "Nasty ones."

"Are you sure you want to go in?" Midas cupped her cheek. "You don't have to do this."

"Yes," she said, withdrawing with a wane smile. "I do."

Part of her stubborn determination stemmed from a responsibility to her family, and he respected that. A larger portion of her disliked leaning on anyone, him included, out of fear everything she had worked for would be snatched out of her hands if she showed any signs of weakness. That part broke his heart.

The shadow reappeared in a blink and stabbed through her temple, causing her to wobble to one side.

Midas sent Ford ahead to scout, and to cover for her.

"Bastard," she growled, impressing him with its grit. "I hope you choke on your bonbons."

After flinging candies into the void, she took a moment to get steady.

"There's a ward up ahead," she gritted out between her teeth. "He's confirmed the magical signature."

"The coven's work?"

"Oh, yes."

Magic was outside his realm of expertise, but he trusted her skills. "Can you bring it down?"

"The question is almost never *can I*, but *should I*." Her expression tightened. "Ambrose eats the energy. That's what causes the wards I disassemble to fail. He's at his deadliest on a full stomach, and it gives him enough power to sway my thoughts toward actions he wants me to take. Nothing major, I would catch on too quickly, but minor things I might not notice until it's too late."

The line he was asking her to walk was thin. Too thin. "Can he tell if anyone is in there?"

"The ward is too repellent for him to get a deep read."

"We can still call Linus or Grier," he offered. "They could be here in a half hour or less."

"Waiting is too risky now that we're here. We're racing the clock. We have to move forward."

Either Ares was in there and things were about to get bloody, or she wasn't and things might be about to blow up in their faces. As much as he hated to put Hadley at risk, he agreed with her assessment.

"How can I help with Ambrose?" He fell in step with her as they caught up to Ford. "If it gets bad?"

"Force me to expend the energy. Once he's drained, he'll be docile again. Well, as docile as he gets."

They got within spitting distance of Ford, and Hadley fell silent on the topic of her shadow half.

"I'm picking up two familiar scents," Ford reported to them. "Ares and Liz have been here. Recently."

Proof the couple was working together? Or evidence Ares had taken Liz as a hostage? Or as a host?

Drawing in deep breaths, Midas confirmed Ford's assessment. "Do your best to minimalize casualties."

"Stay alive." Ford gave each of their shoulders a squeeze. "I expect to live to see mini Hadases."

Hadley blinked at him. "Mini what?"

"Midleys?" Ford tried again. "Do you not know what happens when a boy gwyllgi and a girl—"

"We're not having this conversation." Hadley slapped a hand over his mouth. "Focus, Ford, or we'll start ribbing you about mini Lisords."

"Or Forbeths," Midas tacked on. "Get your head in the game, Ford."

"I don't know if I can." He appeared disturbed. "It sounded like you said *lizards*, and now I keep picturing Lisbeth and my heads on baby lizard bodies." A shudder rolled through him. "Thanks for ruining procreation for me."

Tipping the brim of an imaginary hat, she drawled, "You're welcome, partner."

Brows lowered, he glowered at her. "Cowboy jokes, really?"

"Hey," she countered, "it got your mind off the lizard babies, didn't it?"

FOURTEEN

We all knew what the others were up to, but we indulged one another in procrastinating a minute longer. It was easier to joke than to focus on whatever awaited us. It was easier to pretend than to face an ugly reality. But we didn't have time for it, and my impatience won out in the end.

Certain they would follow, I strode toward the building. I didn't slow to unsheathe my swords from Ambrose's nebulous mass. I couldn't risk stopping now that I had gained momentum. The urge to put off what I was about to discover about my family, about my friend, preyed on me.

The ward registered as a tingle over my skin, a gentle force nudging me back and away.

Ambrose strode beside me, curious, and I didn't trust this weird dynamic duo vibe he was going for.

The shadow pointed a long finger, and I felt a magical pressure increase before I grasped his meaning.

The coven had used concentric wards at the meat packing plant too. If it ain't broke, don't fix it, I guess.

"Don't come any closer," I told the guys. "Let me see if I can get this ward down first."

The space was also necessary to chat with Ambrose without giving myself away to Ford.

"Do you see the anchor?" I walked the perimeter as Ambrose searched. "Let's go deeper."

We passed through two more layers, each more viscous than the last, and then I felt a primal tug.

"There." I crouched near a crumpled soda can. "That's it."

Polite as you please, Ambrose knelt beside me and waited to see what I wanted him to do.

"Take it down." I flicked my hand. "We have no choice."

Rather than his usual antics, Ambrose simply placed a hand on the can's shadow and inhaled its essence. He took his treat for good behavior then went to clear the rest of the area for magical traps or alarms.

Ears popping as the ward dropped, I rubbed them before turning to Midas and Ford. "We're clear."

Midas took my elbow a second later and helped me stand. Ford wasn't far behind him.

There was a dawning knowledge in Ford's eyes that worried me, but it faded so fast, I figured it must be paranoia catching up with me again. As if it ever left my side these days.

All too soon, I was cupping the doorknob in my palm and wishing it was locked or bolted or welded shut. I wanted more time to *believe*, to hope, but it was warm, dented, scratched, and...it turned easily when I twisted my wrist.

Hot air exhaled in my face, and I gagged on the stench. I wished I couldn't identify the scents, but I knew each by heart. People had stayed here, in the heat, their bodies ripe, with no access to working facilities. That didn't mean it was the people we were searching for, not in this neighborhood. The homeless had a tendency to den up wherever they could for as long as they could, until they got caught or arrested, and this place had all the earmarks of having been used for just that purpose.

The lobby had tears filling my eyes from the onionlike foulness, but it got worse the deeper we ventured into the clinic until I wished I had brought Vicks to wipe under my nose. I didn't know how the gwyllgi could stand it. It must be killing them to keep going while their keen senses were assaulted by squalor.

We cleared the restrooms, which were…yeah…about as disgusting I had expected with no running water to flush the multiple contributions that had been made over the last few days or weeks.

A large room that might have been an office yielded better results, or at least less disgusting ones.

Supplies were stacked high against the far wall, several cases of water and wholesale protein bars. Toilet paper, wet wipes, and basic hygiene materials. That might have sparked hope, had any of them been opened. I reminded myself they were delivered yesterday, that they might not be needed yet, but I was appalled by the conditions around me and terrified of what else we would discover.

Midas gripped my shoulder in silent support then jerked his chin toward the hall.

I nodded back, tightened my hands on my swords, and began kicking open doors to the individual exam rooms. The first three were cramped, filthy, and empty of everything but waste—human and otherwise. The fourth held strong beneath my shoe, and contact sent a zing of recognition through me.

"Ward," I mouthed to Midas, then I swept out my arm to usher the guys behind me.

I didn't have to ask Ambrose twice. He attacked the door with gusto, feasting on its residual magic. Energy tingled under my skin when he finished, and he rubbed his belly with satisfaction. For his power to be spilling over into me, he was flush, and that was more dangerous than anything we had faced yet.

Bracing for the worst, I kicked open the door, and it slammed against the wall, pinned by the knob piercing the sheetrock. Across the room, propped in a corner, sat Addie.

Pupils blown wide, her eyes unfocused, Addie trembled. Her hands shook in her lap, jittery like an addict in withdrawal, and her shoulders twitched. Her teeth chattered, and she shivered as if she were freezing in the muggy room.

No two ways about it. She had been drugged into a stupor and didn't recognize help had finally arrived.

A hard lurch of my heart propelled me forward while Midas growled a warning at my back, but I couldn't leave her there. I couldn't bear to see her so drawn and pale. I rushed to her, hit my knees at her side, and stifled a yelp when she punched me in the jaw hard enough I saw stars.

"You're not Hadley," she snarled. "Get the fuck out."

Perfect. Wonderful. Fantastic even. Just marvelous.

The coven must have cobbled together a shoestring glamour to play mind games with their prisoners. The simple illusion wouldn't fool anyone who knew me for long, and it wouldn't trick a gwyllgi nose at all, but drugs, depravation, and darkness went a long way toward smoothing out the wrinkles in any disguise.

"I *am* Hadley." I touched my cheek. "I think you broke my jaw."

"Prove it," she spat with enough vehemence I knew they had used my face against her.

"Tell me how." I kept out of range of her next punch, though the fight had drained out of her. "What can I say or do to prove to you I am who I say I am?"

Midas walked in, but she snarled at him too, her fingers curving into claws on her lap. "Hello, Addie."

"Come one step closer, and I will bury my foot so far up your butt you'll be tasting my toenail polish."

"We need to move this along." I rolled my hand. "I would like to find my brother, if you don't mind."

Plus, if this place was rigged to blow, I would prefer to not be in it when that happened.

A flicker of uncertainty passed over her features before she blanked them. "Say it."

"Say what?"

"You know what." A sisterly scowl cut her mouth. "If you're Hadley, then say it."

Embarrassment singed me clear to the tips of my toes, but I mumbled, "I am enough."

Head lolling back, she focused on me. "I couldn't hear you."

"I am enough," I muttered a fraction louder. "Do you believe me now?"

"Yes."

"Will you punch me again?"

"I'm sorry about that."

"Don't be." I crouched, more carefully this time. "You gave them hell." I checked her over. "I'm proud of you."

"I warned them my little sister would come for me." She shut her eyes. "Told 'em they'd be sorry."

"I'll take it from here." Ford swooped in and began a more thorough exam. "Find the others."

Goddess, please let there be others to find.

"I'll be right back," I promised her. "We're getting you out of here."

Leaving her behind physically hurt, even though Ford was with her, and I trusted him.

If ever I doubted that I loved her, I had my confirmation in spades.

Screw blood ties.

Addie was the sister of my heart.

Midas's steady presence gave me the nerve to try the next door, but the room was empty, and I wanted to hurl. I was lucky, so lucky, Addie was more or less okay. It was a selfish thing to pray, but I wanted my brother too. I wasn't sure what I would do without him to annoy the living daylights out of me.

The door after that rebuffed my heel, and I didn't have to summon Ambrose for him to begin gobbling.

The ward burst like a popped bubble, and I kicked in the door before I could think too much about what might be waiting for me on the other side. It rebounded off the wall then swung almost closed in my face. I didn't see anyone, but we had lost the element of surprise when I started yanking down wards and smashing down doors. We wouldn't take anyone unawares.

"Hello?" I took a cautious step into the room. "Anyone here?"

A low murmur drew me to a figure curled beneath a ratty blanket, their face bloody from long gouges. In the dim light streaming in from the hall, I noticed the shortness of their matted hair and determined it to be Mr. Whitaker. Picking my way to him, I crouched to get a better look.

The gouges were from fingernails, and when I checked his hand, I confirmed he had done it to himself.

"He's in bad shape," I told Midas. "He needs immediate medical attention."

"Unconscious?"

"Yeah." I was afraid to touch him, worried I might hurt him worse. "He's out cold."

"Let's clear the rest of the building," Midas decided. "We can leave his door open."

There weren't enough of us to guard everyone in their individual rooms, but I couldn't wait around for help to arrive. I wanted to see my brother with my own eyes. I wanted to know he was okay.

Please, please, please let him be okay.

"All right." I backed into the hall, making sure the way stayed clear. "There are four rooms left."

The next door slammed me with a ward that made my back teeth ache, but Ambrose devoured it.

Midas smashed it in with his shoulder, since I was limping from one too many blows to live wards.

I was on my back, staring up at the ceiling, admiring the stars twinkling there, before I registered the hit.

Hit? No. *Bell-ringer?* Yes. That fit better. I had met stone trolls with softer fists than my brother's.

The right side of my jaw throbbed in time with my heart, and a crunching noise filled my head when I closed my teeth. This is what I got for joking with Addie about breaking my jaw earlier. *"Ouch."*

"Where is Addie?"

A hard kick made my ribs crunch.

"Where. Is. Adelaide?"

Boaz stood over me, weaving in and out of view. I couldn't tell if pain was making me woozy or if weakness made him wobble. Either way, I couldn't let him land another strike. My brother was a tank.

Ambrose curled protectively around me. Too little, too late in my opinion, but he was here now.

"Addie is two doors down," I wheezed. "Same side of the hall."

Wild laughter poured out of him, his disbelief palpable, and he lifted his foot to stomp on me.

A blur of blond fur, sharp teeth, and claws nailed Boaz square in the chest and knocked him into a wall.

Crimson magic splashed through the room, and Midas, back on two legs, towered over Boaz.

"I didn't expect the sucker punch, but I should have seen it coming." Midas curled and flexed his hands down at his sides. "I let you land the kick, even though I would rather snap off your leg and beat you with it than allow you to harm my mate. All because Hadley loves you and didn't want it to come to this." Midas unsheathed claws in his fingertips and held them to Boaz's throat. "Hurt her, and you won't ever hurt another woman."

Leveraging up into a sitting position, I waited until my head stopped spinning to address them.

"Midas."

Poised on the brink of violence, he didn't tear his gaze away from Boaz.

"He didn't know what he was doing."

A bitter laugh worked up Boaz's throat.

"Okay, he knew what he was doing but not who he was doing it to. Remember how Addie reacted?"

That eased a fraction of the tension in Midas's shoulders.

"She clocked me and good, but she thought I was coven."

As Midas was about to lower his hand, Boaz had to go and open his big mouth.

"I'm really enjoying the play." He clapped slowly. "Stellar performances from the entire cast."

"Boaz, I'm Hadley. Your sister."

"You're out of your goddessdamn minds if you think I'm buying what you're selling."

Standing sucked donkey balls, but I got to my feet. "What proof do you require?"

"Ah." He chuckled. "This is the part where I ask you to tell me something only Hadley would know."

"Whatever it takes to get you out of here before your captors return."

Boaz clammed up, set his jaw, and settled in for an interrogation that wasn't coming.

"Ambrose," I said, hating how he jumped to my command with eagerness. "Take a little off the top."

"Ambrose," Boaz echoed. "How do you know about...?"

One good swoop through his midsection put Boaz out like a light, and he slid to the floor in a heap.

"I am the worst sister in the world." I watched my brother's chest rise and fall. "The absolute worst."

"Yes," Midas agreed dryly. "You're horrible for preventing him from harming himself or others while you finish rescuing him." He glanced toward the hall. "We're still missing one."

Yeah.

We were, weren't we?

I was trying hard not to think how satisfying it would be to walk out on her without looking back.

I wondered how she liked the dark, the bugs, the fear of never knowing when the next strike would land. I wondered if she had used her time to reflect on the bad things she had done, if she had promised the goddess she would make amends to anyone she had wronged, or if she had spent her confinement cursing Hecate and asking why a paragon such as herself had been brought so low.

"Stay here with him." I swallowed the bile welling up my throat. "I have to do this alone."

Midas clenched his jaw. "All right."

Exiting the room, I stood in the hall and counted the remaining doors then recounted them.

I was tired, I was sore, and Ambrose loomed over me, crackling with power.

That ought to frighten me, but I was more afraid of this, of facing my mother.

The shadow rested a hand on my shoulder, and his energy spilled into me, giving me a boost.

Puzzled and exhausted, I glanced over at him. "What was that for?"

Ambrose made a heart shape with his fingers that he thumped against his chest like it was beating.

"Um." I had no idea what that meant. "Thanks?" He kept going, and I reached in my pocket. "Here."

Unsure what else to do, I flung chocolate at him, which he swallowed without a hitch.

Linus and I would definitely have a talk about this peculiar behavior.

And...I was back to stalling.

Anything to stop myself from identifying the final door and opening it.

The door beside Boaz's exam room opened with a twist of my wrist. It was clear, but that made the next doorknob that much harder to grip. It too expelled a stale breath of fetid air that built a knot in my throat because I couldn't tell if I felt relieved that I hadn't found her yet or guilty for hoping I didn't find her at all.

Power tingled in my hand when I reached the last door in the hall, and Ambrose took his time with it. As much as I wanted to claim he was building the suspense so the reveal would be that much more brutal, I couldn't fault him there. He was full as a tick, swollen with power, even after sharing with me, and he had little appetite left.

A breath of magic hit me in the face, soft as an exhale, and then the ward collapsed on itself.

This knob hurt when I gripped it, like cupping broken glass, and I half expected blood to spill through my fingers.

Ambrose set his hand over mine, a jolt of energy tingling through the contact, and I turned my wrist.

"I don't know what you're up to," I told him, "but please don't make me regret this."

The room was dark, darker than the others. Or maybe my vision tunneled when I saw her sitting there. It hit me then, her age. Her fragility. The lines around her mouth cut deeper these days, and the hollows in her cheeks stood out in stark detail. Her cracked lips were thin, hard lines gone white from pressure.

On the floor, she sat with her spine rigid and her legs folded beneath her. I noticed tracks in her makeup where tears had fallen, but I wasn't foolish enough to assign their cause to any emotion other than rage. Her clothing was neat, if soiled, and she regarded me through sharp eyes that cut me to the quick.

Without saying a word, she conveyed her utter disappointment that it had taken me this long to find her.

Not enough, not enough, not enough.

Of all the monsters I had battled, I feared this one the most.

At least she hadn't come out swinging like Addie and Boaz.

"I'm here to get you out." I lingered in the doorway. "Can you stand?"

"I can." Mother rose to her feet with a hand braced on the floor. "How are the others?"

"They're alive." I wavered on whether I ought to offer her my arm. "Do you need help?"

"No, thank you." Her chin rose higher. "I can manage."

With her the most lucid of the four, I decided I would question her. "Who took you?"

"One of your friend Tisdale's mongrel gwyllgi." She limped around the room, palm flaking paint as she dragged it along the wall. "I didn't catch her name."

"How do you know she belongs to Tisdale?"

"I recognized her from the Faraday."

The next question left me with a dry mouth. "Was she working alone?"

"There was another woman." She paused to catch her breath. "She gave us the injections."

"She drugged you."

"Yes."

That confirmed my suspicions. "Can you describe her for me?"

Dragging in a sharp hiss through her teeth, she did, and my heart plummeted at her description of Liz.

Dropping my chin until it almost bumped my chest, I muttered, "Frakking hell."

This as good as confirmed that Ares, or whoever wore her, had enlisted Liz for her skills.

But was Liz working with her by choice or by force? Usually, it was a no-brainer. This time, I had doubts. The coven had kept my family alive, though they were as yet untested. Who was to say they hadn't done the same with Liz? Maybe she had been acting as the unwitting warden of this place all this time.

Either way, the pack had suffered a critical breach, and I had worked alongside Midas long enough to have endangered my team through exposure as well.

Alone, Ares and Liz each held enough power to fracture the pack with intel they had accumulated while occupying sensitive positions. Both of them? If they were working together? The information they could supply the coven on the inner workings of the pack were catastrophic. Worse, the odds of them using their positions to place more of the coven's agents within the pack was astronomically high.

We had to assemble an impartial panel dedicated to clearing each individual pack member, like yesterday, and Abbott would have to jump on creating another device or two so that we could arm our panelists and key persons in the field.

We had passed the point of allowing traitors the luxury of time to reveal themselves. We had to root them out and rip them from the pack before they choked the life out of us all.

"Addie is outside," Ford said from behind me, and I absolutely didn't jump at the sound of his voice. "I came to help with Matron Pritchard."

Angling toward him, I peered down the hall. "What about the others?"

"I passed Midas on the way. He's evacuating Mr. Whitaker then heading back for the lug."

"What about my son?" Mother pulled herself taller. "What about Boaz?"

"He's the lug," Ford said, rare annoyance in his tone. "He'll be outside waiting for you."

"Take me to him." She hobbled faster. "Bring me to my son."

Mother had always preferred Boaz to me, but she was the pragmatic sort who never forgot she had options should she require a spare heir. With me out of the way, the dubious honor of *break in case of emergency* fell to our little brother, Macon.

Ford quirked a brow when I didn't offer her my arm to steady her, but he was too much of a gentleman to follow my example. He cocked his elbow and smiled his country-boy smile. "Would you like some help?"

"I don't require your assistance." She smoothed her clothing. "I can manage on my own, thank you."

"Yes, ma'am." He got out of her way then lowered his voice. "That woman is a…" His nostrils flared, gaze cutting to her back, and he rooted himself to the floor as she exited the building. "Did you touch her?" He scented the air. "Did she touch you?"

"No." I couldn't bring myself to, even to help her, and she wasn't the touchy-feely type. "Why?"

"That's not Matron Pritchard."

The sour taste from earlier flooded my mouth with water. "Come again?"

"I've been nose blind since we walked through the door, but even I can smell black magic up close."

Midas would pick up on it in a blink with the fresh air to clear his head, and he would confront her.

Goddess.

I shouldn't have been such a frakking coward. I barely looked her in the eye longer than to identify her. I, who stood toe-to-toe with alphas and future alphas, glanced away first. Had I paid her closer attention, I might have noticed something, anything, but I had been too eager to do my duty and be rid of her.

I should have known they would exploit my greatest weakness. Goddessdamn it. I should have *known.*

I shoved Ford aside and sprinted down the hall, bursting through the door into the moonlight.

Mother swooped down on Boaz, radiating concern, and I screamed at the top of my lungs. *"No."*

Midas whipped his head toward me, but I was too late.

The woman, whoever she truly was, murmured softly to Boaz, lovingly, but it was all *wrong.*

Gaze searching the area for threats, Midas tensed, crimson sparking in his eyes. "Hadley?"

"That's not Matron Pritchard." I stumbled forward as she lifted her head. "Who are you?"

"Did you know that when we claim a skin, we harvest its memories too?" She petted Boaz's hair, smoothing it in place. "I know who you are, Amelie *Pritchard*, and I know what she did to you."

The blood drained from my face in an icy rush that left me woozy. "Step away from him."

"Hmm." She glanced around the gathering. "You told them your secret?"

I swallowed hard, and she saw it, her eyes gleaming with malice.

"Not all of them, I see."

"Back away from him, nice and slow." I ignored her taunting. "This doesn't have to get ugly."

"Like the scars on your back? On your buttocks?" Her grin stretched wide. "What does your mate think of it? The stippling?" A throaty laugh Mother never would have made escaped her throat. "Can he bear to look at it? At you? Or do you keep the lights off and your clothes on when you make love?" Her lip curled. "As if animals were capable of more than scratching an itch."

"Get...away..." a faint voice rasped, "...from my...son."

Unable to turn my back on Boaz, I trusted Ambrose—goddess help me—to vet the danger behind me.

The shadow molded itself into my mother's tall and stately figure as I watched, and my brain spluttered.

I'm not proud the first thought tripping through my head was that two of them was worse than one.

"I found her in the dumpster," Ford said quietly. "She smells okay. Well, bad actually, but untainted."

"Why, Hadley." The woman in front of me shimmered like a heat mirage and sat back on her heels. "You look shocked."

No, no, no.

I had the sight. I could see through glamours. Midas could too. That was the point of the bargain I struck. That was the cost of the risk I took. Tricking me with illusion should be impossible, and yet I had no other explanation for how two Annabeth Pritchards had coexisted in the same space at the same time.

"I don't get it." As shock set in, I came near to babbling. "Why didn't you take her?"

Frak.

That made it sound like I wanted her to kill my mother and wear her like a pantsuit.

"She has no power, physical or political." She watched me, and she saw too much. I could tell by her feline smile. "Her only value to us was her worth to you."

The woman began a transformation that ended with her as an identical copy of Liz, but that didn't mean she wouldn't snap her fingers and become Ares. Glamour was elastic, and I couldn't tell if she was using it or her closet to change forms.

But if she became Ares, did that mean she was the one who had been on a caffeine binge lately? Hiding in plain sight, masking her scent with strong coffee, smoothing her social gaffes with the excuse of sleep deprivation?

The twisting path that possibility carved through my brain left my gray matter sliced too thin for this.

"Imagine my disappointment when I learned she was not your mother, but your abuser. Your tormenter. Your own personal boogeyman." Pity darkened her eyes, and that a monster felt sorry for me made the past that much harder to stomach. "Once I determined her uselessness, I did us both a favor and tossed her in the dumpster out back. The heat would have killed her in another day or two, but it worked out in the end. The perimeter wards warned me you were here, and I took her place in her room. There was no time for anything else. Your dogs would have hunted me if I ran."

The question drumming in my ears let me ignore the woman behind me. "Why keep them alive?"

"Wouldn't you rather know how I know? About the scars? About the ants?"

A familiar shiver danced along my spine, a premonition I developed as a child that warned me when Mother was near.

"She told me," the woman announced. "In great detail. Without much coercion." She searched my face. "Do you want my honest opinion?"

"No."

"She hates herself, and you're a mirror image of her younger self, so she hates you too." She tapped Boaz on the nose. "I bet she never raised a hand to him, did she? He was a boy, and he took after his father I'm guessing. She didn't see enough of her in him to bother. Your little brother, though." She wet her lips. "He's a meld of your parents, isn't he? Little of Dad, little of Mom. How long before he learns the sting of the brush? The sting of the ants? The sting of knowing his mother despises the parts of herself she sees in him?"

"She will never lay a hand on him," I snarled. *"Never."*

"How can you stop her when you're here and he's there?"

"Hadley." Midas stood watch over Addie. "Don't let her get in your head."

"Yes, *Hadley*, don't let me get in your head. It's so dark in there I might not find my way out again."

The barb struck true, and I flinched. "Who are you?"

"That's a question with an answer you might not be ready to hear."

"Are you wearing Liz," I demanded, "or is this more glamour?"

"I'm not wearing anyone." Her smile grew toothier. "Does that clear things up for you?"

Crimson magic sparked out of the corner of my eye, but Midas and Ford were both accounted for.

"Oh dear." Liz, or whoever—whatever—she was stood. "Now you've done it."

A vicious snarl rattled my bones as the gwyllgi who had shifted on my periphery prowled closer.

With heartbreaking clarity, the earlier pretzel of my thoughts unraveled as the truth revealed itself to us.

There were two of them.

A pair.

Ares and Liz.

Dead women walking.

"Ares." I cut off the twinge of regret before it took root. "What are you doing?"

"Protecting her mate." Liz waited for Ares to come to her side then petted her. "Good girl."

"You can't be serious," I demanded of Ares, as if a firm scolding could fix this. "That's not Liz."

"That might not be Ares," Ford reminded me, and Ares pinned her ears against her skull.

"This is not how I pictured tonight ending." Liz scratched Ares's head. "I banked on the abuse twisting you up, making you doubt yourself. All I needed was a second alone to disappear into the background." She glared at Ford. "You should have kept your mouth shut." She flicked her gaze over him. "You just won't die, will you?"

"Momma expects grandkids." He shrugged. "I try not to disappoint my momma."

While Liz bumped her gums, Ares nudged her back, away from us and immediate danger. Uncovenlike behavior by any metric. They tended to attack, brutally, in whatever form guaranteed the most damage to their adversaries. They didn't tuck tail and run, and I had only ever seen them protect one member above the others, but that had been during battle when they sought the element of surprise.

This wasn't right. Ares was acting like a gwyllgi defending her mate, not a coven lackey, and that made no sense. None at all. There was no way she was that good of an actor, that she could have faked being Midas's friend for so long without getting caught out.

"Ares," I tried reasoning with her. "You don't have to do this."

The gwyllgi hung her head but kept backing away slowly, herding Liz behind her.

Ares was still in there. *She was in there.* Why wasn't she fighting back?

"Ares," Midas commanded, his eyes tight when he used his power as beta against her. "Stop."

A hard shudder wracked her frame, but she slung her head and shook off his compulsion.

"She's not pack," he said, dumbfounded. "She couldn't disobey me otherwise."

Again, I questioned what we were seeing. And again, I couldn't shake the sense Ares was present.

There was no other excuse for the deep sorrow in her eyes or the shame in her posture.

Pressing my shoulder against his in a show of support, I asked, "How does that happen?"

"She forsook her alpha," Liz told me then winked at Midas. "She's mine now, Beta."

A soft whine escaped Ares, but she didn't slow their retreat.

The transformation engulfed Midas, crested and splashed, washed away his humanity and left a beast in a lather standing before us. He lunged for Ares, who rose up to protect Liz, and they clashed with bone-crunching force.

"Bring her down," I told Ambrose quietly. "Whatever it takes."

Understanding I meant Liz, who was attempting to flee while Ares distracted us, he streaked across the craggy lot aiming straight for her. He punched through her, inflicting small hurts, but he was too full to slow her down.

Calling him back to me as I ran after her, I dipped my hands into him and retrieved my swords.

Then I prayed I didn't trip, fall, and skewer myself. I was getting better, but I was no Jedi Master.

As I got within striking distance, an engine rumbled to life, and a truck streaked past me. Liz waited until it got even with her then leapt into the bed as nimbly as a doe. She popped back up, grinning, and waved goodbye before climbing through the window into the cab with the unfamiliar driver.

The truck squealed onto the main road. Next stop, the interstate. After that, I would never catch them.

Pulling on Ambrose's reserves, I pushed my body to its limits to pace the truck. I brushed the tailgate with my outstretched fingertips, but they glanced off as I rung a pothole with my foot.

A sickening crunch filled my ears, my balance wobbled, and I flung out my hands to stop the fall. I hit the asphalt. Hard. I didn't look down. I knew my ankle was broken. I could tell because of the loud snap, the agonizing pain, and—oh yeah—the fact my foot was still wedged in the hole a bit too far behind me.

Water poured from my eyes, but I had this much in common with my mother. The tears were borne of rage and fury.

Not fifteen seconds later, Midas skidded to a halt next to me, assessed my injuries while dragging a hand over his mouth, then cursed in a language that I would have found beautiful at any other time.

Crouching beside me, he stabbed the air in front of my nose with his finger.

"Don't—" he bit off the word, "—move."

"I didn't plan on it." I noticed the phone in his hand. "Who are you calling?"

"Abbott."

"Grier can fix this," I whined. "I bet Linus could patch me up too."

"Abbott can be the judge of that."

Given how the air vibrated with barely leashed violence, I decided to pick my battles and whispered, "Okay."

"I don't trust your tone," he admitted, "but you aren't budging without help."

The shadow, who hummed with energy, poked my ankle then skittered away when I yelped at him.

"We found them," Midas said into his cell. "I need medical transport for five."

Five meant Ares had escaped, which meant we had no fresh leads with Liz in the wind too.

On the other end of the line, the voice grew more heated until Midas held it away from his ear.

"Yes." He flicked his gaze down my leg. "I can send you a picture."

Quick as a flash, he did just that, and the volume on the other end of the line increased then cut out flat.

"You hung up on him," I realized. "You actually hung up on Abbott."

"There's poor reception out here," he lied. "I've already called Bishop. He's on his way to meet us."

"We need to test the Pritchards and the Whitakers." I forced my brain to be more productive than screaming in agony. "Make sure there are no other surprises."

"Who do you think Ares was protecting?"

Ares.

The momentary distraction kept the pain from overwhelming me. "Is she...?"

"Alive." His lips twisted. "She's heavily injured and unconscious."

But was she herself or a skin or a host or some new and terrible creation?

I had already gotten my miracle—*miracles*—with Boaz and Addie. I was afraid to hope for more.

"She was the fifth person in need of transport." I let that settle. "How am I getting home?"

Crimson flecked his eyes, and they shone. "You're lucky I don't make you stump it back to the Faraday."

Unfortunately for his tough-guy act, a gleaming white pickup with a familiar face behind the wheel rolled to a stop beside us. Lisbeth hopped out of Ford's truck then slapped a hand over her mouth when she got a good look at me.

"Your ankle..." She turned green. "How...?"

"You're an LPN." I wished I could scoot to one side or another. "Don't you dare barf on me."

"I'm not an ER nurse." She breathed in deeply through her nose then exhaled through her mouth. "I saw more paperwork than patients on my last job, and no one shows up to their family doctor with their foot hanging on by a thread. They call 911 and hitch a ride to a hospital in an ambulance."

"Okay then." I flapped my hands at her. "How about you stand a few paces away?"

"Yeah." She bobbed her head. "I'll just be over there, admiring the honeysuckle vines."

Near a ditch that wouldn't mind if she threw up in it.

"I can't believe Ford let her drive his truck." I watched Midas head to the tailgate. "He never let me drive his truck." I frowned when he reached into the bed. "I probably would have needed a booster seat anyway."

"Lisbeth is his girlfriend," Midas pointed out. "They've also lived together off and on."

Their relationship had started out as nurse to patient. Well, a nurse with a raging Ford crush to a patient. Then he repaid her kindness when she needed it. I hadn't framed their relationship as roomies, but Midas was right. They might as well have lived together, given how long one had been providing live-in nursing for the other.

They were moving fast. *Really* fast. For a human. Not so much for a gwyllgi. But Lisbeth had crushed on him from afar for so long, I imagine they were on the same page. She might even be a chapter ahead of him.

Trying my best not to move an inch, I glared up at him. "Why must you insist on using logic against me?"

"I have to get you in the truck bed and to Abbott." Hands on his hips, he surveyed his makeshift ambulance. "It's going to hurt."

"Yeah." I stopped trying to distract myself with Fisbeth, my favorite couple name for Ford and Lisbeth to date, and I focused on my own problems. "Do you think it will fall off when you lift me?"

"Your foot? Or your leg?"

"Both? Either?" I flinched on reflex when he touched my shoulders. "Do I have to pick just one?"

"It won't fall off," he promised me. "Keep as still as you can."

Teeth gritted, I nodded the go ahead and let him unstick my foot from the hole, which cost me my shoe.

"Okay," he said, his face pale. "Now I'm going to put you on the air mattress."

"Air mattress?" I huffed out a laugh. "Now that's fancy."

I would like to say I (wo)manfully endured as he gathered me into a bridal carry, but without Lisbeth to brace my ankle, it just sort of... hung there.

As soon as the full weight of my foot dangled, a lightning bolt of nerve-singeing agony struck me in the brain ten times harder than Ambrose ever dreamed possible.

The lights in my head blinked once and then went out.

FIFTEEN

"I've never seen anything like it."

"Are you saying what I think you're saying?"

"Interesting."

That last voice sliced through the fuzzy cocoon between my ears, and I cranked open my eyes.

"Linus?" I squinted at the blurry ceiling. What was it with ceilings lately? Were they stalking me? "What are you doing here?"

"I came to offer my assistance, but it appears you don't require any."

"Grier?" I unstuck my tongue from the roof of my mouth. "Did she...wave her...magic wand?"

"I have one of those?" She made a wistful sound. "How cool would that be?"

"More like a magic churro," Lethe scoffed. "Instead of pixie dust, you sprinkle sugar everywhere you go."

"Midas?" I twisted my head but couldn't spot him. "Where...?"

"Right here." He jogged into the room. "I was updating Mom on your condition."

That all but guaranteed she would put in an appearance and gang up on me with Abbott riding shotgun.

"I broke my ankle, not my head." I swatted away cobwebs. "Why is my brain so cottony?"

Silence enveloped the room, and all eyes turned toward Linus, which couldn't be a good thing.

"Ambrose healed you," he said, when no one else made a peep. "He also spoke through you."

"That last part sounds less than ideal." I braced for the worst. "What did he say?"

"To set the ankle so he could heal it."

"That's it?" I glanced around but didn't spot him. "What did he say *exactly*?"

Not since Linus inked a binding tattoo that joined Ambrose to me had he verbally communicated with anyone. Even when he took control of my body to keep me safe while the coven's charm sent me walking into the city streets unconscious in the daytime, he had held his tongue. He and I couldn't talk directly, not precisely, so I was as curious as I was incredulous and, well, terrified to have lost control over myself.

"'Set the bone,' he quoted, 'and I will mend her.'"

"That's it?" I watched him hard. "That's all?"

"That's it," he assured me. "That's all."

"I don't get it." I mustered the courage to finally look at my ankle. "I'm healed?"

"Yes," Abbott said, clearly disturbed. "I've never seen anything like it."

"He didn't ask for a favor or for chocolate or my immortal soul?" I clarified. "He wanted nothing?"

Linus didn't answer, but the amusement in his eyes told me he was allowing me to process it all.

"I don't understand why he did it." I was suspicious as frak about it. "And it's not like I can ask him."

If he could speak through me, he could manipulate my physical body. He could have said or done anything, and not many would have recognized I wasn't the one in control. Why not press his advantage? Why not break out of the infirmary and go hunting? Why not, I don't know, ask for a case of Amedei Porcelana or a box of La Madeline au Truffe?

The others left the room at some cue Linus must have given them while I gingerly tested my ankle.

"Your greatest fear has always been that Ambrose would influence your thoughts and actions."

Forgetting my self-exam, I twisted onto my side to face him. "Yes."

"Have you ever considered his ability to influence you is a two-way street? That residing in you, as a part of you, has affected him in ways we couldn't anticipate?"

"Are you saying he's...grown a conscience?"

"I wouldn't go that far." Linus chuckled. "I would venture that he's grown attached to *you*, in more than the literal sense."

"He has been acting weird lately," I confessed. "I've been joking he wants to be a dynamic duo."

"You fed him a considerable amount of power tonight, but he stored it, like a battery. He could have used it against you and done you irreparable harm, but he chose to reserve his strength. For this. For you."

The other small touches throughout the night drifted to the surface of my thoughts, the way he kept feeding me extra punches of energy when I began flagging.

"This isn't the first time he's acted in your best interests," Linus reminded me. "He protected you from the coven's charm under your pillow."

"He did." I gave credit where it was due. "I didn't trust his motivations then either."

"You're unique, Hadley. There's never been another dybbuk, to our knowledge, who has survived longer than a year. You're charting new territory that will help pave the way for others who've made mistakes and wish to rectify them." He rose and pulled the cover back, exposing my bare leg to the knee. "No one believed a dybbuk could be redeemed, but you've proven that's not the case."

A sudden tightness in my throat made it hard to speak. "I couldn't have done this without you."

"Don't sell yourself short." He examined the tattoos on my ankle. "All I did was bind Ambrose to you for life to prevent him from killing you to escape into a new host. That was the work of a few hours. You're the one who fights to maintain your identity every day. That's the work of a lifetime."

Uncomfortable with his subtle praise, which from Linus was like any other mentor pinning a gold medal on their student's chest, I gave myself permission to ask after the others. "How are they?"

Accepting the change of subject, since he was as uncomfortable with praise as me, he smiled. "Good."

"They're going to be okay?"

"Adelaide is awake and talking. We've flushed the drugs from her system. We're working on rehydrating her now." He sat back in his chair. "Boaz punched Abbott, called him a witchy bastard, stumbled into the room with Adelaide, then passed out on her floor."

"That's...romantic...I guess?"

"Abbott had a second bed put in her room, so they're together. Boaz is, however, cuffed to his bedrail to prevent another assault on the staff." Linus tapped his fingers on his knee. "He must have put up more resistance than the others. He was pumped full of drugs, a lethal amount, and his progress has been slower." He stilled his drumming. "Honestly, I'm not sure how he survived as long as he did with that particular cocktail in his system. If you hadn't found him when you did, he would have died. I doubt he would have lived the day."

A cold lump hardened in my gut, and I wet my lips. "He's going to be okay, though, right?"

"Grier has been working on him." He smiled tightly. "He's in very capable hands."

"That's good." I twisted the sheet into knots. "How is Mr. Whitaker?"

"He's in a medically induced coma. He didn't handle withdrawal from his drug of choice well. He inflicted a lot of damage on himself, so he's restrained. The drugs he was given interacted with ones already in his system, but we expect him to make a full recovery."

"I knew he drank, but I had no idea he used anything harder."

"Adelaide was also unaware he had developed other tastes, but she says it explains where some of their money has gone. She plans to check him into rehab once he's stable enough for transfer."

"If you see her before I do, tell her not to worry about the cost. I'll pay for it. All of it."

"I'll do that." A deep line furrowed his brow. "Matron Pritchard is also in good health."

"Good," I said sharply, and wished I had taken time to dull the edge first. "I'm glad everyone is okay."

"Your mate is pacing a hole in the floor." He rose and patted my hand. "I'll leave you to it."

Linus nodded to Midas in passing, but I don't think Midas noticed with his entire being focused on me.

It didn't bode well that Midas shut the door behind him to keep us from being overheard by the others. I had an idea of where this conversation was heading, and I would rather sew my mouth together without anesthesia than talk about this. But the feral cat was out of the bag now.

The mattress dipped when he sat beside me. "Do you want to talk about Liz's allegations?"

"No."

Taking my hand, he toyed with my fingers. "Any idea how to locate her?"

"You would really let it go, just like that?"

"Do you know how long it took me to work up the courage to share what happened to me in Faerie?" He let that sink in. "Do you know how long after I told Mom and Lethe I held it all in until I told you?" He cut me off before I could answer. "You're young, Hadley. It's okay if you haven't made peace with your past. We have the rest of our lives for you to decide what you do and don't want me to know."

"Except now I'll be paranoid every time I'm naked in front of you that you're staring at them. The scars."

"You don't gawk at mine." He rubbed a hand down one cross-hatched forearm. "Why would I fixate on yours?"

"You heard what she said," I whispered. "You know how I got them."

Honest confusion tugged his lips down. "What's your point?"

"You've dedicated yourself to empowering women who have suffered abuse." I hadn't consciously had a clue I felt this way about us until it popped out of my mouth. "What if that's what attracted you to me?"

"You're not wearing a scarlet letter, Hadley. You don't telegraph your abuse simply by existing. You fight against your perception of yourself, against *her* perception of *you*, every day. It's only natural you would think others see the conflict in you, but they don't, I promise you that."

"You did." I had been too flighty around him at first, too nervous he would unmask me. "Quickly too."

"Did I wonder at times? Yes. I've been around enough survivors to recognize the symptoms, and you evidenced several of them. I had no idea it was your mother, or what she did to you." He laughed harshly, but it was self-directed. "I thought a boyfriend might have done it."

Scrunching up my face, I asked, "Why is that funny?"

"Abuse colors the world survivors live in, and I chalked up *your* problems to *my* issues." He hesitated as I studied him. "I laughed at the reminder of how twisted up we all get in our own heads, in our own pasts. We view everyone else through the clouded lens of our own life experience. That's how assumptions get made, and they're generally wrong. We apply our experiences to others in an effort to understand them and their motivations, but we rarely get it right."

"Liz said something..."

"...designed to get under your skin."

"I was happy to take it slow, physically, with you." I wasn't sure how to fit the rest of the words in my mouth without choking on them. "You were working through some stuff, and I didn't want to pressure you." He looked at his hands, his features unreadable. "I put it all on you. In my head, I mean. I convinced myself I was content waiting for your benefit."

"You think you were subconsciously avoiding sex with me to avoid a conversation on your scars."

"I've never dated anyone who mattered. I've never cared what the guys I was with thought of me. I had plans. I had school. Dreams. Guys were warm bodies when I felt like having dinner out or watching a movie or...*that*." A slow burn moved through my cheeks. "But you matter. I care very much, maybe too much, what you think of me. I still have plans. I still have dreams. They just all include you now."

"You can't believe it would make any difference to me."

"We're all twisted up in our own heads, our own pasts," I quoted back to him. "What do you think?"

"I want to see your scars." He placed one hand beside my pillow and leaned over me, his delicious heat sinking into me. "I want to see you." He ducked his head, pressed his lips to mine, and kissed me slowly, with such tenderness tears threatened to swamp me. "I want you, Hadley."

The way he tasted me, with a hungry growl revving up the back of his throat and a sharp edge to his kiss, turned my knees—and more interesting places—liquid as I patted the mattress. "There's room for two."

"There are also half a dozen people with their noses pressed to the glass."

"Frak, frak, frak." I peered around him. "Tell them to go away?"

The crowd dispersed to make way for a woman with instincts that bordered on downright terrifying.

"Your mom is here." I smoothed a hand down my chest. "Does she know? About...?"

The ants. The scars. The pantry.

"I didn't tell her." He twisted around to scan the newcomers. "I won't tell her without your permission."

Feeling small, I gripped his wrists. "Ford?"

"I can't see him mentioning your private business in his report." Midas rubbed his jaw. "He wouldn't betray you unless he felt you had been compromised and the pack was in danger." He dropped his hand. "Mom could have pressed him for details, without understanding what he would confide, but I doubt it."

"Okay." I wiggled myself upright. "Let her in."

The door had barely cracked before Tisdale wedged herself through it and strode to me. "Sweetheart."

"Hi." I waved like a dork. "I'm fine. You don't have to—"

Gwyllgi are strong, and their hugs can be fierce, but Tisdale's was downright ferocious.

"Hush." She cinched her arms tighter until spots danced in my vision. "I'm so relieved you're all right."

Midas grinned at me when I slid a panicked glance past her shoulder.

"It was just a broken ankle." I patted her lightly on the back. "Seriously, I'm good."

"Abbott told me you healed yourself." She pulled back, and I sucked in air. "That's remarkable."

A queasy sensation writhed through my gut when it hit me that she and I hadn't been alone since she learned who and what I really was the hard way. We weren't alone now, with Midas here, but it left me itching to hunch away from the blow that was sure to come.

Tisdale hadn't had a problem with Hadley Whitaker, future Potentate of Atlanta, as a daughter-in-law.

But I wasn't her, exactly, and now she knew it.

"I took the liberty of familiarizing myself with your history," she said, plucking the creeping fear right out of my head. "For the pack's sake, I have to be well informed on any matter that might blow back onto us in the future."

Lips gone numb, I managed to fumble out, "I understand."

"That history will not be made public, sweetheart. No one will learn of it from me. I wouldn't betray you or your secrets." She cupped my cheek. "You understand you are pack now. This was as much to protect you as the rest of us."

Again, Midas grinned at me, and again, his mother practiced her anaconda-style hugging technique.

"I might be out of line in supposing that your reluctance to spend time with me and the pack stems from the betrayal from your own mother and family when they disowned you." She tightened her thin arms, I don't know how, and my vision tunneled. "You're ours now, and we'll fight for you. I don't only mean myself, or Midas, but all of us. Pack means you never walk alone."

Tears pricked the backs of my eyes, and I blinked at the ceiling to clear them. "Thanks."

"I understand Liz is still at large." She withdrew slowly. "Ares hasn't woken yet, but she will soon."

Even without the vow she just made me, I would have to be blind to miss how much the losses hurt her.

"I'm hoping Ares will have answers for us." I leaned back before she trapped me again. "Nothing about it makes sense to me." I smoothed my sheets. "They took high-value targets but didn't ransom them. They had days to..." I swallowed hard, "...but they didn't add them to their closet. They fed and watered them and had more supplies that hinted at their plans to keep them alive for an undisclosed purpose and amount of time. Even the drugs were meant to keep them docile enough they wouldn't harm themselves, or their captors."

Not that Boaz let their best intentions stop him from causing enough trouble to force them to take lethal measures to contain him.

"You'll figure it out." She patted my thigh. "I have faith."

A knock on the door brought her head around as Lethe strolled into the room. "Time to go, Mom."

"Leaving so soon?" Midas intercepted her with an arm slung around her shoulders. "Are you two headed back to the den?"

"Yep." Leaning her head against him, she growled, "The Knoxville debacle is eating my soul."

Withdrawing a bit, he looked down at her bright blue hair. "Do you need any help?"

"If two alphas can't fix this," she reasoned, straightening, "then two alphas and a beta can't either."

"What's causing the problem?" I glanced between them. "I thought we had worked out a solution."

The former alpha had been kicked to the curb, and Tisdale was open to absorbing the rest into her pack.

"With the pack itself?" Lethe met my gaze, and for once it was absent of hostilities. "They're cool with whatever. Honestly? They've been beaten down so often they don't much care what happens to them." She twitched her shoulder. "The issue is other packs who have a bone to pick with Atlanta seeing guests of ours come to harm. They're spinning the incident into an attack on neighboring packs instead of what it is—an attack on *us*—in the hopes it gives them a foothold to social climb."

"You said *ours*," Midas pointed out with a little-brother smirk.

"Shut up your face." She palmed his forehead and pushed him back. "Old habits die hard."

"Call if you need anything." Tisdale went to break up the shoving match between her kids. "And do try not to get yourself maimed, mauled, or generally murdered, won't you, sweetheart?"

"I will do my best," I promised her. "Let me know if you need any help on your end too."

Tisdale and Lethe made their exit, leaving Midas and me alone together.

For all of a second.

"You've got to be more careful." Remy bounded into the room. "You're the face of our company, and it's not a great look when you're black and blue."

"It warms my heart to hear your concern."

"If I didn't care, I'd have brought the paperwork you owe me and made you do it while you're laid up."

"That would have been cruel."

"But effective."

I smiled when she produced a steaming café mocha and thrust it at me.

"There is a favor I need to ask." She flopped onto the bed with me. "Can I have your apartment?"

"Uh." I did a double take. "Come again?"

"Your old apartment. Can I have it?" She bristled. "I'll pay rent and everything, but it's the only open spot in the whole building. Mostly because it's not really open. It's still in your name. So can I have it?"

"You want to move into the Faraday?"

"I need a place of my own, and somebody's got to watch your back. It'll be easier for me if I'm only a few floors down."

"Okay."

"Okay you agree with me, or okay I can have your apartment?"

"Okay to both." I took a sip and sighed happily. "I don't need two apartments."

Midas and I were in a good place, a great place, actually, and I was ready to let that bit of my past go.

"Excellent." She clapped her hands. "Then I'll let you get back to your scheming."

Scheming was more of a Remy thing, but her business plans—which bred like rabbits in the dark corners of her mind—kept her too busy to get in much trouble these days, for which I was grateful. The apartment would be yet another project, and Atlanta was always a bit safer with her mind occupied and her car off the roads.

"Thanks."

Giving Bishop a high-five as she passed him, he took the opening and joined us.

"Hey, kid." He sat on the bed. "Why are you still lazing about? I thought your ankle was fixed."

A low sound poured into the room and lifted the fine hairs down my nape. "Midas."

"He. Blew. You. Up."

"This again?" Bishop threw his hands up in frustration. "She told me to do it."

Wincing at Midas's scowl, I raised a finger. "I did tell him to do it."

Midas dripped beads of red magic onto the floor. "He also tran-quilized you."

"For her own protection," Bishop argued, "you lunkhead."

"He's not wrong," I said quietly, whispered really. "I've been tranqed before and probably will be again."

Turning away from the bed, Midas stared through the glass door into the now-empty hall.

Intellectually, I knew he wasn't turning his back on me. He was tuning out Bishop, and the reminder of how fast things could and did spin out of his control. He was fighting against his instincts to give me room to breathe, but it was hard for him to suppress the urge to coddle and protect me from every thorn destined for my side. But it required conscious effort not to cringe from his temper, when he would never hurt me.

Thanks, Mom.

"Linus performs a necessary function for Hadley, and I do too. Neither of us wants to hurt her, but we're both responsible for doing whatever it takes to de-escalate any behavior that might cost her her life. I get it's hard for you. Guess what? It's hard for us too. She's our friend, and we care about her. It's not fun to always have the fear of what might happen if she ever slips wedged into the back of your mind like a splinter. Actually, it fucking sucks."

"I'm sorry, Bish." I covered his hand with mine. "You shouldn't have to police me."

"Kid, you're not listening." He layered his other hand on top of mine. "You're my friend, and I care what happens to you. That's why I do it. I'm not worried about what havoc you unleash. I'm worried about the consequences to you if your control slips." He shrugged. "I'm selfish like that."

"You're with the OPA," I reminded him. "You're supposed to protect the city first and always."

"Guess what?" He chucked me on the chin. "Protecting its protector accomplishes that very goal."

"Does Linus know you've developed a rebellious streak?"

"Who do you think inspired it?" He chuckled. "You have to believe in something, or it's all for nothing. I believe in you. You're the good I want to see in the world. You're not perfect, and you don't try to be. You do the best you can, no matter what it costs you, and that's all any of us can do."

"I'm sorry." Midas addressed the wall, but there was little doubt he was talking to Bishop. "I won't make any promises, but I will try harder not to want to murder you every time I see you."

"Hey." Bishop winked at me. "What else can a guy ask for?"

"You have entire notebooks full of wish lists." I shoved him. "However, a gal could ask for a lead on Liz."

"She's in the wind." He shook his head. "We've got a few ideas, but nothing's panned out yet."

"Ares is our best bet." Midas turned to face them. "She'll know where Liz is denning."

"Then we need to go talk to her." I swung my legs over the side of the bed. "Here goes nothing."

Sliding my toes onto cool laminate flooring, I tested my ankle and found it held my weight without buckling. It didn't exactly hurt so much as it was brutally tender, but I stood and walked without keeling over. That was definitely progress.

Hunting Liz while Midas pushed me in a wheelchair with my

ankle in a cast would have seriously dinged my street cred. It was hard to look intimidating with one leg elevated and a golden god steering you where you need to go.

"How do you feel?" Midas hovered, but he didn't swoop in to save me. "Can you manage?"

"It hurts, but nothing like it did. I can walk on it without my eyes crossing in pain."

The door opened then, and like a messenger sent from biblical heaven, or a healer who eavesdropped on his patients, Abbott descended upon us with a plastic contraption in his hand that he pointed at me with the conviction of an archangel wielding his holy blade.

SIXTEEN

"Y ou're going to wear this." Abbott slapped an ankle brace across my palm. "You're going to like it."

"I won't," I countered only to be contrary, "and you can't make me."

A quick trip to the storage cabinet produced my tennis shoes, one of them rather bloody.

"These are ruined." He clucked his tongue. "I'm throwing them away."

As I gaped at him, they thumped the bottom of the can. "What do you think bleach is for?"

"You don't have time to bleach and dry the shoes if you're going toddling off into danger this second."

Toddling off made me sound like a baby, and I was in age compared to most gwyllgi, but *grr*.

I bought bleach in bulk for a reason, dammit.

"I took the precaution of having Remy procure another pair." He returned to the cabinet. "Here we are."

The sneakers were still in the box and smelled overwhelmingly of *new*.

"These aren't my shoes," I grumped. "I like my old shoes better."

Midas rubbed a hand across his mouth, but it didn't smudge his grin.

Abbott ripped out the sole in the right shoe, slid the contraption in, then replaced it with a scowl.

"I'll make you a deal." He crouched in front of me. "Lift your foot, please."

I wrinkled my nose at the top of his head, but Midas crossed his arms over his chest.

No help there.

Bowling Abbott over and hobbling to the elevators, to freedom, wasn't happening without an accomplice. I cooperated like a co-beta ought to, but I wasn't happy about it. "What's the deal?"

"Be a good girl, wear the brace for the next week, and I'll bag your old shoes for you to bleach later."

"Fine." Gripping the bedrail, I lifted my foot and let him slide the shoe contraption on me. "I'll do it."

"We shall see," he muttered. "In the meantime, I'll keep the shoes until you fulfill your end of the deal."

"What?" I grimaced as he Velcroed the straps into place around my tender ankle. "That's not fair."

"I'm not saying I don't trust you." He leaned back to admire his handiwork. "I'm just saying motivation is a good thing." He rose. "You don't have to wear it around the house, but keep it on while you're at work for the next seven days. Seven, Hadley. Not six. Not five and a half. Not four. *Seven*."

"Why did you become a healer when you enjoy inflicting pain on others?"

"We all must play to our strengths." He stood back. "Please be careful."

Remy had also brought me a change of clothes, which was nice. The black yoga pants were heaven and stretched over the itchy brace. The bright-pink racerback sports bra was not my favorite thing, but the white oversized Metallica tank might end up in rotation for my runs in the Active Oval.

"This isn't as horrendous as I feared." I pulled my hair into a high ponytail. "Remy didn't do too badly."

"It's tame by her standards." Midas raked his heated gaze down me. "It's hard to go wrong with you as her model."

"You're adorable." I pinched his cheek. "Can we spare a second for me to look in on Boaz and Addie?"

"Sure." He took my hand. "Grier and Linus are still at our place. It'll take them a minute to get downstairs."

Our place.

Music to my ears.

"You texted them?" I made stiff progress to the door, but my ankle was loosening. "Good deal."

"Grier is our best bet for getting information out of Ares without resorting to the usual methods."

The usual methods being torture, which no one would want to inflict on her, even a shell of her, least of all him.

"I'll keep my fingers crossed she can work her magic then."

Midas stopped a few yards down from my room in front of a door with a cutout identical to mine. I pressed my face to the glass and ignored the slight hitch in my breath.

Boaz and Addie each had a bed, as reported, but he had hauled her onto his, and she slept draped over the top of him. His arm, the one not cuffed to the bed, circled her waist, and he held on as if afraid someone might take her from him again. Her face was turned toward the window, and she was smiling even in her sleep.

Yep.

She was a goner.

We might be hearing wedding bells this year after all.

"They're cute." I resisted the urge to tap the glass like they were fish swimming in an aquarium. "Right?"

"They love each other." He rubbed my shoulders. "They might not have realized how much."

"Boaz is a loveaphobe, and a commitmentaphobe. She's got her hands full with that one."

"Yes." Midas twisted me away from the window before I registered the squeak of my shoes on the tile. "She does, literally." He captured my face between his palms. "No." He held me still. "Don't look back."

"Eww, eww, eww." I threw up a little in my mouth. "Get me out of here."

We hit the elevators and rode up to the lobby then crossed it to reach the enforcer's on-site HQ.

An uncomfortable silence fell when I entered, which I would have blamed on the intrusion of an outside authority figure in their personal space, if not for the fact I had bought their loyalty with pizza, donuts, and fried chicken over the last several months. No, the quiet wasn't my fault. It was *our* fault.

Midas and I had caged Ares. We were hunting Liz. And we couldn't exactly make an announcement to put everyone at ease. From the outside looking in, we had done the unthinkable in turning against a packmate, and it smarted. They understood protocol better than most since they had hands-on experience dealing with gwyllgi-on-gwyllgi crimes, but it sucked all the way around.

"She's in A2," a slight female told us. "We have four guards on her."

Midas nodded then escorted me through a reinforced steel door into a dim observation area with one-way mirrored glass overlooking a mini prison-style pod with two levels of cells that must extend into the basement and might explain the cramped underground parking deck. The facilities belonged to the Faraday, not the pack, and were rigged to hold every flavor of resident should they become a problem for the rest of the building.

There were four cells on each floor for a total of eight. The top row was outfitted with metal bars, two in silver and two in bronze. They were meant to accommodate shifters. Gwyllgi and wargs in particular. The bottom row were solid gray boxes of undetermined material outfitted with clear polycarbonate doors to contain vampires, humans, and fae offenders until their faction leader arranged for their release.

The enforcers on guard duty snapped to attention at our arrival, but none of them looked at us, and not just because of the dominance factor.

"We need a few minutes alone with the prisoner," Midas told them. "Grier Woolworth and Linus Lawson will be joining us. Escort them back when they arrive, please."

"Yes, sir," they echoed in unison then pivoted on their heels and marched out in a single file.

"The pack isn't happy about this," I stated the obvious. "How do we smooth things over?"

"When enforcers hunt one of their own, it reminds the pack what can happen if they ever step out of line." He gazed through the door into the bright cell holding Ares. "We're supposed to take care of our people, and we do, but the punishment for breaking trust with Mom is brutal. Often, it's fatal too. It has to be or else there's chaos. We are predators, and predators don't respect weakness."

"I'm sorry it's come to this." I joined him in watching her sleep. "She is—*was*—a good friend to have at your back."

"I always thought so." He cut his gaze to mine. "I hope I wasn't wrong about that too."

His meaning sank in, that he might never have known the real Ares, and my heart pinched. The witchborn fae hadn't made their move until I was one year into my apprenticeship, but that didn't mean they hadn't infiltrated the local packs well before then.

Ares might have cozied up to me as I hit it off with Midas in the hopes she could worm her way into my confidence, which she had, and learn my weaknesses. She might have never been my friend, and that sucked. We'd had rough patches, but she always came across as genuine, and I liked her. I liked Liz, what little I knew of her, too.

But then again, I was sure plenty of folks—my brothers included—believed Matron Pritchard was a good woman.

They were wrong about her.

We had been wrong about Ares.

Watching her sleep under present conditions felt ghoulish, so Midas and I settled in against the wall to wait on Grier and Linus. I leaned my head on his shoulder, shifted the weight off my right foot, and gave myself a moment to process before things got hectic again.

What felt like seconds later, I jolted awake, having fallen asleep standing. All that had kept me from melting onto the floor was the warm arm Midas had wrapped around my middle to keep me wedged between him and the wall. The noise that had stirred me was the outer door opening then clanging shut behind Linus and Grier.

The couple approached, hand in hand, but neither carried their kits stocked with necromantic implements. Their low conversation echoed, and I listened in once I realized what they were discussing.

"The guard warned she's not restrained," Grier was saying. "Sigil or zip tie?"

"Sigil." Linus awarded her his full attention. "Bind her wrists and ankles first."

This must be how gwyllgi felt all the time, doomed to listen in without meaning to, but it felt rude to me.

"He's right." As much as I hated to be harsh on Ares, she wasn't Ares anymore. "Take all precautions."

Neither of them started at my verbal intrusion, but they would have noticed the echo too.

"Okay." Dipping her chin, Grier shook out her hands. "Let's do this."

A tad concerned by her apparent lack of preparation, I asked, "You've got everything you need?"

"Yep." She withdrew an antique pocketknife with a lethal edge. "I'm ready."

"I'll go in with her," Midas volunteered. "I'll secure Ares until Grier restrains her."

"Works for me." I checked with Linus. "You okay with that?"

"Yes." He tucked his hands into his pockets. "I trust Midas with her."

A greater endorsement had never been spoken, and even Midas appeared taken aback.

"Abbott told us she was sedated." Midas removed a card from his pocket and swiped it through the lock. "We burn through drugs in our systems quickly, so stay on your guard. She might be playing possum."

"Okay." Grier pulled on her game face. "Wrists first."

Once the door swung open and the path cleared, a few things happened all at once.

Ares jackknifed off the bed.

Midas charged her.

Grier cut her palm.

And Ambrose stretched to wakefulness inside me, spreading dark tendrils that seeped across the floor.

From the corner of my eye, I watched the familiar tattered cowl envelope Linus's head and his dark cloak unfurl to his ankles. The scythe that often haunted my dreams appeared in his hand, and he strode to the door with lethal purpose.

A braver woman might have reached out, but my fingers curled, nails biting into the meat of my palms. I would never not be afraid of him like this. I wished I could say otherwise, but it was the truth. I saw him all in black and wanted to wet my pants, run, scream, sink into the floor, vanish into thin air, or some combination of all those things.

The crack of meat against bone jerked my head back toward the cell in time to witness Ares's head snap to one side and her eyes roll up in her skull. She collapsed at Midas's feet, and he flipped her onto her stomach, planted his knee on her spine, and waved Grier in.

She rushed in, dipped a finger in her blood, then drew binding sigils at Ares's wrists and ankles. "Done."

Hauling Ares up and onto the cot where she had been lying, Midas arranged her in an upright seated position. Gwyllgi can take a beating, and they heal fast. She was already coming around, her eyes twitching behind their lids.

"The way this works is—" Grier caught sight of Linus in Grim Reaper mode and sighed. "Linus."

That she could watch him approach in full nightmare regalia and simply sigh at him...

Yeah.

That was love for you.

The tattered edges of his cloak fluttered one last time then vanished along with his cowl and scythe.

"Thank you." Grier blew him a kiss. "I've got this."

Joining me, which gave me the heebie-jeebies after that display, Linus murmured, "It never gets easier."

Skin attempting to crawl off my body and hide, I impressed him with my ready wit. "Hmm?"

"Watching someone you love put themselves in harm's way for the sake of another."

"Oh. Yeah." I got myself under control. "I'm starting to see that."

A tiny smile tugged on one corner of Linus's mouth. "I believe Midas is seeing it too."

"I can't be anything other than what I am." I spread my hands. "I tried to warn him off me."

Never taking his eyes off Ares, Midas rumbled, "Don't make me come out there and bite you, Hadley."

I made a noise halfway between a laugh and a cry of indignation.

"He's very bitey," I confided in Linus, aware Midas would overhear. "Must be a gwyllgi thing."

"Grier is very bitey too," he confessed in an equally low tone. "But then, her father was a vampire."

"I can hear you." Grier glowered at him. "I won't bite you again if you go around advertising it."

A slight pinkness tipped his ears, and I was very uncomfortable all of a sudden.

"So." I clasped my hands together loud enough to ring in my ears. "Are we ready to get started?"

Amusement bright in her eyes, Grier waved us over to them. "Yes."

Careful not to get too close in case Midas made good on his threat, I focused on Ares. "How does this work?"

"This sigil loosens her tongue and guarantees she'll talk to us." Grier pointed to Ares's forehead and then her chin. "This one indicates whether she's telling the truth." She shrugged. "Sadly, they're not mutually exclusive. I haven't worked out the quirks combining the two yet."

"Does it hurt when she lies?"

"There's a slight twinge, but it's no worse than a bee sting." She glanced at Linus. "Or so I'm told."

Since I didn't want to know why she would have interrogated Linus, or what it led to, I erased it from my memory. I'd had no idea Linus was so kinky, and I wish I had stayed ignorant. It was called bliss for a reason.

"Would you like to handle the interrogation?" Grier watched me. "She can answer anyone."

No, I didn't *want* to hammer away at her façade and watch it crack, but it was my job.

"Where can we find Liz?"

"The old meat packing plant."

A red sheen, brighter than gwyllgi crimson, rolled across her eyes.

"She's lying," Grier interpreted. "Try again now that you know what you're looking for in a response."

"Where is Liz?"

"She's my mate."

Green.

"That doesn't change the fact she's killed a lot of innocent people."

"It changes everything," she said tiredly. "I can't let you hurt her."

Green.

As much as I hated the certain knowledge bubbling in my brain, I had no choice but to ask. "You're not coven, are you? Not a host either."

The dark circles under her eyes creased when she smiled at me. "I'm a worse monster than that."

Green.

The test hadn't failed. The results weren't flawed. Abbott hadn't given himself enough credit.

Midas couldn't keep his silence. "You're helping Liz of your own free will?"

"Free will?" Ares's misery was palpable. "She's my *mate.*"

Green.

"We're your pack." Midas curbed his growl. "Your family." He glanced at me. "Hadley is your friend."

"I protected Hadley as best I could," she whispered, "but it was only a matter of time."

Green.

"You were luring me away from the sites Liz chose, or detonating them early when you couldn't."

"Yeah." She rolled her shoulders. "It was the best I could do."

Red.

Down deep, she didn't believe that, and neither did I.

Mate bonds were powerful things, but you couldn't let love blind you to the cost of dozens of lives.

On the heels of that revelation ran another one. "You kidnapped my family."

"Liz was pissed you kept slipping through her fingers, so she targeted them to put you off balance." The lines creasing her face made her appear older, as if the past week had aged her. "I booked the dining room for a private party and put it under their names. That's how I cleared the restaurant of patrons."

Green.

Patrons were only half the collateral damage. "What about the staff?"

"There was no staff present when I arrived." A certain grimness tightened her mouth. "There were no bodies either. I checked. I'm not sure what Liz did with them before I got there."

"Liz was present?" I verified. "How did you get my family past her?"

"I spooked her off with a lie about you being on your way to join your family."

Midas keep the ball rolling when I couldn't find the words. "What happened next?"

"I drugged the Whitakers and the Pritchards then brought them to the old clinic until I could figure out what to do with them."

Green.

"Why wouldn't she have waited for Hadley to join them and then taken them all out at once?"

Midas made a good point, and I lent weight to his argument. "That would have fixed all her problems."

"I think..." Her mouth stretched thin. "I think she figured out what I was doing, minimizing the damage, protecting Hadley." She wet her lips. "I think she wanted them as hostages all along, but she was happy to let me believe I was getting one over on her as long as the job got done."

Green.

That made no sense. "Why not just kidnap them and be done with it?"

"She needed Ares to commit a crime against the pack of such severity it would cut her ties to us," Midas realized. "When Ares took your family, she violated the trust given to her as your friend and as a pack enforcer. She struck a blow to her beta and his mate. She forsook her vows."

So that's what Liz meant.

Not that Ares had shrugged off her pack bonds, but that she had smashed them with a hammer.

"She was isolating you," Linus said. "She wanted you alone, with no allies and no one to ask for help."

And once Liz had spent Ares's reputation down to the last penny, Liz would have killed her. There was no point in adding Ares to the coven's closet, not when Liz had torched her credibility. That had to hurt.

Head down, she gave no indication she heard, but the hitch in her indrawn breath made me want to hug her. Right up until I remembered how we got into this mess.

She could have killed my entire family. Wiped them out in a blink. The mercy she showed them would leave scars. I was as grateful for it as I was furious about it. "That's why you left me Boaz's ring."

Guilt had forced her to give me hope, maybe even direction. Subconsciously, she must have wanted the truth to come out, whether it damned her, Liz, or both of them.

"We had hostages, so we might as well use them." Ares's feet twitched with muscle spasms. "That's what she told me when she found me at the clinic. That's when I knew I had been set up since Choco-Loco, the night Boaz and Addie got into town." She tucked her legs under her. "I made them as comfortable as possible. I left them food and water and buckets for…"

The buckets, and their stench, wasn't one that would soon fade from my memories.

"You kept them alive," Midas coaxed, drawing out her confessions. "That matters."

There was one last hurdle to truly understanding how far this relationship had soured, and I tasted the question on my tongue when I asked it. "Liz is coven, isn't she?"

The ambiguous phrasing wasn't intentional, but it worked in my favor.

"I thought at first she was infected. A host." Ares's shoulders hunched even more. "It was almost a relief to believe it was curable. That if Ford had survived, she could too." Tears glittered on her cheeks. "The way she acted, I—I knew she must be coven. That a witchborn fae had… That my mate was…" A sob lodged in her throat. "But it was so much worse."

Green.

What had Liz told me?

I'm not wearing anyone.

I hadn't believed her then, not with so much glamour at her fingertips.

"Liz is a witchborn fae," I realized. "She's a member of the coven, not a skin or a host."

"She quit practicing," Midas said slowly. "Otherwise, we would have smelled black magic on her."

"I thought she was human." Ares shook her head. "I had no idea…"

Green.

"When did you learn the truth?"

"I walked her to work last Friday, like I always do when time permits." Her tears hit her pants with wet plops. "I was halfway back to the Faraday when I noticed I had her ID badge in my pocket, so I circled back to the hospital and hit the help desk. I had them page her, but she didn't show. An older man, another surgeon, came to explain she had been on leave for a month."

Green.

"What did you do next?"

"I thought maybe if she got fired, she would have been too embarrassed to tell me. The hormone therapy was hard on her, and she got written up a few times for losing her temper. I checked our apartment in case she had gone home. She knew I was working, so she would have had the place to herself, but she wasn't there."

Green.

"Where did you find her?"

"She came home at dawn, still dressed for work. I confronted her, but she made all these excuses." Ares shifted on the bed to get more comfortable. "She told me stress was bad for the baby, and I was driving her nuts with all the questions. I was worried she was right, so I let it go."

Green.

"You didn't really let it go," I asked gently, "did you?"

"I started staying up days, following her. Liz—" She shut her eyes briefly. "*My* Liz wasn't the type to have an affair, but I couldn't turn a blind eye. She was finally pregnant, and I became obsessed with tracking her. I had to *know* the child didn't belong to an ex-boyfriend or..."

A current one.

How much simpler infidelity would have been compared to all this.

Green.

"You were there," I said, prying her heart open wider, "at Choco-Loco."

"There was no reason for Liz to be there that night, so I followed her inside." Ares swallowed. "Chef Daaé... He was already dead. A stake through the heart. I didn't understand. I stood there, but I..." It was clear she still struggled with it. "That's when I got it, what she meant to do. I begged her to stop, but she wouldn't listen. I couldn't fight her..." She turned bloodshot eyes on us. "The baby. I couldn't risk the baby. Not after we tried so hard."

Quiet sobs broke the harsh lines of her shoulders then, and my heart shattered into razor-sharp pieces.

"Have you considered Liz didn't want a baby?" I hated to twist the knife, but it was already in my hand. "That she never had trouble conceiving?"

The lowest of the low wouldn't wield a woman's desire for a child with her mate against her, but Liz had used the struggle to bring them closer, to tie their goals tighter, to blind Ares to what else she might be doing under her nose.

Watch the left hand while the right balls into a fist and punches you into next week.

Classic misdirection.

"She lied to me, used me, but it doesn't change the fact I loved that woman with everything in me." Ares laugh-cried and sniffled. "The Liz I loved doesn't exist, but this one moves like her, talks like her, and it makes me a coward, but I still tell myself *my* Liz is in there."

Green.

Guess this time I was the right fist staring down the barrel of next week. "Are you sure she's pregnant?"

A slow breath shuddered out of her. "Yes."

Green.

A gwyllgi nose would be impossible to fool. They would pick up the subtle changes in scent in their mate, but I wore a ring to fake mine. Who was to say Liz hadn't done the same? She was a doctor, of that I had no doubt, given her service record among the gwyllgi. But that meant she had access to pregnant gwyllgi females and could craft a disguise based on their natural pheromones. "Help us then."

"I can't."

Red.

"What do you think will happen to your child if Liz goes free? The coven will help her raise it. What kind of life is that for a kid? What kind of mom would you be if you let it happen?"

"I'll never see it," she breathed. "I'll be killed for my crimes, and I'll deserve it."

Tisdale was a wise alpha, and a good mother. Both of those required a streak of ruthlessness.

"Are you saying because you won't be there to see it, that makes it all right?"

"What's worse? That the child grows up orphaned or is raised by at least one parent?"

"Depending on the parent," I said with absolute certainty, "an orphan would be luckier."

Ares looked at me then, and I could tell she had overheard Liz's long talks with my mother. "You hate your mother that much?"

A dull black sheen veiled her eyes.

"No question answered," Grier murmured an interpretation of the new result.

"I loved my mother. That's what you have to understand. I *loved* her. I bent over backwards to live up to her standards. I did and said whatever I thought would make her happy, or at least not make her angry." I stripped the hurt from my words and pressed on. "All I wanted was to make her proud." I swallowed hard. "I just wanted to not hurt."

Midas crossed to me and took my hand in his, reminding me I wasn't alone, that love didn't require pain.

"I thought if I was good enough, smart enough, pretty enough, that she would love me back. I thought if I was a better daughter, she would find me worthy." I stared at Ares, but she had to glance away. "I tried. So hard. For so long." I watched my shadow pacing, as if he too were upset. "I had no idea who I was or what I wanted. I had no identity outside of being the empty vessel I had become for her to fill with her anger, and I cracked the day I realized I would never be enough in her eyes."

And then I went and bargained with Ambrose, still thumbing my nose at her, and ended up in the same place as where I started. Empty of self and yet overflowing with another's purpose for me.

The choice to move to Atlanta, to *survive*, was the first one I had ever made fully for myself in my life.

"We're all responsible for our own actions and for the consequences of those decisions. That sucks extra hard if you have a crap role model and don't comprehend up from down or left from right. But you can't afford to let yourself off the hook, not even once. Otherwise, you'll keep excusing your behavior until you never find a reason to swallow the blame for anything you do ever again."

"I'm sorry for what she did to you," Ares said. "No child should have to fear their parent."

Black.

More tears, harder tears, cut tracks down her cheeks as she visibly struggled to come to a decision.

"There are two places she might have gone."

Green.

"A warehouse in Buckhead or a condemned auto parts store in Alpharetta."

Green.

"Thank you." I shot to my feet. "You're doing the right thing."

While Midas collected more detailed information, I stepped outside the cell, and Linus followed me.

"What you said in there..." black swallowed his eyes from corner to corner, "...I had no idea."

"No one did." I rolled a shoulder, but it hitched under his steady regard. "I made sure of it."

As if unable to resist, he tossed out, "Not even Boaz?"

"Especially not him." I sawed my upper teeth over my bottom lip. "He's always been the one good thing in my life. Bright, funny, outgoing." I wasn't sure if I was explaining it right, but it wouldn't matter in the days to come, when I had harder questions to answer. "No matter how bad it got, I could go to him, and he was always there with a quick hug or an idiotic idea guaranteed to get us grounded or just a shoulder when I was tired and sore and hurting." I blasted out a sigh. "He's not perfect by any means, and I would never encourage anyone to date him, but he's the best big brother a girl could ask for and then some. He loved me, *loves* me, no matter what."

For me, he had squared off with our mother after she disowned me.

For me, he had given up on the dream of something *more* with Grier.

For me, he had wooed Addie so I could claim Hadley's name as my own.

And he had done all those things out of love, not guilt. *Love.* However misguided his actions might be, he always battled his heart over his head when it came to those he loved most. I was the chink in his armor, the exception to his rules, and he had no clue how often he had saved my life with a well-timed hug that convinced me tomorrow would be better than today.

"Despite our issues," Linus said gently, "I will admit he's not without his redeeming attributes."

"Don't go getting soft on me." I punched him in the upper arm. "I won't know what to think."

Ducking his head, he huffed out a small laugh. "How do you want to handle this?"

"I'll take the warehouse." I had a feeling about it. A bad one. "Are you up for tackling the store?"

"*We* are happy to help any way we can," Grier chimed in before he could answer. "Right?"

"Right," he said, the black of his eyes fading to dark blue with her near.

The two of them went to prepare for their drive, and I stood in the hall to wait on Midas to finish. I could have gone back in, checked to see if he needed any help, but it was as if every word I had spoken lingered in the air of that room, and it threatened to choke me if I reentered it.

"Did I hear right?" Midas tugged the end of my hair. "You picked Buckhead for *us*?"

Oh, yes. He had been eavesdropping. He was almost as sneaky as Grier.

"You do that a lot now." I readjusted my ponytail. "Touch me."

"I like touching you."

"I like that you like touching me." I smiled. "It's nice. Different. But nice."

"I haven't acted on instinct where women are concerned in a long time." He walked with me down the hall. "I was always afraid of what would come of it." He placed his hand at the small of my back, like I had cracked something open by verbally approving his more tactile side. "I don't have to worry with you."

"Because I can kick your butt."

"Yes." He rolled his eyes. "That."

"I mean, I could. I don't have long legs, but they'll stretch that high."

Midas dug his fingers into my ribs, and I burst into giggle-snorts that horrified me to my core.

Future potentates weren't ticklish, and they didn't respond to personal assaults with giggle-snorts.

Since it needed saying, I fended him off with my elbow. "I would never use that power against you."

I'd had enough power stripped from me in my life to never do it to another person without grave cause.

"But you could."

"If I had to."

"If I had to," he repeated with the solemnity of a vow. "I'm beginning to understand the appeal of what you have with Linus."

"Oh?"

"It's nice to know there's always someone there to pull you back from the ledge."

Rising onto my tiptoes, I kissed him gently. "Failing that, I'll be your parachute."

He took the kiss but looked at me funny, not for the first time.

"I made it weird, huh?" I spread my hands. "Honestly? What else did you expect?"

"I can pull you back," he said after a moment. "I can probably manage parachuting too."

I read between the lines. "But you can't be what Linus is for me."

"No." He cupped my face in his hands and smoothed his thumbs across my cheeks. "Never."

"It's cute that you don't think you could murder me to save potentially dozens of lives."

"You would think so." He trailed his fingers across my jaw then down my throat. "You are so weird."

"But you like it."

"I do." He frowned. "I wonder what that says about me."

Preening for him, I fluttered my lashes Southern belle style. "That you have excellent taste?"

A laugh almost escaped him. "Let's go with that."

Buckhead was too far for the average Swyft, which left us with few other possibilities.

Namely Ford or Remy.

And no one willingly got into a car with her behind the wheel.

We had one other choice that overlapped our usual suspects, and I grinned as I dialed her.

SEVENTEEN

"Hadley," Lisbeth chirped when she answered her phone. "I heard your foot didn't fall off after all."

"It seems to be right where I left it," I agreed. "How's your stomach?"

"Let's not talk about it." She cleared her throat. "How can I help?"

"I like that you assume I'm calling you for help."

"Yes, well, if you're up and moving, then I have the right to be suspicious."

She wasn't wrong. I would be suspicious of phone calls from me too. In fact, I would block my number.

"You sound really chipper." I imagined I heard her blush. "What's up with that?"

"Ford kissed me," she sang. "Full on the mouth and everything."

Because I was a terrible person, I couldn't help poking at her. "And everything, huh?"

"I'm *not* that kind of girl." A loud groan escaped her. "I lied, Hadley. Oh God, I am that kind of girl. I want to climb that man like a Christmas tree and plant a star on top of his head."

That was a new one for me. "Thank you for ruining Christmas."

A loud snorted laugh blasted the receiver. "Like you don't want to—"

"Whatever you're about to say, don't. Hold it in. If you can't do it for me, do it for Tiny Tim."

"You're an innocent babe in a manger, aren't you?"

"Do *not* bring Jesus into this."

As a necromancer who attended public school with humans, I was well versed in Christianity. I even picked and chose from their bigger holidays to celebrate as much for fun as habit. Lisbeth's fixation on Christmas trees didn't mean she was a Christian, but she often wore a pair of earrings with small golden crosses, which implied that's how she leaned spiritually.

I showed others' religions the respect I showed my own, even that one guy who worshipped—I kid you not—a package of beef franks whose brand stickers had peeled off since it hit the dumpster where he found it. He swore it was a divine message on not labeling others, and no. That didn't stop him from eating his gods a week later. Then almost dying from food poisoning. Under the circumstances, it counted as divine retribution, I guess?

That said, I hoped she didn't think I was being flip about her religion. Then again, she started it.

Jesus would know that, right?

"Okay, I'm seriously not that kind of girl." Lisbeth tried for prim. "I'm not going to bring baby Jesus into this conversation."

"You just did."

"Dang it."

Laughter felt good. Scratch that. It felt *great*. But we had work to do. "Can you borrow Ford's truck for a drive out to Buckhead?"

"Let me ask." She muted the call for a heartbeat. "He says yes but wants to know if he can come too."

The fit in the cab would be tight, but we could manage. "The more the merrier."

With that settled, Midas and I stepped outside the Faraday and bumped right into Lisbeth.

"What are you doing here?" I scanned the street from left to right. "Where's Ford?"

"I was coming to meet him on his break." She shrugged. "This sounds like more fun than a taco."

"Nothing is more fun than a taco." I slanted my eyes toward her. "Are you sure you're not a host?"

"What?" Jerking back, she touched her throat. "Why?"

"Tacos occupy a somewhat holy level on the food pyramid for Hadley," Midas explained. "You're fine."

"Hey." I spun on him. "How would you feel if she turned up her nose at extra rare steak?"

Teeth sparkled as his smile spread. "More steak for me."

Thirty seconds later, Ford pulled up in his truck and rolled down his window. "Need a lift?"

Lisbeth wiggled her fingers at him, and he wiggled his right back.

"Thanks for this." I opened the door and crammed Lisbeth in beside him. "We appreciate it."

"We felt better about you guys having backup anyway." Ford kissed Lisbeth's check. "Food can wait."

It hit me then, that between Ford and Lisbeth, they could track every breath Midas and I took then report to one another, or their factions, on it. We needed to draw hard lines on what information could be passed between the pack and the OPA in any official capacity ASAP.

Midas climbed in next, leaving me for last. I bumped his hip with mine, but he didn't scoot. Instead, he hauled me onto his lap, and his warm breath hit my nape. "Let me get the door."

With his long legs taking up most of the space, I banged a knee on the dash when I spread mine over the outside of his. I also managed to bang my head against the light protruding from the ceiling and bumped the funny bone in my right elbow on the glass. I fought the urge to suck in a pained breath between my teeth, but it was a close one.

For his part, his legs were trapped in an awkward bend to give mine room. He thumped his head on the window behind him trying to give me space to lean back against his chest. His arms wrapped around my waist better than a seat belt, and his elbow slid off the armrest to whack the door with every pothole.

Comfortable, it wasn't.

But sitting in Midas's lap wasn't a bad place to be.

"Where are we headed?" Ford pulled out into traffic. "Lis said Buckhead, but where?"

Midas gave him the address then settled in to nibble on the right side of my throat.

Chills peppered my skin, and I angled my chin to give him better access, all the while hoping Liz or her ilk would assume the hickeys he was bound to be leaving were bruises from fighting chupacabras or something more badass than me spending a good half hour as a blissed-out gwyllgi chew toy.

"We're here."

Jolting awake, I hadn't noticed myself drifting, but I had definitely gone to sleep mid make-out session.

Frak.

Magic exacted a price for its use. *Always.* Ambrose had paid the bulk of it to heal me, which depleted his reserves, but he and I were one and the same. Despite his very generous gift, I was feeling the drain too.

Chuckles moved through my back as Midas cinched his arms around mine to keep me from flailing while I remembered where I was and what I was doing on his lap. Good thing too. I almost elbowed Lisbeth in the jaw trying to work the tingles from my arm. I had fallen so deeply asleep, I couldn't feel the pins and needles. Yet. They were biding their time, I was sure.

"How do you want to handle this?" Ford threaded his fingers through Lisbeth's. "I have ideas."

"Your ideas involve me staying in the truck." She snorted. "I've been with the OPA for years. I can handle myself in the field. I'm aware of my limitations, and I've learned to work around them."

"Your limitations put the rest of the human race to shame," I praised her, because it was true, "but we've got to watch our butts in there. The coven doesn't play fair. They play to win."

It was easier for me to erase the Liz who had never existed by lumping her in with the rest of them, but Midas and Ford would struggle. She had been pack. She had been Ares's mate. She had been family.

And it had been a lie.

Sometimes it wasn't all bad, being a world champ at compartmentalizing, but I couldn't recommend the years of training required to reach my skill level. Not even to my worst enemy.

"Are we hoping to contain or eliminate?" Ford kept his voice cool, and I could tell I wasn't the only one who was shoving thoughts into neatly labeled boxes. "One will be infinitely more dangerous than the other."

"We let her make that call," I decided. "She's more useful to us alive, but we'll put her down if she gives us no other choice."

Midas held me closer while he opened the door then spilled me gently out onto my feet in the gravel.

Once we had all exited the vehicle and worked out the kinks from the drive, we stood together, taking in the objective.

The building was smothering beneath vines and crumbling at its foundation. The windows had all been shattered, and the doors had sheets of plywood nailed to their frames to seal them shut. It was creepy, remote, and decaying.

Basically, it had *super-secret witchborn coven hideout* written all over it.

Sliding my hand into Lisbeth's, I gave her a reassuring squeeze. "Make no apologies."

Fingers tightening around mine, she smiled at me. "Survive."

The guys traded glances then shrugged at one another.

"It's an OPA thing," Lisbeth sassed Ford. "You boys wouldn't understand."

Ford popped her on the butt, and she swallowed a yelp, her eyes bright with laughter.

Midas palmed Ford's shoulder. "This isn't the time or place for...*that*."

"Have you seen Hadley's neck?" He cocked an eyebrow. "It looks like a swarm of pixies took turns throat-punching her."

"We need to focus now." Reaching up, I found tender skin already healing. "We can all make out later."

An awkward silence ensued, during which I replayed my words then debated shutting my head in the car door. Never let it be said I lost my ability to make things weird in the face of danger. "Um."

The others stared at me as if I had sprouted three heads and two of them were arguing. In German.

"I'll go in first." I summoned Ambrose, eager to escape, and he coiled around my shoulders. "Clear the way and all that."

Midas let me get a head start before falling in behind me, with Lisbeth and then Ford on his heels.

Careful to keep my voice low, I checked with my shadow. "Do you sense anything?"

Ambrose shook his head then zoomed ahead to search for magical remnants.

The uneven terrain made my ankle twinge, but I wasn't complaining. I was too grateful for the mobility. I still had trouble framing why Ambrose had given up his stores to spare me from pain and a few weeks in a cast. I would have to look into that, but it could wait.

Within seconds, Ambrose sharpened his form to an arrow he shot through my temple.

Apparently, his altruism had its limits.

Hissing through my teeth, I sorted through the information he'd collected for me.

There were wards here, concentric ones, which the coven favored in my experience. Powerful ones too. That didn't mean we had cornered our prey. The coven tended to keep their properties defended with active wards whether they were home or not, but I had yet to crack a ward that didn't yield some fruit.

The outermost ward tingled over my skin as I walked through it, its subtle push telling me I should go. It would be effective on humans or the unwary, but I expected it, and I didn't let it bother me.

The second ring gave me a harder nudge back than I anticipated, and the warning jumped to a higher threat level than usual so early on. That was both promising and annoying.

The third ring smacked me in the face, and my ears popped when I bulled my way through it.

The fourth struck fast, right on three's heels, almost knocking me unconscious when I blundered into it.

"I can't get past this alone," I told Ambrose. "I need your help."

Puffing out his chest, the shadow snapped out a crisp salute then began searching for the anchor.

While he scoured the areas I couldn't access, I glanced over my shoulder to find the others trapped in the second ward ring, unable to get closer until it fell. All my backup was yards away, and it might as well have been miles for their inability to reach me.

A sizzling jolt struck me in the chest, and I blamed Ambrose until the quiet in my head convinced me he wasn't at fault. As a matter of fact, I couldn't see him anywhere. And as the throb eased, I couldn't feel him either.

That was...not good.

"Ambrose?" I pressed my hands against the barrier in front of me. *"Ambrose?"*

A wisp of blackness hissed and crackled as it passed through the ward in front of me to stand by my side.

"Can you bring it down?" My darker half didn't look so hot. "Or do we need a Plan B?"

The shadow rallied and pointed a finger at a glass Coke bottle positioned near the employee entrance but shook his head, indicating he couldn't reach it to devour it.

What he had done for me when I needed it most gave me an idea.

Probably a very bad one.

"Take from me." I ignored the tremble in my voice. "Get to that anchor and destroy it."

The bond between us had never flowed only one way. That had been the greatest danger of it, that he could feed on me, weaken me, and take over my body. But I had gained enough experience that—with help from Linus's tattooed bindings—I could prevent Ambrose from siphoning off me.

This was the first time I'd offered myself to him freely, and it was frankly terrifying, but he could return the favor after he finished devouring the anchor. The same couldn't be said if he took from Midas or Ford, and Lisbeth's humanity made her an impossible food source.

"We're in this together, right?" I extended my olive branch with care. "I'm trusting you here."

The shadow reached a tentative hand toward me and stroked my hair. The sensation was peculiar, like a shiver traipsing down my spine or walking through a cobweb. I couldn't feel him, but I wilted slowly like an ice cream cake left too long in the sun until I puddled on the concrete.

I don't think I fell, exactly, or maybe I did, and I just couldn't feel it.

That...also couldn't be good.

As darkness closed in, I swore I heard voices screaming my name, but I'd probably left the TV on again.

Midas and I really ought to invest in a new couch. This one was hard, the material was rough, and it stank. Its warranty was still in effect. Maybe we could get the manufacturer to send us a replacement. That would be nice.

The sluggish beat of my heart filled my ears with strange music, blotting out the distant cries, and I decided I would take a nap even if the couch wasn't as comfy as the futon or the bed. I would sleep anywhere as long as Midas...

...was with me.

EIGHTEEN

Oxygen stabbed my chest with the sharpness of a dagger, and I screamed into consciousness.

"You have nothing to fear."

Gulping huge breaths, I got my lungs going again, and then I attempted to figure out the rest.

"Who..." I gasped out, still struggling, "...are you?"

"I am your shadow self."

"Ambrose?"

"If you like."

"How are you talking to me?"

"You stand on the precipice between life and death, and that affords me a certain leeway."

"What?" I jolted upright. "I'm dying?" I pressed a palm to my chest. "Maybe lead with that next time?"

"Not yet, no."

"Not yet is good." I kept sucking in air, but I wasn't getting enough. "Then why am I stuck here?"

The space was gray and warm, bleak, its fabric shifting and twisting. Gaunt faces dotted the mist beyond where I sat, and

Ambrose stood in profile, his hands shoved into the pockets of his slacks, a caricature of Linus. I drank in the sight of him, my curiosity finally sated, and I couldn't fault him for his artistic license.

His skin was as pale as the first full moon in winter, his hair a ravaging flame around his head. His lips were so blue they were almost violet, his eyes full of shadows so deep no light had hope of penetrating them. Mist swirled around his ankles, black tendrils that resembled a wraith's tattered cloak, another of his Linus-like affectations.

There was a reason Ambrose had hooked me from the start. No good could come of us meeting like this. Creatures like him homed in on the insecurities and desires of their potential hosts, and I had been ripe for the plucking. They used what they gleaned to seduce prey into leaning on their strength, their knowledge, their power, until the prey—now a host—toppled without their support.

Most of the time, their prey even thanked them for it.

I know I had, in the beginning.

"I wished to tell you that I am not what I once was and not yet what I will become."

A bitter laugh twisted its way out of my throat. "Sure thing."

"It has been an age since I learned a thing I did not already know."

"Was it the Star Trek or the Star Wars trivia that won you over?"

"You have taught me compassion. I had none in life, and I have had none in death. You are a lens through which I see the world more clearly. Your perception fascinates me. Therefore, I propose an alliance."

"Why now?" I coughed, the air too thick and cottony. "What brought this on?"

"You trusted me," he said simply. *"You placed your life in my hands and believed I would cradle it softly."*

"Yeah, well, you've been on good behavior recently."

"I enjoy the chocolates," he said solemnly. *"I have never tasted the likes of which you treat me."*

A rattling cough moved through my chest, and I covered my hand only to pull away bloody fingers.

"You must go before it is too late."

"Will we be able to do this again? Talk, I mean?"

"Only if you find yourself on death's door may I hold it open for you."

"I'll take that as a no." I wiped my hand on my pants. "Thanks, Ambrose."

"We have centuries ahead of us, Amelie. Our kind may step in and out of time as we choose."

A hard thump against my ribs stole what breath I had from me. "How long will we live?"

"We will live until we die."

"As long as Midas?"

"No."

"Oh."

"You will surpass him into eternity."

Frost swept through me, chilling me to the bone. "I don't want that."

"We are bound to him."

"How are we bound to him, exactly?"

"We are what we are, and we take what we need."

"Are you saying our mate bond is...*parasitic?*"

No wonder it didn't work right. Midas and I weren't soul mates. We were conduits. For Ambrose.

"We are symbiotic."

"What does he get out of it, then?"

"The bond flows both ways."

"I don't follow."

"He may take from us and live, or we may take from him and die."

"He can live with us forever," I said slowly, wrapping my head around it. "Or we can die with him?"

"Yes."

"Can I get back to you on that?"

"Take all the time you need."

Amused by his own wit, he laughed, velvet-soft and inviting, the way I sometimes heard in nightmares.

"All right." I rubbed the tender skin over my breastbone. "In that case, I'll—"

Light exploded around me, piercing my eyes and shredding the misty gray landscape like tissue paper.

Lifting a hand in silent farewell, Ambrose watched over me until he too was ripped to tattered nothings.

"Hadley."

Compressions strained my ribs until they creaked.

"Hadley."

Warm lips covered mine, and oxygen swept into my starving lungs.

"Hadley."

The voice murmuring my name like a prayer cracked as Midas attempted to save my life.

"Hadley."

"We've got a pulse," Lisbeth announced, her delicate fingers on my wrist. "Give her room, guys."

No surprise, the guys did not give her room. I woke with both of them leaning over me. Plus Ambrose.

"What happened?" Midas held fists of my curls like that might have held me to life. "You were…"

"Dead," Lisbeth finished for him. "Your heart stopped for a full minute."

"The ward," I mumbled. "Kicked my butt."

"Help me sit her upright." Lisbeth tugged once before Midas shrugged her off and lifted me into his arms. "Um, that's not what I had in mind." The edge of his mouth twitched at her in the promise of a snarl. "But I like your idea better."

Ford positioned himself between Lisbeth and Midas, but he let the threat pass. He understood the murky area where courtesy and instinct collided in gwyllgi and that it wasn't always a line consciously crossed.

Basically, he saved us a lot of time by opting not to posture, and I was grateful for it.

"Help me stand." I wiggled in Midas's grasp. "We can't fight if you're carrying me everywhere."

Reflex curled me tighter against him before he forced himself to relax his grip and ease me down.

Certain I was about to have egg on my face from collapsing at Midas's feet, Ambrose stroked my hair, and lightning struck in its wake, jolting me awake and alert, flooding my system with adrenaline…and every last drop of the power he had borrowed from me.

"Thank you." I patted Midas's chest. "And they say men can't be trained to follow simple instructions."

A low growl was my reward, but it got his mind off Lisbeth and Ford. It was a win in my book.

"Death hasn't improved your sense of humor," he grumbled. "You're still not funny."

Smoothing my thumb over the beat of his frantic heart, I begged him with my gaze for patience.

"I'll explain later," I promised him in a low voice. "It's not exactly what you think."

Expression tight, he exhaled. "Then it's probably worse."

"You are a little ray of sunshine." I frowned at him. "I've always considered you a Grumpy Bear on the Care Bear scale, but maybe I'm wrong. Maybe you're a Funshine."

"Hadley." He pinched the bridge of his nose. "I—"

"—love you too," I finished for him. "Now let's go adventuring."

"You are—"

"—wonderful and amazing and have great taste in side dishes?"

"You're doing it again." He clamped his hands on my shoulders to hold me still. "You're deflecting."

"I'm sure I don't know what you mean."

"I will get frustrated, I will get angry, I will get worried, but I will never hurt you."

The impact of what he'd caught me doing staggered my wobbly legs, and I hated how deep the hooks of insecurity had sunk into me until I couldn't let the man finish a sentence out of fear what he might say next.

Mostly, that he would say *goodbye.*

That I wasn't worth the headache.

That I wasn't worth the hassle.

That I wasn't worth...anything.

"I don't always realize I'm doing it," I confessed. "I hear people start to criticize, and I just want to slap my hand over their mouth before they say something they can't take back." I tugged on his arm. "I'm sorry. I trust you with my life. That ought to prove I can trust you with my heart too."

"We've got time for you to get there." He kissed my forehead. "All the time in the world."

Poor guy had no idea how literal his words were, if Ambrose was to be believed.

That was definitely a conversation for later.

"We're presenting a tempting target out here, folks." Ford glanced around us. "We need to move."

"I'll go in first." I checked with the shadow beside me, who nodded. "There could be more wards."

Muscles worked in Midas's jaw as he chewed over all the things he wanted to tell me, but he swallowed them down with visible effort and trusted me to lead them.

Turning my back on my friends, I stalked toward the front door, shadow in tow.

"They spent a lot of time on these wards." I checked the knob, and it turned in my hand. "Too easy?"

Then again, if no one could reach the door, did it really matter if you bothered locking it behind you?

Once inside the cavernous building, I slumped with disappointment. A wide-open space with nowhere to hide that I could see, I doubted this was where Liz had gone to ground. There were no supplies, food or otherwise. Nothing about the space explained what warranted the heavy security measures set outside.

As that doubt surfaced, an ounce of certainty trickled in that there must be something here worth protecting if they had it locked up so tight.

With a flick of my wrist, I sent Ambrose to scout the interior while I stood there, careful not to trip any traps I might not sense. We had to wipe this place clean before the others joined us. They didn't have a handy-dandy shadow to taste the magic and report back like me.

Moments later, Ambrose returned and waved me deeper into the building.

Normally, he would have stabbed me in the brain to share his findings. "What is it?"

Again, I doubted myself. I had almost—no, I *had* killed myself, temporarily, to gain entrance. For what?

Placing his palm on the wall, he glanced back to make sure I took the hint.

"You want me to touch it." I did as he instructed. "Okay, now what?"

A frisson of power sped through my hand where it touched the wall, and it rippled, wavered, as if I had dipped my fingers into a still pond and disturbed its surface. "What is it?"

An elegant shrug rolled through Ambrose's shoulders.

That was helpful. "Any idea why I can't see through it?"

He spread his hands wide.

"They know I have the sight," I realized. "This is like the glamour Liz used at the clinic."

For them to switch it up, I must have proven myself too adept at locating their safe houses and allies.

Frak.

Maybe I should have been a smidgen less competent.

"For what it cost me, I'd hoped to get more use out of it."

Ambrose made an encompassing gesture, a question, and waited to see what I would decide.

"We don't have much choice," I told him. "We can't go in blind." I stood back. "Strip it down."

Rubbing his hands together, Ambrose did that. He punched his hand through the illusion and yanked it out in curling ribbons he slurped like spaghetti noodles. The bond between us hummed as he filled his stomach, and the excess spilled over into me, better than a shot of espresso.

The illusion shattered into a million points of light that blinded, and the insidious whisper that I was in the wrong place, that I had come to the wrong conclusion, evaporated along with it.

"That was one heck of a compulsion." I rubbed my forehead as my thoughts finished clearing. "It didn't hook me, exactly, but not for lack of trying."

Given more exposure, I would have bent to its will, decided I was wrong, and left without looking back.

The space hidden behind the false wall gobsmacked me, and my jaw scraped the poured concrete floor. Except, it wasn't concrete, or a floor at all. It was a yawning maw that stretched from corner to corner, a good twenty feet across, and this was the cusp.

"Goddess," I breathed, then wished I hadn't sucked in the sulfurous mist lapping across my ankles.

A staircase made of oxidized metal spiraled *down, down, down* until it vanished from sight. It touched on multiple floors, allowing residents stairwell access. Hundreds of individual doorways nestled in tidy rows like apartments. Their chiseled stone façades reminded me of the Lycian tombs of Turkey.

The sentiment pulled me up short.

Tombs.

"What the frakking hell is that?" I turned to Ambrose. "Can you tell if anyone is home?"

The shadow gave a definitive nod, and knowing coven milled below us gave me the willies.

Mostly because I couldn't see them.

"Bring the others." I stood watch at the rim. "We'll need all the backup we can get."

Ambrose zipped past me, on his way to Midas, the only one who could see him to decipher the message.

Pulling out my phone, I snapped a dozen photos and forwarded them to Bishop.

This was not good. This was so very not good. This surpassed the realm of super not good.

The coven had an underground city with the capacity to hold hundreds of families by my count.

Had they built it? Had they slaughtered its original inhabitants and claimed it? Or had they done worse?

A vibration in my palm had me checking my phone for updates.

>>*Get out of there.*

>*We're closing in on Liz.*

>>*Check the first picture.*

I did as he said, and I almost swallowed my tongue. I stumbled back, smack into Midas. "Run."

"What?" Scanning the area, he settled his focus back on me. "What's wrong?"

"*Run.*" I took his hand and dragged him. "Ford, get her out of here."

Scooping up Lisbeth, which cost him seconds, he ran after us. "Don't have to tell me twice."

"Get in the truck." I shoved Midas in, climbed onto his lap, and slammed the door behind me. "We need to go now, now, now."

Ford jogged to his side, dumped Lisbeth onto the bench seat, then hopped in and cranked the engine.

Heart a frozen lump in my throat, I waited a good ten or fifteen miles for it to thaw.

"What happened?" Midas pulled me close. "What did you see?"

Rather than tell him, I flashed the screen and let him see for himself.

Ghoulish faces screamed in silent fury, crowding the vast opening like ants swarming picnic food. Blueish light emanated from them without illuminating the darkness around them. Their clawlike hands grasped for the edge where I had stood gazing down at them without realizing the terrible danger I was in.

Midas pinched his fingers to zoom in on the creatures. "What are those things?"

"I have no frakking clue." I dialed Bishop then demanded, "What are those things?"

"That's the closet."

"I'm sorry, but it sounded like you said that was a closet."

"I did, and it is." Keys tapped in the background. "We got big problems, kid."

"Only always." I leaned against Midas. "How did you figure it out?"

"I had help." He exhaled. "I'll meet you back at the Faraday."

"Okay." I glanced behind us, but the road was empty. "See you in a few."

The gwyllgi had overheard both sides of the conversation, as usual, but even Lisbeth sat close enough I didn't have to repeat myself.

"He sounded freaked," she said when no one else spoke. "Bishop doesn't do freaked."

"This is going to be bad," I agreed. "It's hard to get under his skin."

With that settled, the four of us spent the rest of the drive lost in our own thoughts.

Mine kept circling back to Boaz and Addie. I wanted them gone. Tonight. Back safe in Savannah.

I had no idea what we had uncovered in that warehouse, but it promised me nightmares for days.

"We'll meet you upstairs." Ford pulled to a stop in front of the Faraday. "Give us ten."

"Sure." I slid off Midas's lap, and he exited after me. "See you up there."

Hank was polite as you please, but I chalked it up to my sister's kidnapping and not a permanent shift in his general attitude toward me. That would be too weird. Hmm. Maybe he ought to get tested again just to be on the safe side.

No one stopped us in the lobby, but everyone stared, and it creeped me out.

When the elevator doors rolled shut behind us, I slumped against the back panel. "Ares?"

"Yes."

"The pack needs to get over it."

Rather than answer, he pressed a kiss to my temple. "You have a way of simplifying things."

"Mostly I open my mouth and see what falls out. Usually, I'm as surprised as you guys."

Soft laughter moved through him, and I grinned as I buried my face in his chest.

All too soon a ding announced our arrival, and we trudged over to the door and let ourselves in the loft.

Bishop stood in the center of the living room, legs braced apart and arms crossed over his chest. He glared at the couch. Specifically, he glared at someone sprawled on the couch.

The fae who had gifted Midas and me with the sight sat with his arms around a pillow on his lap in what reminded me of a petulant child's pose. Dressed in what I was coming to think of as his standard uniform, he looked the same as he had the last time we met.

Black leather pants encased his legs, and a whip hung from the silver-studded belt wrapping his narrow waist. He wore no shirt, but the oversized pillow shielded us from a view of the pale muscle he displayed as casually as if my living room was his. His heavy boots made the coffee table groan when he twitched his crossed ankles on its edge. But what caught my eye and held it was the blue-black hair that slid over his shoulders in a seductive curtain. His fingers clenched and relaxed on the poor pillow's tassels while he stared at Bishop's forbidding profile, as if his hands would rather be squeezing...

Ahem.

When our guest spotted us, he rose with leonine grace, giving Midas and me an eyeful of a tattoo of bird wings covering every inch of his back before disappearing into his waistband. I hadn't noticed the design on him before, so it could be cosmetic. He did love his glamours. I was no expert on corvids, but I pegged them as belonging to a crow or raven.

"Bishop," I said warily. "Introduce us to your friend."

Once I had known the fae's true name, but the memory of it was slick as Crisco when I tried to grasp it.

"This is..." he hesitated over what to call him, "...a pain in my ass."

"Only if you're lucky," the fae said toothily, fingering his whip. "You may call me Vasco."

"Okay, *Vasco.*" I hit the kitchen for bottled water and tossed one to Midas. "You guys thirsty?"

Vasco slid his admiring gaze down Bishop from tip to toe. "Always."

Grateful for the icy drink after our frantic run, I took long pulls from my bottle as I brought them each a water. Vasco sipped from his, but I worried for half a second Bishop was going to chuck his at Vasco's pretty head.

After checking my phone, I came out and asked Bishop, "Any word from Linus and Grier?"

"They ought to be back in a few hours. Grier lost sight of him in a used bookstore."

I read between the lines: *Keep your eyes open and your mouth shut around Vasco.*

"A few hours?" I played along. "More like a few days."

The elevator chimed out in the hall, and I tossed my empty while selecting two more bottles. Since Midas and I hadn't bothered shutting the door, Lisbeth and Ford invited themselves in.

"Hello," she said, her eyes lighting on Vasco. "Are you a friend of Bishop's?"

"It's more accurate to say Bishop is a friend of mine," Vasco all but purred. "Aren't you a lovely trifle?"

A slight glaze covered her eyes, and Ford wrapped a hand around her upper arm before I noticed she was attempting to walk straight into Vasco's arms.

"Stop playing with my friend," I warned him and dipped my hand into Ambrose, unsheathing a sword. "If you can't behave, you need to leave. Whether or not you do it with your head still attached is your choice."

"He's got information we need." Bishop heaved a sigh. "Leave the head where it is, for now."

"I knew you cared." Vasco traced a finger down the center of Bishop's chest, stopping when the tip brushed the metal of his belt buckle. "Do they know what this is costing you?"

"Leave them out of this." Bishop fit his palm very gently across Vasco's throat. "This is between us."

"Yes." His lids fluttered closed. *"Us."*

"Don't get cute with me." Bishop leaned in close. "Do what you came here to do and then leave."

"As you wish." Vasco rested his palm over Bishop's heart, smiled at what he felt there, then retreated. "All right, children." He draped himself across the couch once more. "Gather 'round for story time."

Given he might have been around to watch dirt born, I didn't object to the insult. Out loud, anyway.

"You found an archive," he began once we had formed a semicircle around him. "That's remarkable, and I'm impressed you're here to ask what it was that almost killed you."

"An archive?" I reflected on what I had seen. "You're saying that hole was an underground library?"

"Bishop tells me you consider that which the coven harvests to be skins, suits that can be worn and then returned to their collective closet. Not unlike what skinwalkers do, though theirs is a more violent path."

There's more than one way to skin a cat.

Guess that grisly old chestnut applied to skinning people too.

"Information on witchborn fae is scarce," I defended us. "We've done our best with what we've got."

"That I don't doubt." He appeared earnest despite the sting of his words. "You're wrong about the visages. They aren't skins. They're souls. Or, if you prefer, they're essences. They're the sum of the person. From the way they looked to the way they talked, laughed, walked, even breathed. The coven fully embodies those they have stolen. There are no spells capable of such lawful insanity, but there are worlds in which the dead walk and the souls linger."

"The archive is a...portal?"

"Yes and no." He smiled his maddening smile. "An archive is a gateway into a world where such things as these witchborn fae do is possible."

A low growl vibrated in the air, barely loud enough for my ears, and Midas snarled, "You mean Faerie."

"I do indeed." Vasco picked lint off the cushion next to him. "Your coven doesn't own a *closet*. They own a world. A corner of it. A pocket. More of a speck, really. Populated by the souls of all those they have taken."

Bishop made a sound of annoyance that earned him a sigh from Vasco.

"For the sake of your necromancer," he said to Bishop, "I will frame it in a way she will understand."

"That would be nice," I volunteered, happy to play dumb to get the full scoop.

"The coven summons what souls they want for any given task and then invokes a voluntary possession. They embrace those long-dead forms, absorb their thoughts and their feelings, before twisting the souls to suit their purpose."

"That's horrific." Numbness spread through my hand where I clutched the sword, and I returned it to Ambrose before I did something embarrassing like drop it in front of Vasco. "How is it possible?"

"You couldn't comprehend it if I explained it to you," he said benignly, then flicked a wrist, "and I would never do that. Such abominations shouldn't be encouraged, they're a blight on all worlds, and I wouldn't offer up the blueprints for free in any case."

"He's saying you would have stepped into Faerie—like *the* Faerie —if you had gone down those steps?" Lisbeth paled. "That's... I mean... Wow." She leaned against Ford. "I know it's a real place, but an access point? That makes it *really* real. Too real."

Understanding slammed into me with the force of a minotaur chasing after a red flag.

The witchborn fae had created actual routes to Faerie from Earth, and Natisha wanted witchborn fae hearts. Her avariciousness began to make more, and worse, sense. We figured she wanted to harvest power from the hearts, but this was next level. She must require a certain number of them to create her own passkey that would allow her to open their existing doors between our worlds rather than forge her own.

Yeah.

That made more sense.

Witchborn fae straddled the divide between witch and fae, Earth and Faerie. I hadn't realized how literal, how *physical*, it was.

Another thought occurred to me. "Can the coven use these archives to traverse our world as well?"

"Yes," Vasco answered slowly. "There are only four at any given time, one established for each compass point. Their tethers can be moved, but it requires great strength and a large coven to anchor them. I had no idea the southernmost one had been relocated to Atlanta until Bishop texted me."

How or why Bishop had him on speed dial wasn't any of my business, so I didn't ask.

"It can't have been here long," he continued. "I would have noticed the smell."

"The archive smells?"

"Like home," Vasco said wistfully. "It will draw fae to it like flies to honey."

"And the coven will kill them," Bishop said harshly. "Or worse."

Meaning they would add the interesting ones to the coven's growing collection and dispatch the rest.

"That explains why they're impossible to find these days."

This might also be the reason Liz blew her cover. She was active prior to my family's arrival, meaning the coven had been willing to sacrifice a critical asset even before they diverted her focus to keeping me too busy to discover what they felt was worth the loss of a well-liked and well-established mole to accomplish.

"You have the sight," Vasco agreed. "It forced them to hide in less obvious places."

"What would have happened if we had stepped into the archive?"

The sound of Midas's voice brought my head up and my attention to him.

"A thing possessed cannot be possessed," he said to Midas while staring at me. "You, however, would have been taken. The souls are hungry, and the wearing of them is all that sates the gnaw in their guts. It's a phantom sensation that only eases when they're working in concert with the coven. That's how the coven controls them. The ravenous things are all too eager for relief when they're called to ever turn down a summons."

Blocking out the horror of their existence, I focused on the details. "You're saying I can go down safely?"

"Down, yes. Safely, no."

"You're incredibly helpful." I slow-clapped for him. "Really. I mean it. A true giver."

"Shadow child, nothing in this life is free." A cruel smile twitched on his lips. "You ought to know the cost of ambition better than anyone. Who are you to judge the price or those willing to pay it?"

Temper on the rise, Bishop intervened. "Enough."

"We've reached the end of our bargain," Vasco told him. "My portion of our business is concluded."

"Agreed," Bishop exhaled. "I'll stop by later with the payment."

Lust glittered in Vasco's eyes as they swept over Bishop's grim face. "I look forward to collecting."

Under his breath, Bishop muttered a response in a language unknown to me that made Vasco laugh.

From the way Midas stared at the floor, I got the sense he understood but wished he hadn't.

I was definitely asking him about it later.

After our guest left, through the window, which had me questioning how functional his tattoo might be, I flopped down onto the couch, sank into the cushions, and debated shutting my eyes until I fell asleep. I must not be the only one wishing I could sleep off the nightmare scenario Vasco had dumped in our laps. The others claimed their own spots, and we all just sat and let this latest revelation settle around us.

"Do we have to poke the hornets' nest?" Lisbeth wondered out loud. "Can't we ward it to keep others out, them in, and leave it be?"

"We could," Ford said, thinking along the same lines, "but that would mean dumping the problem in someone else's lap to solve later."

Oh, how tempting that would be. To drape it around the next potentate's shoulders when the time came. Except for the fact I had untold years ahead of me and no idea how many of them I would spend as champion of this city. The pack was here, so Midas would stay, which meant I would too, but early retirement sounded sweet right about now.

Thanks to Remy, I had a budding sheet empire to fall back on.

Thanks to Midas, I was co-beta and had a pack to help manage.

Thanks to Linus, I had the cash to do pretty much anything I wanted.

But thanks to Ambrose, I was in a unique position to fight back against the coven.

Atlanta was my home now, and its citizens were mine to protect. I had family here. Midas, Tisdale, Remy, Ford, Bishop, and the rest of the team. I had worked too hard to walk away from my duty because it was hard or scary or—let's be honest—likely to kill me.

"We can't," I contradicted him. "Natisha wants those beating hearts for a reason. Seven of them. That's a magical number." I flicked a glance at Bishop, who had warned me realm walking might be in her plans. "Now we've got a much clearer idea what doors she can unlock if we give her the right keys."

"She's right." Midas lent his weight to my argument. "We can't hand Natisha that type of power."

"You must honor the bargain." Bishop frowned in Ford's direction. "You won't like the consequences if you don't."

"We'll honor the bargain," I assured him, since we had no choice if we wanted to keep Ford alive. "We'll just have to find a way around giving her what she wants."

Lisbeth curled into Ford's side. "How do we do that?"

"I don't know yet," I admitted. "I'm working on it."

"I'm sorry." Ford rubbed the base of his neck. "I didn't mean to make more work for you."

"You're worth it," Lisbeth said with quiet certainty. "You're a good man, Ford."

"She's right." I smiled at him, but it was as tired as it was true. "You are worth it."

"The coven is an issue she would have faced regardless." Bishop tossed in his two cents. "The archive is too. Your role in the bargain is one complication in dozens, the proverbial needle in a haystack by comparison."

Brow wrinkling, Ford scratched his chin. "Uh, thanks?"

"Sentimentality aside, we need you," Bishop continued. "You're a solid enforcer with a decent tactical mind. We need all the brains we can get if we're going to figure out how to destroy the archive, the coven, the hearts, and Natisha."

Midas jerked upright, his voice a jagged rasp. "Destroy...*Natisha?*"

"If we can't think our way out of your bargain, we have to void it."

"Goddess," I breathed. "That's a bit extreme."

"And by *extreme*," Ford pitched in, "she means virtually *impossible*."

"All fae can die." Bishop shifted uncomfortably. "That doesn't mean they'll go down easy."

A buzz in my pocket had me fishing out my phone, and I fumbled it when I saw the number. "Hey."

"I'm calling with an update," Abbott said gently. "Adelaide and Boaz are both well enough to go home, and Matron Pritchard is demanding an early release as well." He hesitated. "Linus discussed the arrangements for Mr. Whitaker?"

"Yes." I relaxed in slow increments. "Do you have a facility in mind?"

"I do." He exhaled. "It's not cheap, but it's the best. He said that's what you wanted."

"I can afford it," I assured him. "It's worth it if it gets him well."

"I'll begin the paperwork then."

"Thanks."

"With your permission, I'm going to encrypt all four files and transfer them to my home computer."

That pulled me upright and drew Midas's attention. "Any particular reason why?"

"There are commonalities between Matron Pritchard, Boaz Pritchard, and yourself that would make you more comfortable if they weren't in a database where other staff might access their records in the event of an emergency."

"Oh."

"Especially since you lack similar commonalities with your sister or your father."

"Um..."

"You don't owe me an explanation." He kept his tone gentle. "You're Hadley Whitaker, future Potentate of Atlanta, and the mate of my beta. You're pack. Whatever else you are, whoever else you might have been, doesn't matter to me."

That seemed to be going around a lot lately, and I couldn't help but feel it was too good to be true.

"Thanks, Abbott."

"Don't thank me yet." He laughed. "We'll have to update your medical records. Based on what I've learned, that means I need blood and tissue samples."

"What if I told you I plan on living forever?"

"I would say that's very nice, but that living forever could still get you killed."

An ungrateful noise clawed up my throat that I was too dignified to admit was a whine.

"Fine," I grumbled. "I'll submit to testing." Finger on the red dot, I added, "Eventually."

Needless to say, I hung up before the lecturing started and didn't answer when he redialed.

It wasn't a perfect solution, obviously, because I would have to go down there, as I said, eventually.

Sooner rather than later based on the discovery of the archive and its nasty warren of surprises.

"My what big teeth you have," Midas teased. "The better to torment healers with?"

"If I don't keep him on his toes, who will? Honestly, I'm performing a public service."

As long as he didn't keel over from high blood pressure, I was sure he would adapt and overcome.

"Mmm-hmm." Midas wound one of my curls around his finger. "How kind of you."

"I'm ready for a medal ceremony when you are," I countered sweetly. "Um, Midas?"

"Yes?"

"Is that your phone in your pocket, or are you just happy to see me?"

Brows crashing down, he attempted a flat stare ruined by the amused spark in his eyes. "Hadley."

"The vibrating thing is new." I kept the smile off my face. "But I'm willing to work around it."

Ignoring me, he checked his phone then flashed me a wide smile full of heart-stopping beauty.

Uh-oh.

"What's up?" I scooted closer as his thumbs flew across the screen. "Can I see?"

Leaning away, he kept his head down. "No."

"They're only going to devolve from here," Bishop promised the others. "We might as well go."

"HQ at dusk?" Lisbeth rose and tugged Ford after her. "We'll all think better after we've slept."

"Yeah." Bishop waved a hand. "We'll sleep off today and meet up tomorrow."

Ford draped his arm across her shoulders. "Drive you home?"

She leaned into him. "Only if you don't mind."

They walked out, their sides pressed together, and it made my heart swell to see them happy.

"And then there were three." Bishop leaned forward, bracing his elbows on his knees. "This is big, kid."

"The coven doesn't do things by half."

"The boss can handle it if you need him to," he said with quiet worry, "just this once."

"You heard Vasco." I shook my head. "I'm uniquely suited to this mission."

"That's what worries me." He rubbed his hands over his face. "He's got an angle, but I can't see it yet. That concerns me." He dropped his arm. "Natisha knew you could survive the archive. How she knew it would relocate here and why she needed a spiritually bulletproof pawn worries me too."

Fae plots were onions with layers upon layers upon layers of deceit, ambition, and malice woven in.

"You need sleep," I told him. "We all do."

For once, I wished I could be the friend who walked him home, but he wasn't going home tonight.

Perhaps reading my unease, he threw effort into a smile. "Things are always clearer tomorrow."

All jokes aside, I rubbed my damp palms down my jeans. "Do you think we have that much time?"

"We'll take the time. Otherwise, we'll be making their job too easy for them."

"Linus isn't wandering a bookstore, is he?"

"No." He pushed off the couch and stood. "They found Liz at the auto parts store."

"That's good news." I pondered his grim tone. "That means Grier can interrogate her about the archive." I was missing something, but I couldn't put my finger on what had gotten under his skin. Other than Vasco. "How is she?"

"She got bruised in the scuffle, but Linus and Grier were as careful as they could be, for the baby's sake."

That would put Ares's mind at ease. "Where is she?"

"The infirmary, for now." An uneasy quiet filled him. "Abbott is assessing her health and, assuming the pregnancy is verified, the baby's as well. He mentioned bringing in a specialist to help identify its species. There's no reason to think the baby is gwyllgi. It's more likely Liz chose a fae or witch donor."

The thought had occurred to me, right after I used the baby for leverage against Ares, which was a new low for me. The truth might tear open old wounds, but it was better for us to know than to be surprised. Especially if the fetus's emerging powers, assuming it had any, put the pregnancy at risk.

"We caught the bad guys—gals?—and have a potential insider source on the coven and on their archive. Those are all good things." I was trying for upbeat when I asked, "Why the long face?"

"There's another problem that maybe you haven't noticed yet."

"I'm sure there are dozens."

"Liz cut Ares off from the pack for a multitude of reasons, but this one..." He hesitated. "This one was done out of spite."

Spite was nothing new, motivation-wise, for the coven either. "I don't follow."

"Tisdale isn't judge and jury on this one."

The truth struck me with an unwelcome flash of clarity. "I am."

For anyone else, the punishment would have already equaled an automatic death sentence.

Liz's deviousness might have impressed me, if it hadn't hurt so frakking much to grasp her endgame.

"Goddess, what a mess."

I attempted to sink into the cushions, never to be seen or heard from again.

I didn't get far.

Damn it.

"Shelve it for tonight," Bishop advised. "Nothing has to be decided right now."

Determination carved deep grooves into Midas's forehead, and I could almost hear the wheels spinning as he searched for ways to get me off the hook. With Linus in town, I could pass the buck easily, but that was a coward's solution.

Midas's phone vibrated again, and he answered it this time. "We're on our way."

"What's wrong?" Adrenaline flooded my system, and my fingertips tingled. "What happened?"

"Mom has requested our presence at the den."

I surprised myself, and him, if his expression was to be believed, by agreeing. "Let's go."

Ares was a delicate subject, and I welcomed all the advice I could get before making a ruling.

The three of us walked out together and rode the elevator down in silence.

"HQ at dusk," I reminded Bishop when we hit the lobby. "Do your best to get the whole team there."

"Will do." He snapped out a salute. "Be careful out there."

"You too."

Bishop was adept at maneuvering the treacherous depths of fae bargains, but that didn't mean I didn't worry about what pieces of himself he gave away. I hoped the cost of Vasco's cooperation hadn't been too high.

Déjà vu struck me when Ford guided his truck against the curb as we exited the building.

Waving a limp hello, I glanced over at Midas. "He got called to the den too?"

"Yes."

Ford was an enforcer, and Midas's right-hand man, so it made sense, but I didn't trust his megawatt grin.

Midas and I piled in, me in the middle, and Ford began singing an old country song under his breath.

The peculiar vibe continued the whole trip, which set my teeth on edge, and Midas was no help.

He rested his forehead against the window…and took a nap.

Resting my head on his shoulder, I shut my eyes, breathed him in, and tried not to think too hard about the fact a Faerie portal throbbed on the outskirts of my city like an abscess only I could lance.

NINETEEN

The timing couldn't be worse for what Midas had planned, but he was beginning to think there was never a right time when it came to him and Hadley. They had to fight and scrape to carve out space in their lives for one another, and tonight was no exception.

Ford parked in front of the ostentatious glass house his mother built to host outsiders and formal events away from the den, and they all climbed out of the truck.

"I think I hear my momma calling me." Ford cupped his ear. "See y'all later."

"His momma is in Texas, isn't she?" Hadley stared after him, but her confusion melted as a scent caught her attention. "Whatever that is, it smells crazy good." She smiled at him. "Do you guys cook out often?"

"Every weekend and holiday." He shrugged. "And any time Kroger has a sale on beef."

Linking their fingers, he guided her toward the front door and tried to ignore the sweat on his palms.

"Looks like the smoke is coming from the backyard." A frown knitted her brow. "Are we interrupting?"

"No." He led her up the walkway, and his mother greeted them before they could knock. "Hi, Mom."

"Two of my favorite people." She rushed out to hug him. "How are you?"

"Good," he said, voice low and tight. "How about you?"

"I've never been better." She embraced Hadley next. "Well? How are you holding up?"

"I'm good." Stiffness pinched Hadley's shoulders, but she relaxed into the hug. "It's been a long night." She withdrew. "Is everything okay here?"

"Better than okay." She rocked forward and kissed Hadley's forehead. "Come on, sweetheart."

Hadley shot him a nervous glance but linked her arm with his mom's and entered the house.

He stood close enough to catch her indrawn breath when she spotted the massive gathering in the entry and recognized the closest faces. Boaz and Addie. Grier and Linus. Bishop and Remy. Ford and Lisbeth. Abbott and Lethe.

"What is this?" She whirled toward him, and his mother slipped away like a wolf into mists. "Midas?"

"I made my share of mistakes during our courtship," he said, loud enough his voice carried through the room. "Most of them stemmed from fear. Of losing you, of losing control."

Her mouth fell open, her eyes rounded, and she rocked back a step. All signs pointed toward her bolting. It was then he realized he had done it again, let his cultural needs supersede her personal preferences. It made the knot in his gut pull tight with certainty that he had no idea what he was doing, but he was sure he was doing it all wrong.

"I made my fair share of mistakes too." Exhaling slowly, she slid her warm hand into his and repeated his words to him. "Most of them stemmed from fear. Of losing you, of losing control."

In her voice, he heard understanding and acceptance, and his stomach quit twisting quite so hard.

"I had no clue what I was doing," he said softer. "I followed the rules outlined by my people to the letter, because they gave me guidelines until I could figure out what to do on my own. Except I keep falling back on my customs and neglecting yours. We need to start our own traditions that meld our heritages."

"I don't feel slighted." She walked into his arms. "I'm just glad one of us had a plan."

"You have to hold me accountable for this to work."

"You're doing your best, and I can't ask for more than that." She linked her hands at his spine. "I like that you want to establish our own traditions, but your pack is your family, and I want to be part of it too. We can walk the line between our cultures, but I'm also good with stepping over to your side every once in a while, if it means allowing you to grow and mature into a leadership role for your people."

"*Our* people," he corrected. "You're pack, Hadley." He smiled a tiny smile. "You're mine."

"This again?" She rolled her eyes. "I'm not a thing to be owned."

"I have no problem being owned." He stared down at her. "Everything I am is yours."

"I thought there would be food," someone yelled. "Where are the cupcakes?"

No, not someone. His sister. *Lethe.* Giving him the kick in the pants he needed to drop to one knee.

"What are you...?" Hadley slapped a hand over her mouth. "Oh, Midas." Her eyes rounded. *"Midas."*

"There are children present," Ford called. "Keep it PG."

Fumbling in his pocket, Midas closed his hand around a small box. "I need to ask you a question."

"Okay," she whispered between her fingers. "Um, yeah. Okay. You can do that."

Careful not to let the box slip through his clumsy fingers, he cracked open the lid to reveal a ring.

"What is that?" Grier leaned in. "An onyx?"

"Looks like jet," Linus countered. "A rather large piece of jet."

Joining in the speculation, his mom tossed in her guess. "Black tourmaline?"

Hadley hadn't moved since the hinge squeaked on his palm. He wasn't certain she was breathing.

"It's a Carbonado diamond," he told them then focused on her. "It's made from—"

"—a star," Hadley finished for him, "that exploded before the formation of our solar system—"

"—and fell to Earth as an asteroid over—"

"—two billion years ago."

The Asscher cut black diamond was three carats, prong set in eighteen-karat white gold, and surrounded by a halo of round white extraterrestrial diamonds. More of the same white diamonds studded the band.

The black stone lacked the glint and glimmer of a traditional white diamond, but its origins spoke to him, a tribute to his geeky mate's love of science fiction. He hoped it spoke to her too. Especially when he had lost his voice again.

"Marry me," she breathed then flashed her eyes up to his. "I'm serious."

"Can I handle this part?" He gestured at his pose. "I'm the one down on one knee."

"Oh. Yeah. Sorry." Her fingers clenched and released at her sides. "I just—wow. I got excited."

"Marry me." A smile tickled the right side of his mouth. "I'm serious."

"You're making fun of me, and I don't even care, because *ohmygoddess* that ring is the coolest and most beautiful thing I've ever seen in my whole life." She flung herself into his arms, knocking him to the floor and landing astride him. "I will marry you, but only if you agree to a Star Trek–themed wedding." She bounced on his hips. "I'll be Captain Kirk, and you can be Mr. Spock."

I love her, he reminded himself. *To the* USS Enterprise *and back.*

"Hadley, darlin'." Ford cleared his throat. "I can see you're very excited, but there are still kids present."

Yanked to attention, she noticed their positions, flushed scarlet, then slid onto the floor next to Midas.

Amazed the ring was still snug in the box, he plucked it from its velvet bed and guided it onto her finger.

Raising her hand, she admired the sparkle. "I love you."

"I love you too."

"I was talking to the ring." She slanted him a playful glance. "You're not half bad either."

"Live long and prosper," Grier shouted, and the others raised their voices alongside hers.

"We are going to have the geekiest wedding." Hadley smiled at the ring. "I really do love you."

Midas couldn't help a laugh as he watched her. "Do you and the ring need to get a room?"

"I was talking to you," she said without moving her gaze from her hand. "How about you come stand in front of the ring. I can't seem to look away from it."

"Ha-ha." He rose and brought her to her feet before him. "You're sure you want this?"

"You?" She stuck her palm against his nose. "Or the ring?"

"I should have asked you before I opened the box. Maybe then you'd have given me a straight answer."

"I'm planning a wedding." She squealed with utter joy. "What do you think the answer is?"

"I suspect it depends on whether or not you get to keep the ring if things don't work out between us."

"Stop torturing the boy." His mom waded in, took Hadley's hand to break her line of sight with the ring, and examined the stone. "Tell him what he needs to hear."

Dutifully, she smiled up at him. "Yes, Midas, I will marry you."

"It's a lovely ring," his mother said. "Is the theme negotiable?"

"No," he and Hadley answered together.

This was her wedding, and she would plan it to suit her. He would see to it. The tradition wasn't a gwyllgi one, so it cost them nothing to let her indulge whatever little-girl fantasies she harbored about her big day.

Even if it meant wearing pointed ears, having his eyebrows drawn on, and learning to make his fingers cooperate in the Vulcan salute.

Hadley was worth it. All of it. She was worth everything.

THE OUTDOOR PARTY wound down as bellies filled with burgers, steaks, and brats, and little ones' eyes got heavy. The night had gone better than he could have dreamed, and he couldn't wipe the dopey grin off his face each time Hadley nearly poked out the eye of anyone who asked to see her ring in her eagerness to flash it at them.

That she had known about Carbonado diamonds didn't surprise him, and she was quick to educate anyone who asked (and some who didn't) about how scientists theorized their scarcity was due to a single asteroid impact.

"You did good." Boaz clasped him on the shoulder. "I've never seen her this happy, and I took her to her first Dragon Con when she was eight."

Wreathed in a proud smile, Mom never left Hadley's side as they navigated the room.

"Thanks." Midas soaked up how the pack embraced her, and she embraced them right back. "That's all I want. To make her happy."

Boaz watched them for a moment longer but glanced away as if the sight of Mom and Hadley hurt him.

"I didn't know," he said quietly. "How did I not see it?"

Midas had wondered the same thing, at first, but he knew his Hadley. She would protect those she loved at any cost, especially to herself. She had suffered in silence most of her life, and nothing he could say to Boaz could make him feel better or worse about the agony clawing him up inside when he looked at her.

"Don't treat her like she's broken." Midas studied him. "I'm not saying turn a blind eye to her past. She's going to want to talk to you about it someday, now that you know. She'll also want precautions taken on Macon's behalf. But don't let her catch you staring at her like you are now. She's worked too damn hard. I won't let it all to have been for nothing."

"You really do love her, don't you?"

"I agreed to be Mr. Spock, didn't I?"

Boaz snorted out a laugh. "Sucker."

"You're her Man of Honor," he said toothily. *"Dr. McCoy."*

"Goddessdamn it." Boaz recoiled. "You're not serious."

"As a Vulcan." Might as well get in character. "Better practice your *I'm a doctor, not a...* one-liners."

Adelaide waved to him as music spilled into the backyard from speakers mounted on the porch.

Guess the party had caught its second wind, now that the littles were tucked safely in their beds.

"I'm being summoned." Boaz lingered a moment longer. "Just a friendly FYI, Addie is heavy into Keanu."

"Reeves?" Midas frowned. "Are we talking a *Speed*-themed wedding?"

"More like *Constantine* with a splash of *John Wick.*"

Hadley waved her geek flag proudly for all to see, but Addie hadn't unfurled hers around Midas yet.

"She's that into him?"

"Hadley is a geek in the broadest sense of the word. She lives and breathes her fandoms. Addie isn't that into any particular franchise, so much as the man himself." He frowned. "She blames her best friend for it, but I've seen the body pillow in her closet with him screen-printed on it."

Giving up on Boaz's ability to take direction, Addie came to collect him. "Come on."

Midas gave them ten minutes before Abbott noticed they were physically exerting themselves, intercepted them, and sat them at a table where they could be monitored for the rest of the night.

Until then, they rocked gently in a slow dance while other couples moved to the upbeat tempo.

"Hadley's eyes are glazing over," Mom warned after hitting a cooler for a can of beer. "She won't last much longer without caffeine or sugar."

Meeting the entire pack was overwhelming, especially when they were welcoming you to the family.

"I understand Mr. Whitaker is bound for rehab," she said. "Otherwise, I'm sure he'd be here."

"He would," Midas agreed. That was the nature of the bargain Hadley had struck with him.

"Matron Pritchard, on the other hand, has already left Atlanta."

That bit of news jerked his attention to his mother. "That was fast."

Mom watched Hadley, a faint smile arranged on her face that clashed with the furious storm in her eyes. "She plans on returning to Savannah, where she will pack her husband and her belongings, then relocate to upstate New York."

Careful of his tone around the woman who was his mother *and* his alpha, he asked, "Why would she do that?"

"She won't be Matron Pritchard much longer, and she's not the type to sit idle. She has family there, and she's decided to take a position with their firm."

"What about Macon?"

"They don't know it yet, but Boaz and Adelaide will be signing guardianship papers within the hour."

"And if Mr. Pritchard balks?"

"He's welcome to secure lodgings in Savannah, if that suits him better, but he has been evicted from the Pritchard home effective immediately. The Pritchards will be allowed supervised visits with Macon, after a time, but they are to have no contact with any future grandchildren."

Mom wasn't much for empty threats, and Hadley was pack. Mom could take the law into her own hands if she deemed it necessary. Neither the Grande Dame nor the Lyceum could protect the Pritchards now.

"He may not have raised his hand against his daughter," she added, her voice arctic, "but he didn't stop his wife, and that's unforgiveable. The elder Pritchards are about to receive an all-expense-paid education in what happens when you harm *my* children."

"What will you tell Hadley?"

"I'm hoping she will choose to believe her mother had a come-to-Jesus moment in that clinic and decided to get her life right."

"You're getting soft in your old age," he teased. "You let her mother off with a warning."

"Yes, well." Mom ran her tongue along the edge of her teeth. "I thought about ripping out her throat."

Amused, though he knew it for the truth, he still asked, "What stopped you?"

Wrinkling her nose, she curled her lip. "Can you imagine how that bitter woman must taste?"

Ford waltzed up to her as the music changed and held out his hand. "May I have this dance?"

Flushed rosy with pleasure at having been asked, she accepted with a smile. "I would be delighted."

Males in the crowd who would dare approach her were few and far between. She preferred the distance most of the time, but she enjoyed the occasional spin around the dance floor, and she lit up when males worked up the nerve to help her forget her duties for a song or two.

Skimming the crowd, he searched for Hadley, but she was nowhere in sight.

"I have something to show you." A warm hand slid into his from behind. "Quick."

Midas let Hadley tug him from the yard, through the house, and out the front door.

"Where are we going?"

"*Shh.*"

Laughing under his breath, he followed her into the woods and understood in minutes where she meant to take them. Sure enough, the cabin came into view, and she let herself in without knocking. It was a safe bet no one was home thanks to the party at the house, but he performed a quick search to be sure they weren't intruding.

"Who left candles burning?" He blew out the first one then turned back to her. "That's a fire hazard in this dry—"

Soft light caressed Hadley's bare skin, and the second candle's flame was spared only by virtue of him forgetting how to breathe.

TWENTY

Halfway through our surprise engagement party, I got struck by inspiration and drafted Lisbeth for cupid duty. That is to say, I bribed her to sweet-talk Ford into bringing her to this cabin and setting the scene. I might have had more success with the whole seduction thing if I hadn't stripped buck-naked the instant Midas turned his back. Instead of aroused, he looked kind of, I don't know, peaked. Like he might faint.

Thank the goddess, I had also bribed Ambrose into disappearing for the night so he couldn't mock me about this for all eternity.

"I can't not make it weird." I covered my face with my hands. "I'm sorry I—"

"Hadley." Midas pried my fingers apart then lowered my arms to my sides. "You're beautiful."

"I'm naked."

And I was covered in contraceptive sigils that smelled of blood and crushed herbs, a quickie engagement gift from Grier.

"I noticed."

"I'm really sorry about that."

"Why?" He trailed his gaze down my body, and my stomach quivered. "I'm not."

"I'll put my clothes back on." I shifted my weight from foot to foot. "This is just too awkward."

Midas captured my wrists and pinned them behind my back. "How about I take mine off instead?"

"Sure." I wet my lips. "Yeah." I stopped fidgeting. "That would work for me."

"Don't move," he cautioned then released his hold. "I will chase you if you run."

Heat flashed through me, pooling low in my belly, and I darted a glance toward the door.

"Hadley," he growled in warning.

The challenge proved too much for me, and I feinted toward the exit.

Midas was on me in a heartbeat, his arms locking around my waist, his breath hot in my ear. "Behave."

The oxygen inside the cabin took on a syrupy quality. It was too thick and moved too slowly through my lungs. Sliding his rough palms down to cup my butt, he lifted me, and I linked my ankles at his spine.

"You're a butt guy, huh?" I wrapped my arms around his neck. "Why does that not surprise me?"

"I'm a Hadley guy." He nipped the side of my throat. "I like all parts of you equally."

"Even that wonky little toe without a nail?" I scratched his scalp. "You like that as well as my butt?"

"Yes," he sighed. "Even that wonky little toe without a nail."

His shins bumped the bedframe, and he tossed me onto the mattress. I bounced once then rolled off the edge onto the floor. I landed on said butt with a grunt then rocked back into the wall, smacking my head.

"*Oomph.*"

It does not get sexier than this, folks.

Midas wiped a hand over his mouth. "Are you all right?"

"Are you *laughing* at me?" I rubbed the back of my skull. "Seriously?"

Hooking his thumbs into the hem of his shirt, Midas pulled it over his head and tossed it aside.

"Your abs won't make me forget what you've done, mister."

Anchoring his hands on his hips, he managed to flex muscles other guys would have to photoshop on.

I was definitely still mad at him. He had done...something. Yeah. Something.

Goddess, the man's abs had abs. How was that fair?

And he wasn't striking a pose...

He was hooking his thumbs into his belt loops and sliding his jeans down his lean hips.

A zipper and button must have been involved at some point, surely, but I had been too distracted by the way candlelight played across his rippled abs to notice. Maybe he removed his underwear with the same economy of motion, or maybe he had gone commando tonight. All I knew was once he kicked the pile of denim aside, he was gloriously naked, and I had trouble recalling my name. Either of them.

Midas was beautiful. I forgot that. I *made* myself forget it. Or else I would stammer and blush and never be able to speak to him without humiliating myself every time I opened my mouth.

Naked Midas made it impossible to forget or overlook or look away. *Frak.* I was doing good not to drool.

Between the two of us, we were road maps of life experience, scars upon scars upon scars. Exposing our bodies, our histories, took courage. I wanted him to know I saw *him*, and not only the marks left by his past. Even if it made me sound like an idiot. "You're gorgeous, you know that? How are you even real?"

Bright pink splashed across his cheeks, and he shifted his weight like he might grab for the sheets to hide from my frank assessment. "Thanks?"

"You're welcome," I said primly, and used the wall to help me stand. "Now come here and kiss me."

Happy to oblige, he leapt across the bottom corner of the bed and landed in front of me.

Surprise and shock mingled in a super-attractive snort. "Showoff."

Midas set his hands on my shoulders then smoothed them down my arms until he held my hands. It was ridiculous, standing there with him, neither of us with a stitch of clothes on, while he made such a tender gesture. He wore a silly little grin while he rolled his thumb over the knuckle above my engagement ring.

The sweetness of the moment burst like ripe summer berries on my tongue when he finally kissed me, and heat swooped through my middle as he walked me back until my knees hit the edge of the bed. I fell, and he came down with me, covering me, his mouth never leaving mine.

The hard length of him pressed against my stomach, the friction between us maddening, and I trembled. I longed to wrap my hand around him, to hear his breath catch as I explored him, but he had similar plans.

I gasped for air once he broke our endless kiss, but his lips were already traveling my jaw, my throat, my shoulder. Lower. He peppered my skin with stinging nips then soothed the bites with gentle swirls of his tongue that made me shiver.

He kept going until he knelt on the floor, his palms spreading my thighs wide, and he wet his lips. But it was all too much. I was done with anticipation. Foreplay could wait. I swatted his hands aside, and he growled, but I didn't care. I followed him down, my knees split to either side of his hips, my weight balanced on the balls of my feet.

Crimson sparked in his eyes, his question clear, and I nodded that I was ready.

A pained groan rose in his throat as he reached between us, and finally, *finally*, sheathed himself in me.

A ragged breath burst from my lungs, and I sank my nails into his shoulders.

It had been a long time for me, and Midas was...not a small man in any sense.

Burying his face in my neck, he let me adjust to his size as shivers rippled through his tense muscles.

He pressed loving kisses to my throat and face, and his lips were salty when they met mine. I'm not sure when he lifted me or how he got my upper body back onto the bed, but he stood between my legs, his hands hooked beneath my knees, *waiting, waiting, waiting.*

Rolling my hips against his, I urged him to get a move on, and his control fractured as he thrust into me. I writhed under him, unable to escape, unable to think, unable to do more than *feel.* Piercing his skin with my nails, I fought the delicious tension coiling tighter and tighter in my core, but Midas was ruthless in his pursuit of my pleasure.

Teeth scraping my throat, my jaw, he breathed in my ear, "Let go."

The orgasm exploded through me, tearing a sob from my throat, and I clawed at him, pulling him closer.

"Beautiful," he panted, his lips curving. "So damn beautiful."

Arching my neck to reach his shoulder, I sank my teeth into the tender skin where my nails had been.

Midas came apart in my arms, my name a ragged prayer he chanted under his breath, over and over, his hips swaying as they lost their rhythm, his weight crushing when he went boneless above me.

I didn't say a word, and not just because I had no oxygen to form them.

With a grunt of effort, Midas rolled off me before I suffocated, not that it would have been a bad way to go. I'm not proud that I considered rolling him again—right onto the floor. Payback was coming. Oh yes. But it would have to wait, seeing as how my arms were the consistency of Jell-O cubes.

"Thank you," he murmured, his eyes drifting closed, his chest rising and falling in slow breaths.

Unable to resist, I brushed my fingertips across his cheekbones. "You don't have to thank me for sex."

"I meant for loving me." A slow smile spread across his face. "The sex was good too."

"Good?" I squinted at the ceiling. "Yeah." I lifted a hand and wobbled it. "It was okay."

Flecks of crimson sparked in his eyes when they opened, and he trained them on me. "Okay?"

Teeth cutting into my bottom lip to hold in a laugh, I shrugged. "It was fine."

"I thought we agreed not to grade each other on our performances."

"I was kidding." I reached for him, hating I had ruined the moment. "Tell me you know that."

Midas shifted his gaze out the window, but the telltale twitch of his lips ruined his act.

"You're fishing for compliments," I realized with delight, pinching his arm. "Put away your pole, sir."

"What if I'm not done with it yet?"

Throaty chuckles bubbled up in me, and I covered my face with my hand. "You did *not* just say that."

His weight landed on me, his knee wedging between my thighs before I recovered from my laughing fit. He palmed my leg, wrapped it around his hip, and slid back into me. The shock of sensation dropped my hand onto his shoulder, and I dug my heel into his spine to let him know I was with him.

Always.

ABOUT THE AUTHOR

USA Today best-selling author Hailey Edwards writes about questionable applications of otherwise perfectly good magic, the transformative power of love, the family you choose for yourself, and blowing stuff up. Not necessarily all at once. That could get messy.

www.HaileyEdwards.net

Moment of Truth #5

Black Dog Series

Dog with a Bone #1
Dog Days of Summer #1.5
Heir of the Dog #2
Lie Down with Dogs #3
Old Dog, New Tricks #4

Black Dog Series Novellas

Stone-Cold Fox

Gemini Series

Dead in the Water #1
Head Above Water #2
Hell or High Water #3

Gemini Series Novellas

Fish Out of Water

Lorimar Pack Series

Promise the Moon #1
Wolf at the Door #2
Over the Moon #3

Araneae Nation

A Heart of Ice #.5

A Hint of Frost #1

A Feast of Souls #2

A Cast of Shadows #2.5

A Time of Dying #3

A Kiss of Venom #3.5

A Breath of Winter #4

A Veil of Secrets #5

Daughters of Askara

Everlong #1

Evermine #2

Eversworn #3

Wicked Kin

Soul Weaver #1